ON THE WINGS OF THE RED-TAILED HAWK

Gail Combs Oglesby

DEDICATION

This book is dedicated to all the women in my family who came before me. I have spent the last forty years learning your stories and this book represents an amalgamation of those historical experiences augmented by my own imagination. In their lives these women endured heartbreak and sacrifice that can never be truly acknowledged. Yet, their gifts of tenacity and strength have flowed down to me across the generations, and for that I am most grateful. I hope I have done justice to your voices and helped you to live on in the hearts and minds of all who read your stories.

This book is also dedicated to my daughter Taylor, who is by far the most wonderful woman I have ever known, and it is my life's biggest reward to be her mother. Also, my sincere thanks to all the women in my life who have supported and uplifted me in both my career and personal life. Your love, support, laughter, and friendship have meant the world to me. I would be remiss to not also acknowledge my wonderful husband, without his encouragement, love, and unwavering faith in me, this book would never have come to be.

The Story Tellers: We are the chosen ones.

In each family there is one who seems called to find the ancestors, to put flesh on their bones and make them live again, to tell the family story and to feel that somehow, they know and approve. To me, doing genealogy is not a cold gathering of facts but, instead, breathing life into all who have gone before. We are the story tellers of the tribe. All tribes have one. We have been called as it were by our genes.

Those who have gone before crying out to us: Tell our story! So, we do. In finding them, we somehow find ourselves. How many graves have I stood before and cried? I have lost count. How many times have I told the ancestors you have a wonderful family? You would be proud of us! How many times have I walked up to a grave and felt somehow there was love there for me? I cannot say.

It goes to pride in what our ancestors were able to accomplish. How they contributed to what we are today. It goes to respecting their hardships and losses, they're never giving in or giving up, their resoluteness to go on and build a life for their family. So, as a scribe called, I tell the story of my family. It is up to that one called in the next generation to answer the call and take their place in the long line of family storytellers.

Excerpt from the poem The Story Tellers attributed to Della Joann McGinnis Johnson

CONTENTS

Chapter One
So It Begins...

The moaning wakes me up, a sound like an old woman in the last moments of her life—gasping, writhing, a torment of body and soul. It is a sound that is now so familiar it is almost comforting; it means we are still afloat. I lean over, careful to not wake Jonathan, who lies ever so still next to me. So still, in fact, I watch for a moment to see the comforting rise and fall of his chest. On his other side, his brother Abraham lies flat on his back, arms over his head as young men do. I press my cheek against the cool, musty wood of the hull, the dampness a welcome relief from the oppressive air filled with the smell of lamp oil, sweat, and vomit. How many days now? I'm beginning to lose track. Fifty-eight? No, sixty, I think I overheard Mrs. Fowler say this morning. Sixty days from England, sixty days farther from the life I've known, from the people I love, from the life that, while not perfect, was nearly perfect for me.

The ship is small, and you could easily see end to end if it were not for the cloths hung to provide a small modicum of much-needed privacy. We are all here in this one cabin, which would normally transport wine or cheese, not people. The musty odor of past cargos lingers like the shadow of a ghost within the timbers, seeping out of the woods pores from time to time to taunt us. There is room to stand for most everyone but a few of the tallest men, who must lean over slightly, always looking like they might topple at any moment. The oil lamps and candles have left smoky stains on the ceiling that drip acrid-smelling black, tarry droplets on us in heavy rain or high seas. We use chamber pots as privies and sometimes must leave them for several days if the seas are rough. The stench can make you want to vomit, and between that and the tossing of the sea, I do often.

I close my eyes, leaning against the cold wood, and think of Leiden. It seems so far away now, an ocean away. We were mostly happy there, at least I was. The people of the Dutch Republic had been kind to us, welcoming even, but still we were outsiders, which I know was troublesome for so many. I think we should have stayed, but Jonathan and the other men felt it could never be our home. We were misfits, farmers in the city with not even a church to call our own, and we couldn't go back to our little village in Lancashire. Sadly, England was no longer a safe place for us. As Separatists, we were a threat to the crown and to the Church of England. I'm unsure what the King thought this small group of outsiders might do, but lack of obedience to the crown is a threat no matter how small. The Church, the creation of the disgruntled King Henry VIII, left many wondering what had become of England. We left for good when we went to Amsterdam.

Whispers began slowly, just a faint murmur in the crowd at the market. But over time they grew more frequent, rumors about the settlement at Jamestown in a place called The Americas. A new land, they whispered in hushed but excited voices, a new place, a place where we could worship freely and build our own lives. I couldn't help but laugh to myself. Did the men really think such a place would exist? I had my doubts, worry gnawing at my heart to match the hunger gnawing in my belly. Surely Jonathan and the others are right, but…

A large wave suddenly hits the ship, bringing me back to my senses, and I stretch out my arm to steady myself against the hull. This is not the kind of gentle wave that makes sleeping on a ship so lulling but rather the sudden slamming that makes you take in a sharp breath, wondering if this is going to be the one, the one that breaks the ship apart. I've learned to watch the men. When they stir and look about, you know there is trouble, and the lamps are to be put out to avoid a fire should one get knocked off its mooring. But for now, almost no one stirs. "Sarah," Jonathan says sleepily, not even lifting his head. "Why aren't you sleeping, my dear? All is well, get some rest." If only I could. I can barely make out the others in this dim light, just shadows on the thin burlap that separates our small pallet from the others. The Strangers on one side of our cramped space and us Puritan Saints on the other, with little more than enough space to lay oneself down assigned to each person. Children sleep on their parents' laps or with a half portion of space allotted to them. One-hundred and two people on this level of the ship, with provisions and animals below and the crew above.

When the last wave hit the hull it began to leak, as I am used to now, but I move closer to Jonathan to avoid the bracingly chilly water now seeping through the cracks. The wind has become colder of late as it whistles through the wood ruffling the burlap dividers. I've not been on deck for a few days, but I can tell from the smell and the mist in the air that it is damp and cold and overcast, with the sky and sea the same solid grey it's been for weeks. Beyond Jonathan and his brother Abraham, I see the outline of my friend Mary Crippen through the thin fabric. She is my dearest companion on this journey, and I don't know what I would do without her here. We are nearly the same age, she just a few years older than I am. Her husband, Edward, and son, Daniel, lie next to her and her parents just beyond them. Mehitable, their new and most precious daughter, swaddled carefully between her parents, cries out ever so softly. Mary reaches out and gently rests her hand on her belly, and the crying stops.

Despite having been married for nearly three years, Jonathan and I have not been blessed with a child. Jonathan says it will come in God's time, but the time goes slowly while others of my age have full homes and precious babes to hold in their arms. I have nothing. My parents living in exile in Holland still, our family estate long ago lost to the crown for unpaid taxes, no babe to hold, and now this journey a further trial to test my faith. Thirty days, they said, and we would be in the new world, but the journey has been unexpectedly long and is becoming more treacherous. The constant storms make it difficult to allow us on the deck, as the crew is always jumping here and there in response to orders barked by Captain Jones. While he has been kindly to us, with the crew I've heard he is a harsh taskmaster, no doubt to ensure our safe passage.

Provisions are running low, no water with which to clean ourselves and precious little ale left to drink, and much of that goes to the crew to revive them from their heavy labors. The days and nights seem to blend in the monotony that has become our life. How much longer? No one seems to know, or if they do, they are not saying. The light is beginning to filter through the narrow slits in the upper edges of the walls, sending small shafts of yellow into the hazy darkness. It will be time for morning prayers soon. I lie against Jonathan's back, warming myself with his heat that radiates through his clothes. "You couldn't sleep again?" he whispers softly.

"I slept for a few hours. I didn't mean to disturb you," I whisper back, burrowing my face into the hair at the back of his neck.

"You are never a disturbance, my dearest," he says as he turns to wrap his arms around me.

I've nearly fallen back to sleep when the cabin begins to stir in earnest, and I am fully awake again. I see Mary sit up,

Mehitable at her breast cooing and waving her fat little fists in the air. Mrs. Richards, Mary's mother, is also up and attempting to comb Daniel's thick head of curly hair, and so the day begins. Another day of this stifling air and endless routine. The sounds of the day filter through the cabin with the moaning of the ship an ever-present companion. Clanking of tin cups, occasional laughter, and hushed voices begin to carry ever so slightly over the sounds of ropes and sails and loud voices from overhead. As always, we do our best to clean and make the cabin as tidy as possible, but it is an effort in futility and frustration.

The seas have calmed enough for the men to take the chamber pots up to the deck and empty them, which will help reduce the pungent smell of the night's urine filling our nostrils. I work to push away any dust and dirt that's accumulated around our bedding, but it is a hopeless task and the chronic dampness cakes everything to the floors, the walls, our clothes, my hair. I brush off my clothes as best I can and tuck back under my cap the few strands of dirty brown hair that have come loose during the night. I've learned to sleep with my cap on for warmth and protection from the fleas, which often bite at night. I can only imagine what it will be like to wash again.

There is little to eat and nothing to cook, as only hard tack and dried meat are left in our provisions. Nursing mothers like Mary, children, then the men, younger women like me, and then the oldest women are fed with ever-decreasing portions. The older women are expendable it seems. No longer able to bear children or to put in a full day of hard labor when the time will come, they eke by with the barest of rations. "Thank you kindly, Mrs. Fuller," I say, holding out my hands for my day's allotment, which is smaller than yesterday's.

"Bless you, child," she murmurs. "May God nourish your body and soul."

"Indeed," I reply, not sure that these hard pieces of meat and bread in my hand are what God intended we should eat. In fact, I have moments where I think this voyage is not what God would have intended at all. *Blasphemy*, I think and quickly push those thoughts away. Jonathan must know we are doing the right thing; he prays so fervently and with such devotion I'm sure there is never any doubt in his mind that this is what God intended. Jonathan trusts the voice of God, and I trust Jonathan.

I saw him for the first time at the weaver's near where we were living in Leiden, outside of Amsterdam. He was bringing in wool to be made into cloth. His boots were covered in mud, and he smelled of dirty sheep and hay and had a smile that melted my heart. His eyes the palest of blue, his hair not quite brown but not red either. I was smitten instantly. My mother looked sideways at me to find me staring like a fool at this man whose name I did not even know. "Sarah, are you well?" she asked slyly.

"Yes, yes of course, Mother," I stammered, my cheeks flushing a deep crimson.

She could hardly stifle her laugh. "I'm Elizabeth Hodgkin," she said to the handsome man.

"M'lady." He smiled back at her. "I'm Jon, Jonathan Bailey."

I nudged her foot ever so slightly with the toe of my shoe, and she said, "This is my daughter Sarah."

I raised my head to meet his gaze, he smiled at me, I smiled at him. We were married in our gathering church just three months later. A small ceremony, but perfect in every way. I wore my best blue dress, truthfully the only good dress of the three I had left. My younger brother, Richard, and my little sister, Margaret, picked small flowers from the yard around our house for my hair. My father shook Jonathan's hand with a fervor I had never seen before. "You should be very humbled and grateful to God that he has blessed this marriage to my Sarah," he said with more pride than God would have probably liked.

"I am, dear father, and I will be a kind and loving husband to her and a good father to our children." I wanted to giggle, my heart bursting with pride at them both, but I managed to restrain myself to only a smile. Father would not have thought that laughing about something as serious as God's blessing was appropriate. Mother was beaming, and I could tell she felt it was a good match. It was a wonderful day, a happy day, and happiness was often hard to come by.

"Let me help you," I say to Mary, reaching for baby Mehitable as the Saints of the congregation gather around for morning prayers.

"Dear God, I thank you this morning for my friend Sarah," Mary says, hugging me close. The babe is warm, and I brush my cheek against the faint wisp of hair peeking out from under her cap. Despite the stench of the cabin, she still smells of that sweet mother's-milk smell that only babes can have. I hold her a little too tightly as we sit down on the floor, gathered around Elder Brewster for the morning prayer. Mostly it's just the Saints for prayers, but this morning I notice one of the Strangers leaning against the hull, close enough to hear but not so close to intrude. I'm sure even the Strangers want God's intervention for our safe passage after so many days.

The Strangers scare me; the men seem rough and worldly in a way the men of the congregation are not. Merchants, craftsmen, carpenters, and the cooper, John Alden, who had made friends with Jonathan, Captain Standish, Mr. Martin, Mr. Rigsdale, and their wives and several children. "And so, we ask God's blessing today as we have done every day for our continued safety on this journey," Elder Brewster's deep voice intones, and I realize I haven't been paying attention. I blush, hoping no one noticed, but Mary is clearly hiding a smile behind her hand.

"Amen," we say in unison as we slowly rise from the floor to set about the day. I reluctantly hand the baby back to Mary.

"Where did your thoughts take you, dear Sarah?" asks Mary.

"Not far." I laugh softly. "Just thinking about the Strangers. What do you think they think of us?"

"That we are the source of their livelihood," says Mary confidently. "They will help us build a town, a church, and schools so we can have a real life in the new world."

A real life—I'd had a real life in Leiden. Had we really needed to leave? The atrocities that took place in the name of the Church of England had started well before I was born; my parents told me often of the struggles. The closing of the monasteries, the destruction of sacred books, even burning at the stake for those Catholics who refused to leave the Roman church. King Henry had created the Church of England for his own purposes, but when he died, the Church did not, the crown having realized the Church could be used for its own interests. By the time Queen Elizabeth took the throne, conflicts between Catholics, Protestants, and the Church of England were commonplace. For a while under Elizabeth things seemed better, but the reforms begun under her reign stopped when James I came to the throne in 1603, and once again the steel bands of the Church of England enclosed the country. Now there is no forgiveness, no concession, just fear, punishment, and death.

By 1607 many of our congregation were meeting in secret, some having already been imprisoned or fined for straying outside the confines of the Church of England. It was time to leave, so our group made its way to the Dutch Republic. My father, mother, younger sister and brother, and I fled to Amsterdam, to what we thought would be a better life.

The Dutch were very open about religious freedoms and people from countries all over Europe flocked to this seaside town. Germans, Jews, and many people from Flanders, both Protestants and Catholics, lived side by side, mostly peacefully. But Father had trouble finding work, and while we found religious freedom, we were still treated as outsiders. When he did find work, it was barely enough to sustain the five of us and it exhausted him in both body and soul. Mother helped by taking in washing for the many sailors who came in and out of the port. I did my best to help when I wasn't studying, and Margaret and Richard helped by fetching water from the town well and gathering firewood in the forest beyond the city gate.

After a time, we moved to Leiden, a lovely smaller town further inland, where things began to improve. William Bradford, one of the leaders of the congregation, had come into his inheritance, and he bought a home and opened a weaver's shop that made cloth for men's clothes. Many of the group found work there, including Father and Mother, and so for a time, things were better. Some of the group even began hat making and became tailors. William Brewster opened a printing shop with some of the other men and began to print religious books, which proved a great source of income for both his family and the congregation. Still, there were fears that the children were becoming too Dutch; even in my own house, my parents worked hard to teach us English ways and customs. The men would gather at night in the closed shop to pray and talk about the future. Mr. Hopkins, having been to the Americas, would regale the other men with stories about the lush, rich land that lay beyond. If only we could get there.

Home, what would home be like for me? Jonathan and I would have a child, by the grace of God, and then we would be a family, but living how and where I surely did not know. "You and Jonathan must go with the Congregation to the new world," my father said sternly.

"But father," I moaned, sounding more like a ten-year-old than a woman married nearly three years. "I don't want to go without the rest of you, please can't you and Mother come with us, please Father?"

"Sarah, I would like so much that we could, and I believe God would bless our going, but your mother…" he trailed off.

Since my brother had died the previous year in the winter sickness, Mother had been lost inside her own mind, her own thoughts. I knew she blamed herself for Richard getting cold and wet working to help with the wood for the fire. Yet they say it is in God's own mind who stays and who goes. We cannot know and cannot influence his decisions. "Margaret is also hoping to marry the Anglesey boy, and I know they will not be able to afford the journey. But you, you and Jonathan need to be our future, to raise our grandchildren in the peace and freedom your mother and I have seldom known," Father said with conviction. I could feel the hot tears building up in my eyes, my face flushing as if I were sitting by the fire. "Do not be afraid, God will protect you and provide for you and grant you mercy. Your duty is to Jonathan as his wife, not to your mother and I."

In my head I knew he was right, but the aching I could already feel in my heart made me fear it would tear from my body. How could I possibly leave my mother like this? How would Father care for her without me? Would I ever see them again? I turned and buried my head in Jonathan's chest, no longer able to hold back the sobs that I let freely flow. "Sarah, please don't cry," said Margaret, barely holding back her own tears, "I will be here to help Father, and I will come to you when the time is right if I can."

"Oh, Maggie." I hugged her tightly. She was nearly as tall as me, a woman, no longer a girl, yet still my little sister, always my little sister. She needed me, they all needed me. I looked into Jonathan's eyes, searching for the answer, the answer I so desperately needed to be *We will stay if you wish.* But deep in my soul I knew it would not be so. Jonathan believed it was God's desire that we find a new home, a place to worship him the way we chose. I couldn't let Jonathan go alone; I couldn't leave my family. I couldn't…

I help Mrs. Fuller bring up a small barrel of dried pork from the stores below to begin parceling out for the evening meal. "My child, why so quiet?" she says.

"Oh Mrs. Fuller, do you think we will starve to death before we get off this ship?" I say with more fear in my voice than I would have liked.

"Oh, my dear, we will find our way, it's just the storms, all the men say it will be soon, any day now," she says soothingly.

She reminds me of my mother, and I so want to bury my head in her shoulder. "I know I should be strong, and I trust the men know the truth, but sometimes, I am so afraid," I confess to her.

Her eyes soften as she holds both my hands in hers, looking deeply into my eyes. "You are strong, my child. If you were not, you would not be here." She squeezes my hands tightly in hers and smiles, and I feel my burden ease a bit. She is right I know; it took a strength I had never summoned before to board this ship two months ago in Plimouth Harbor, and yet here I am.

Someone saw a bird…or so they say, perhaps it was just a shadow in the clouds. I hope it is true, but my heart cannot take the disappointment if it is not. The sun has been shining now for a few days, the seas seem a bit calmer but still very cold, and the wind is icy and damp. Every passing day makes me doubt more and more that we will ever find our way. "Good morning, Saints," says Elder Brewster in a more cheerful voice than I have heard since we left England. "Based on the sighting yesterday by one of the deck hands of a bird over the sea, we believe we are getting close to Virginia." The cheers and excited screams rise with a joy and relief that is nearly palpable.

"Sarah, we made it, we made it," Jonathan exclaims as he hugs me tightly, pulling Abraham in to enjoy the moment, much to his disdain.

"Let go a me," he squeals but only half-heartedly, as even he can't contain his joy.

"Not yet you two, not yet," I caution, but I also feel as though a weight has been lifted from my chest and I can breathe again. It is day sixty-three at sea.

The difficulties of this voyage cannot be overstated. The constant motion of the ship with nearly half the people sick at any given time, and the stench, the never-ending smells of people and animals in a space meant for neither. A deck hand died two days ago, washed into the sea, God rest his soul. We are nearly out of food, and it has been too rough for the deck hands to even attempt to get any fish. Captain Jones has been coming down several times a day to speak to Elder Brewster and William Bradford and some of the other men, concerned about whether our rations will hold. I know they think that the women cannot hear them, but in this cabin, nothing goes unnoticed, and nothing is private. Little to drink, little to eat, exhausted, and fearful, we cannot come to the end of our voyage soon enough.

Later that night as I lie next to Jonathan, I allow myself to dream, just a little. "So, when will we have our own house?" I ask hopefully.

"We must talk with the settlers already there to see what arrangements can be made. Most likely we will build the common buildings first, which we will move into as a congregation, and as soon as they are finished, and this could take a few months depending on the weather, we will start on each home in turn. But I promise you Sarah, I've not brought you all this way with all this difficulty not to give you a house of your own." He smiles and looks into my eyes intently.

"So, what will we do while you are building?" I wonder out loud.

"We will continue to stay on the ship, of course."

I recoil, aghast at the thought, before he can even finish the last word.

"No, no, Sarah, it will be fine," he says, kissing my hand. "We will spread out more and move the animals out to the pens already on shore. Some of the men will probably stay on shore to watch over things and to work with the colonists. You will be able to go ashore during the day to wash and help gather food and to relieve yourself. Things will be better, but be patient my dear, it will take some time."

More time on this ship, I can barely contain my disappointment. I had imagined sailing into the port in Virginia and walking off to our new life right away. I have played that day over and over in my mind these last two months. Just as a I play in my mind the day when we will hold our child in our arms.

It's been difficult to sleep the last two nights. The men have been helping the crew take watch on the deck, and snow has been swirling through the air, delicate flakes of white dancing on the currents of air, neither going up nor down but simply sailing along with us. The skies are gray and overcast and the seas are a tempest of waves crashing against the ship. Mary and I and most of the other women are bent over our needlework, struggling in the dim light to make last minute repairs to our clothes in anticipation of making landfall soon. "I must confess, Sarah," says Mary, "I'm struggling to contain my excitement! After years of talking and years of planning, we are finally here."

"Aren't you at all frightened?" I ask.

"No, of course not, what would I have to be frightened about?"

In my mind I run through all the terrors I see in my dreams, ferocious wild animals, savages, raging rivers and vast forests in which to become lost, all the things Mr. Hopkins talked about in his nightly stories. "I don't know." I hesitate. "Just so many things that we don't know and don't understand, like the savages or wild beasts." It may be best not to share all my fears for want of also making Mary afraid when clearly, she isn't.

"That is why we have the Strangers, and Edward and Jonathan and all the other men, to keep us safe." She smiles cheerfully.

"Yes, of course, I'm sure you are right." Would we be safe? So much is unknown. I wonder how the colonists will feel about having new people in their midst. Will they welcome us, or will we simply become outsiders in a new land, again?

Above us it suddenly becomes louder, and we hear heavy footsteps and shouting. "Land, land!" the cry goes up, and now we are on our feet. I so desperately want to go up to the deck, but we've been told to stay below, to stay out of the way as the men work. Is it real? Is it true? We wait. More shouting, the sounds of ropes being thrown upon the deck, but no one comes. We wait in silence, straining our ears to try and pick up words shouted over the wind. No one comes. "I'm going up," I announce to anyone listening.

"No, no, you can't," come various protests from the other women.

"My dear child, we must ask God for patience, perhaps we should pray," says Mrs. Fuller. "Dear God, we ask that you grant us your peace and instill in us the patience required in this difficult hour. Bless and keep the men of this ship safe in their duties, and bring us safely to the land and home which you have so graciously promised."

"Amen," I say, although my eyes are still on the stairs when a pair of boots appears.

"My dear women, I have come to tell you that we have spotted land," says Mr. Bradford in a voice calmer than I might have imagined for this moment. "We are still some hours away and the seas are rough, so coming into the harbor may be difficult. Please prepare the cabin so that you, your children, and your belongings may be most secure." All at once the cabin is a flurry of activity as we gather up our few belongings and pack them away into the one small satchel we have each been allowed.

"I think we should pack up the belongings of the Strangers," says Elizabeth. We all turn to look at her. "Truly, I do think we should, they are above working with our men, and their belongings must be secured as well…don't you think?" she says hesitantly.

"Yes of course Elizabeth, you are right," says Mrs. Fuller.

"Mary and I will do it," I volunteer. "Abraham and Daniel can finish preparing our things, can't you, boys?" They both nod in agreement

"Where shall we begin?" asks Mary.

"Let's just start on each end," I suggest. "I will go to the forward space if you go aft."

"Agreed."

As I make my way up toward the front of the ship, I realize I've never been in this area, and though it's only fifteen feet from where we sleep, beyond the myriad of hanging cloths it feels far away. I begin with Mr. Warren's things. It's strange to be touching the clothing of a man not my husband. He has very little—one shirt, one pair of breeches, a bible, a few tools used to make barrels and casks. A small pencil drawing in a frame, a lovely woman, clearly someone he loved. I put everything into his bag quickly, feeling suddenly that I am looking into this man's life in a way I have no right to. "Mr. Warren, I beg your forgiveness for this intrusion," I whisper softly.

In just a few minutes we are done, as no one has much in the way of personal belongings with them in the cabin. There are trunks in the hold below, but not many even of those. A few precious things—so little with which to build a new life in a new land. There should have been more space, but when the *Speedwell* was not able to make the trip at the last moment, nearly fifty of its passengers joined us on the *Mayflower*. If we'd known leaving behind some provisions to make room for additional passengers would have put us in danger of running out of food and ale, I wonder if we would have made the same decision.

At last Jonathan comes into the cabin, but I can see immediately the fear on his face. "What is it, I can see something is wrong," I say, trying to keep the quaking from my voice.

"Not here," he says sternly, and my heart sinks. He is never stern with me. Jonathan guides me through the maze of hanging clothes until we are in the small space under the stairs.

"What are you doing?"

"I don't want the other women to overhear, and you must not speak to them about what I tell you," Jonathan says in hushed tones.

"But Mary, I must tell Mary if there is something she should know."

"No one. It is up to Edward if he decides to speak to Mary, but I do not think many of the men will tell their wives just yet."

"Jonathan, please, what is it?"

"We are lost," he says bluntly. I can feel my knees buckle and he grabs me by the arm to steady me. "Sarah, you must not react, we can't risk having all the women and children in a panic."

I try hard to steady myself as I feel the small amount of food from my breakfast sitting just at the top of my throat, and I will myself to keep it down.

"What are you saying? I don't understand Jonathan, you're scaring me."

"I know, and you have every right to be scared. We expected to make landfall in an area of Virginia where there is already a Colony, but the land we can see has no such settlement. There is nothing and no one." He shakes his head uncomprehendingly.

"How could this have happened?" My voice quivers, and I feel the tears coming despite my best efforts.

"Sarah, you mustn't cry, the other women will know something is wrong, you must compose yourself."

I feel as if I can't catch my breath and my lungs and chest are about to burst. I gulp for air as I struggle to slow my breathing and to stop the tears. "What does this mean?" I ask cautiously.

"It's not clear yet. We are going to try to move south to see if we can find the place we intended to land, but the currents are not in our favor and the going will be rough," he says quietly.

"But we will find the settlement, and we will manage… won't we?" I can barely bring myself to look in his eyes.

"I hope so, I believe so, but it is in God's hands now and all we can do is that which we can. We must make land soon, we have almost no provisions left," he says frankly.

I barely sleep; I am torn between appreciation for Jonathan's honesty and wishing that I could sleep as soundly as the other women, not aware that a disaster could be unfolding in front of us. I wonder who else knows? Has Edward told Mary? Mrs. Fuller? Elizabeth? I'm assuming all the men must know, since all of them were up on the deck all day. How do they sleep knowing this terrible truth? If we can't find the settlement, that means there is no help waiting for us on shore. No pen in which to offload the animals, no stockade to keep us safe from the savages, no stores of food or grain. *Dear Lord, please oh please, why have you forsaken us*, my mind cries out in silent accusation and anguish. Have we done something to deserve this desertion by the one who was supposed to guide us, to protect us? Perhaps it is my fault. I know my faith is often not what it should be, I trust more in Jonathan than I should, and I should trust only in God, so maybe this is my punishment…but why punish the others, who are so devout?

All morning we wait quietly in the cabin, trying to focus on the smallest of tasks to occupy our minds and our hands. The voices above are quieter today, and the ship seems to be turning back and forth as if we are not sure where we are going—and clearly, we aren't. I wish I was not so pessimistic; I see Mary smiling and cooing at the baby, she can't possibly know. Then without warning the ship shudders and turns slowly to the left, and we hear the sound of a heavy chain moving across the deck before we come to a stop. The ship has not been still for over two months, and now there is almost no movement at all. We can only look at each other with a sense of excitement and, for me, some dread as to what will happen next. It seems like an eternity before the men file down the stairs into the cabin—all of them, including Captain Jones and most of the crew. We squeeze against the back of the ship to make room for them; there have never been this many people inside the cabin before, and we are packed in solidly with no room to even sit.

Captain Jones clears his throat and looks down at the floor, and for a moment I am not sure if he intends to speak, but when he does every word hits me like a cold wave from the sea. "As you are all aware, we have dropped anchor in a bay just offshore," he says in measured tones. "Our destination was northern Virginia at the mouth of the Hudson River to join the Colony already in place there. Unfortunately, the heavy winds which we have battled for the last few weeks have blown us off course by some distance, the exact amount of which is unclear, and despite our best efforts today we were not able to move farther south." I can't raise my eyes to look at the other women, would they see that I already knew? I hear murmurings throughout the crowd, and a few of the women begin to cry softly as the impact of this news sinks in. "After much discussion with Captain Standish, Elder Brewster, and Mr. Bradford, we have decided to go ashore here to see what we can determine rather than continuing to try and fight our way to another location in these rough seas." Some of the Strangers are clearly uncomfortable with this decision.

"Excuse me, sir," says John Allerton, "on behalf of the those of us onboard who are not with Elder Brewster's congregation, our contracts are with the Virginia Company and if we are not going to be joining them, our contracts are no longer valid."

Not fully understanding what that means, I search out Jonathan's face in the crowd to see his reaction to Mr. Allerton's claim. But I do not need to see his face to know how the congregation feels; the raised voices and shouts from many of the men make it clear. "Now Mr. Allerton, we appreciate your concerns, but it is too soon to know what the outcome will be. Please dear sir, give us a few days to determine our next steps," says Mr. Bradford, with nods of agreement from the other men in the congregation.

"A few days, sir, but that is all," agrees Mr. Allerton.

"For now," says Captain Jones, "we will launch a boat to shore. We must obtain food stores and determine if this area is safe for a hunting party. While we do that, women and children may go on deck in small numbers to get some fresh air, which I know has been sorely lacking, but please be mindful of the crew and the safety of the little ones," he cautions. "We have made it this far by the grace of God and I thank him most fervently," he says as he turns quickly and makes his way back up to the deck. There is near silence in the cabin. No one moves, unsure what to do next.

Mrs. Fuller, as always, takes control. "Gentlemen, please remove yourselves to the deck so that we women may ready ourselves and the children to go up." The men quickly move back to the deck, and the sounds of the small boat being launched are clear even to us below. I am anxious to get to Jonathan—would he be going ashore? He would need his coat, which I have with me below, as well as his sword and his musket. Surely he wouldn't go anywhere without them. I had seen Captain Standish grab his coat before going up, as well as Mr. Bradford, so perhaps they would be going ashore with some of the crew and Captain Jones. "So, women with at least one child over the age of ten will go up first," says Mrs. Fuller, taking charge again. "After which, women with children under the age of ten will go next, but in two groups. I suggest no very young babes go above as the cold may be too much for them, so women in the other groups will stay with your children below while you take in some much-needed fresh air.

"Women with no children and children with fathers only, such as John Cooke, will be in the last group. Please protect yourselves against the cold and borrow clothing from each other, if need be, for yourselves and the children," she concludes with her normal air of authority.

My heart sinks. It could be hours before I am able to see Jonathan, to see the land, to get some air! What am I to do? But Mary would be going up first.

"Mary, you must find Jonathan for me," I say breathlessly. "If he's going ashore, I need to know."

"Why don't you ask him yourself," she says, pointing over my shoulder to Jonathan coming down the stairs. I nearly run the length of the ship to get to him and without hesitation throw myself into his arms.

"My dearest, please." He blushes as he sets me back on my feet but with a smile that says I have not done wrong.

"Oh Jonathan, I'm so glad you didn't go ashore, I'm so nervous about what we will find."

"I am going on the second boat," he says, dampening the relief I had felt upon seeing him. "I came for my coat, sword, and musket." He steers me back to our compartment. Safely behind our curtain, he quickly pulls me toward him and kisses me, a deep kiss, and as I lean into him, I can feel him quaking. "I love you and I will be back before nightfall; I give you my solemn vow as your husband. Now, I must go, and quickly," he murmurs into my ear, the softness of his beard brushing against my cheek.

"Here, take your things, go with a prayer that God will keep you safe," I say quietly. He turns quickly but stops just long enough at the base of the stairs to catch my eye. I know he will be back; he has to come back to me; he just has to… and then he is gone.

By the time I am able to get on the deck, the light is already beginning to fade behind the trees. I had forgotten how beautiful and green trees are, how lovely they make the air smell, and how beautiful the sight of the setting sun can be. Although it is bitterly cold, I could stand here for hours just looking at the cove. The sand, lapped by waves, seems close enough to swim to, but I am sure no man would make it before they should freeze to death in what now must be most frigid waters. A few flakes of snow continue to swirl about us as we all crowd against the rail of the ship to see the land. "It's so pretty," a small voice says just below my elbow, and I look down to see young Hannah peering over the edge of the railing, trying to see what lies ahead.

"Would you like me to lift you up so you can see better?" I offer.

"Oh yes please." She smiles as I lift her into my arms and hold her up over the railing. "It's smells so fresh," she squeals, and I laugh out loud. A very fair observation from such a young child, as our cabin air is some of the foulest I have ever smelled, and at even her young age she must understand it.

We can see the small boats resting on the sand where the men went ashore, but I only see John Carver and his servant, John Howland, standing nearby, keeping a watchful eye on us and the shore. I scan the woods to see if I can make out any of the other men, but the brush is heavy, the light fading, and from this distance it is simply shadows of dark and light. The sun would set soon—why aren't they back yet? Hannah squirms in my arms. "Oh, Hannah, I'm sorry I was distracted, it's a good thing I didn't drop you overboard," I exclaim.

"You wouldn't do that Mrs. Bailey, would you?" she says, wide-eyed.

"No, of course not," I say and sit her back on the deck. "Now go inside, it's getting quite cold."

"Aren't you coming?" she asks as she tugs on my sleeve.

"Not just yet. I'm going to wait just a few more minutes for Mr. Bailey to come back on the boat, you go ahead."

I wait what seems like an eternity.

"Sarah, Mrs. Fuller sent me to get you," Mary says softly behind me.

"Just a few more minutes please, I need to know that Jonathan is going to make it back safely."

"Of course, he will, the men will be fine," she says. Mary always seems so confident. I wish I could feel this same optimism—it must be comforting in a way. Reluctantly I turn to follow Mary below, and as I do, a flash of light on shore catches my eye. It is a torch, the men are back on the shore, but is Jonathan with them? I run back to the railing, peering into the darkness. Where is he? I scan the faces, but in the darkness…a glint of silver catches my eye, a sword reflecting the torch light. It is him; he is there! "See, I told you" says Mary, linking her arm through mine. "Now come below before Mrs. Fuller comes herself to drag you away."

It seems an eternity before Jonathan finally makes his way through the cabin to where I'm waiting on our pallet. Abraham is playing naughts and crosses nearby with John Billington, and we turn our backs to them so as not to be overheard. "So, tell me, tell me everything, did you see savages, were there beasts roaming the forests, did you kill anything for food?" The words tumble out quickly.

"No, a few, and yes," he says, smiling.

"Oh, whatever do you mean?" I say crossly.

"No, we didn't see any savages, yes there were a few animals—some wild turkeys and a fox. Captain Standish saw a deer with a beautiful coat of fur, and yes, we did manage to kill a few turkeys, although it would have been good to have gotten that deer," he explains with a slight grin. "Oh, Sarah, it was so glorious to have my feet on the soil of this land. It's a bountiful place with a beauty I had not imagined even in my dreams."

I can imagine it; that's all I have been doing for two months. "What else did you see? Are we nearing the Virginia settlement?" I ask hopefully.

"We do not appear to be. We saw no signs of prior disturbance other than by the savages near the shore, so it appears we are among the first white men to this place," he says with no real indication as to how he feels about that revelation.

"Well, what does this mean, then? Are we going to pull up anchor and continue trying to find the Colony?"

He thinks carefully before responding. "I'm not sure, honestly. We will see what tomorrow brings, as we will go ashore again and survey more of the area. For now I am most tired and hungry, and I can smell that turkey cooking on the deck." He sighs.

"Let me get you some food, my dear," I say, but as I rise to go, I notice something is different. I study Jonathan's face carefully, but I am not sure… "Jonathan, did you wash your face?"

"I did and it was a blessing from God." He laughs.

"I want to wash too," I chide him.

"Soon my love, soon."

The time has been filled with the busy work that comes from waiting. The men have been going ashore on and off for a few days now, and each time, the news is the same: no sign of the Virginia Colony. I'm very anxious to go ashore, as I'm sure all the women and children are, but the men are reluctant to let us go until we are sure that it is safe. No one has seen the savages that we believe are in this area, but Mr. Hopkins said he did see a trap that he thinks had been set by one of them to catch a large animal, which means they are near. Every evening the men gather in a corner of the cabin talking in hushed voices, the Saints in one group and the Strangers in another. I can feel the tension building between the two groups, perhaps in disagreement about what to do next. Jonathan has said that if we don't come to some resolution soon, *every man for himself* mentality could pervade, which would spell disaster for us all.

At last, it seems a decision has been made, as Captain Jones once again appears in the cabin with all the men gathered around.

"After careful consideration and considerable effort, we have determined that we will stay here, in this bay of Cape-

Cod, to form what we will call the Plimouth Plantation, our home in the new world," says Captain Jones, who is clearly choosing his words carefully. No one says a word. "To that end, we have decided to create a document called the *Agreement Between Settlers of New Plimouth*, reflecting the desire of members of this party to create a civil arrangement between individual men of this sailing who have determined we must commit to each other and work together under the grace of God to ensure our mutual survival," he continues solemnly. "I want to read this aloud for the benefit of all, and then I will ask each man to sign his warrant saying it is so and that they are in agreement."

"IN THE NAME OF GOD, AMEN. We, whose names are underwritten, the Loyal Subjects of our dread Sovereign Lord King James, by the Grace of God, of Great Britain, France, and Ireland, King, Defender of the Faith, &c. Having undertaken for the Glory of God, and Advancement of the Christian Faith, and the Honour of our King and Country, a Voyage to plant the first Colony in the northern Parts of Virginia; Do by these Presents, solemnly and mutually, in the Presence of God and one another, covenant and combine ourselves together into a civil Body Politick, for our better Ordering and Preservation, and Furtherance of the Ends aforesaid: And by Virtue hereof do enact, constitute, and frame, such just and equal Laws, Ordinances, Acts, Constitutions, and Offices, from time to time, as shall be thought most meet and convenient for the

general Good of the Colony; unto which we promise all due Submission and Obedience. IN WITNESS whereof we have hereunto subscribed our names at Cape-Cod the eleventh of November, in the Reign of our Sovereign Lord King James, of England, France, and Ireland, the eighteenth, and of Scotland the fifty-fourth, Anno Domini; 1620."

The men form a line to sign their names or make their marks; all free men over the age of twenty-one are obliged to agree, and so they do.

"So, we are staying here," I say to Jonathan when we finally have a moment alone.

"Yes, my dearest, we must stay, it would be true folly to try and leave now with winter upon us and no assurance that we would make it to the Virginia Colony in one piece," he says with a sigh of resignation.

"But what are we going to do, with no one to help us, with not a building in sight? This seems like foolishness, Jonathan," I say, more harshly than I intended.

"It would be more foolish to try to leave. We are a strong group, and we have the means to provide for ourselves and to wait out the winter using the Mayflower for shelter until we can erect a common building to use on shore."

I lie back on the hard floor covered with straw and stare at the ceiling above, listening to the waves lapping against the side of the ship. I'm not feeling very strong at this moment. Not sure whether I want to cry or scream, I do neither. I turn my head toward the hull and try to think on the past, but my mind wants to turn only to the future and what lies ahead.

Our work is not without cost, and sadly Edward Thompson died last night despite the best efforts of Mrs. Fuller and Mrs. Tilley to nurse him. He was the servant of Mr. White, who now has no one for his aide. The men took his body to shore, and I could not help but feel a tremendous sadness, for the struggles he endured on this journey were just coming to an end as he left this life. Although I did not know him well, I know that he was only eighteen, may his soul rest in peace. I am worried there may be more deaths. Some of the children have been ill of late with a rough cough and aches and pains that small children should not have to endure. It has helped to have some fresh water and the meat of the animals the men have been able to kill onshore, but there are no fruits or vegetables. The winter has already taken a strong hold on this land and there is little to be gleaned from its dormant foliage. We have but a small amount of hard tack left and almost no dried meat, and the winter is only beginning. We should have been here in time to settle in before the cold, we should have been in the Virginia Colony where their stores would have helped to sustain us. But it appears we have the benefit of neither: we are alone, no one to rely on but ourselves.

Today, the women and children will be allowed to go ashore for the first time, but my excitement and relief is tempered by the now bitter cold that has swept across the bay. The men pulled the trunks up from below to allow us access to more clothing, but most of us brought little more than we already have on our backs. I was able to get an additional shirt for Abraham from the small bag of Edward Thompson, as he was close to his size, and his few precious belongings have helped several of the men on board. Jonathan's vest is a bit tattered, and his coat has been mended more times than is wise, but it will have to do until we can get some wool from the two sheep we brought with us to make some yarn. I do my best to layer both of my dresses and wrap myself inside my cloak with the blanket on which we sleep.

As we go down the ladder into the shallop the spray splashes up into our faces, and while the joy of finally having water with which to clean my face is significant, the coldness shocks me with its ferocity, nearly causing me to fall as I recoil from the sting. Sitting in this boat next to the ship makes it seem so big, and yet for two months it has felt as small as a prison cell. John Alden is rowing us to shore— Mary, Daniel, Mrs. Eaton, Mrs. Chilton, and their children. The waves, which seemed small from on top of the ship, now toss the small boat about, and I grab tightly to one of the smaller children to keep them from being thrown into the bay. "Dear God, please protect us," I hear Mrs. Eaton call out as we are battered about for what seems hours but I'm sure is only minutes.

Jonathan and Mary's husband, Edward, are there to help pull the boat ashore as far as they can through the wet sand to get us to drier land. We hand the children off one by one, then Edward scoops up Mary. Jonathan helps the other two women, and finally it is my turn. In a moment, it happens: I am on dry land. My legs scarcely know how to react to the total lack of movement beneath my feet.

"Come quickly Sarah, away from the water, it will be much warmer," Jonathan says as he grabs my hand, and we scurry into the forest like two mice escaping a cat. The trees help to block the wind and I lower my head scarf to get a better look. While still mostly green, some trees are bare vestiges of what was once, I'm sure, the most beautiful of leaves. Lush and fragrant, the evergreen trees with majestic boughs in all sizes and shapes fill the forest, and the world is still at last. The air is crisp like fresh linen and smells of damp woods, old leaves, the slightest hint of a rainy mist descending through the trees. If there is a heaven, this might be it.

Beneath our feet the ground is covered with leaves of every kind, in some places to a depth well over our ankles, and acorns! "Jonathan, we can use these acorns to make flour," I say excitedly.

"Are you sure?"

"Yes, I've seen Mother do it, she taught me all about plants and how to use them for healing and eating. We need cold water to leech them in first, but then we can pound them out into flour."

"Well, there is plenty of cold water," laughs Jonathan as he helps me gather a few handfuls into my scarf. "We will come back tomorrow with a sack and gather more," he assures me.

We wander a bit more through the lush forest, stopping long enough for me to wash my face in a cold meandering stream.

Ice clings to the shore at the edges of the stream, glistening in the bright sun, but there is just enough flowing water for me to reach in and carefully scoop up a handful or two. The tingling cold of the water feels like needles on my face but I feel weeks, months, of dirt washing into my hands. I dry my face and hands on the hem of my skirt. "So, what do you think of our new home?" asks Jonathan, his face close to mine, the steam from his breath billowing in the air between us.

"I think I will love it, and I know I love you."

He kisses me, our first kiss in our new home, and I know there will be many more to come.

The men have determined that John Carver will be the Governor of the Colony. He and his wife, Katherine, are godly people, well known to everyone in the congregation, and so a good choice. It seems he was behind the writing of the document to which the men agreed, keeping the peace between the Strangers and the Saints, for which we are all very grateful. John and Katherine Carver have no children of their own, but with them is Jasper More, who is much younger than Abraham, merely seven or eight, and one of four More children on board. Their presence is the result of a legal dispute between the children's parents—the children eventually became the legal wards of several men in the congregation, including the Winslows and Bradfords as well as the Carvers. The sight of them here in this strange place without their parents often saddens me. I know how often my heart aches for the loss of mine, and I'm a woman of an age where my parents are not a necessity.

A pall has fallen over the ship and everyone speaks in hushed tones, as the dearest wife of William Bradford, his Dorothy, has died, having fallen over-board yesterday and drowned in the frigid waters of the bay. We have been allowed to go on deck at will this last week now that things have been settled, and none of the crew saw or heard anything from her until the sound of splashing, at which time they ran to see what had happened. One of the crew grabbed a rope and threw it over to her, but she had quickly disappeared underneath the dark and murky water. No cry for help, no screams of panic, just simply gone beyond our reach and into the waiting arms of God. "Jonathan, I don't understand, how could this have happened?" I say, a tear trickling down my face and sliding off my cheek onto my skirt below.

"No one knows for certain; it can be slippery, especially along the railing, where ice can form as the spray splashes on deck. We believe she just fell," he says with the sadness we are all feeling.

"Fell, but how would she get over the railing?"

Jonathan looks away, no answer for what seems like a simple question. "Just please be careful when you are on deck Sarah, it can be a dangerous place."

The men have begun to cut trees, clearing a place to build the common store so that we can offload more cargo onto the shore and provide more room on the ship. The work is difficult and the conditions far from tolerable, and the persistence of the men in this effort must be commended. Mary and I are working on creating a dough which we can then take on shore to cook over a fire to make more hard tack biscuits for the winter. The men have been able to find a few other small animals and a few fish, but it's still barely enough to sustain us. "God will nourish our souls, and in that way, he will sustain our bodies as well," assures Mary, her hands covered in acorn flour.

"Oh, Mary I hope that you are right."

"Sarah, it was God's hand that brought us safely here; he's not going to let us just starve to death now," Mary declares, perhaps trying to convince herself as well as me.

I don't dare say what I am thinking, what I've always been afraid to say out loud, that my faith in God is not secure. That I wonder if we really understand his desires for us or what is required to earn our place in heaven when we depart this earth. Did God really want us to come to this place, or was it the ambitions of men who simply did not want to abide by the rule of the King? How can we be sure? Blind faith is never something I have fully understood. In Jonathan, I have abundant faith, in the love and guidance my parents provided, and in the wisdom of the men and women who are on this journey. But I ask myself how much of this is God and how much of this is man, how does one know? Everyone in the congregation is content to say that all that happens is the will of God, and perhaps it is, but if so, I surely wish I knew what God was thinking and planning next.

It does not take me long to find out. My mind is racing with uneasiness and with the ever-increasing sorrow that comes from loss. The child Jasper More died from a fever after being ill for almost a week. His brothers and sister are inconsolable, having already lost so much in their short lives. More loss is almost too much for them to bear. Governor Carver carries Jasper's lifeless, limp body onto the boat as we all gather on deck to hear the prayers offered for his eternal soul by Elder Brewster. I can hardly hear him as the wind whips through the air, carrying his words away on their currents. Perhaps the wind will carry them to God to bless the soul of this poor boy and to bring comfort to the other children and to all of us who now mourn.

The days take on a new routine: the men on shore during the day clearing and building and the women and children on board trying our best to prepare food for the days and weeks ahead. Captain Standish did finally get a deer, and that helped mightily to give us food for several days, but when you are feeding this many people one deer does not go far. The hide will be of great use though; several will benefit from its warmth once it has been tanned.

The work is brutal, and Jonathan comes back to the ship each evening exhausted from his labors, sometimes too tired to even eat. The men are all haggard and beaten, and now the snow has begun in earnest, making it even more difficult to complete the work. While we may be the first Englishmen in this place, it's become known that the savages, or Indians as many of the men call them, were here before us.

"We are fortunate that we've settled in a place where the Indians were living, as they have cleared much of the land beyond the hill to the north for farming, and so we will not have much work to do in the spring to prepare this land," says Jonathan as he leans against the hull eating his small evening meal.

"So where are they now, are they going to come back and chase us from this land?"

"Not likely. We have found many bones which are human remains around the area, and it appears these people, whoever they were, are no more," he says matter-of-factly.

I can't bring myself to say what I am thinking. If this could happen to them, could it happen to us? People, Indians or not, living, farming, raising their families, and then they are just gone? To what end, and why?

"Most likely from a sickness, I would say," says Jonathan, "since it seems to have taken the whole lot of them, children too."

A sickness, like the one that took the child Jasper More or Richard Britteridge, who had died just this morning? Could this be the pox? Are we all going to get it now and die?

"Sarah, you're being overly emotional. I don't think we can catch anything from people who died some time ago," says Jonathan thoughtfully, "but we are cautious all the same, and we don't touch the remains of the people or animals we find, just to be sure."

"We should say a prayer for them," I say.

"No, I don't think a prayer for the soul of a savage who did not know God is of any value to them," says Jonathan with a tinge of hard-heartedness I have not heard before in his voice.

"It can't hurt."

"Perhaps. You can certainly pray for them if you like, but I won't be wasting my prayers on them when there is so much more we need from God than his blessing on those long departed."

Thomas English, Moses Fletcher, and Mrs. Chilton, as well as the son of Thomas Tinker, have all gone to heaven. Even the dog that the Bradfords had brought with them passed one night. Death has become a weekly occurrence on the ship as January looms only a few days away. We have been anchored here a bit more than a month, and seven of our company have now died. We call on God sincerely in our prayers each day to look after and keep in his grace those of us who remain.

The men have made great progress on the stores building, and today they will move most of the gunpowder and many of the tools and building materials still on board to the shore. I can't help but wonder how we can possibly survive this winter. Mrs. Fuller has called the women together to go through the possessions of those who have passed and determine who is in the most need, as we can afford to waste nothing. Mary gets a dress, which is sorely needed as the one she has been wearing every day now for three months is worn through to her undergarments in several places.

The darkness comes earlier and earlier each day it seems, and now there are precious few hours that the men can safely work onshore. We must conserve the remaining oil and candles, so all but a few lights are put out after supper. With the cabin plunged into darkness, the men sleep to rest their weary bones. The women, with no light for needlework or reading, sit in small groups, trying to keep the children entertained with stories and quiet games. Elizabeth, Mary, Susanna White, and I sit together with the babe Mehitable and Susanna's infant boy, Peregrine, born just a few weeks ago.

"Such an unusual name you chose," Elizabeth says, admiring Peregrine on Susanna's lap.

"It is, I know, and while we usually turn to the holy books for inspiration, my husband thought this name, which means 'traveler,' would be perfect."

"A fitting name for one who has journeyed so far," I say, wondering when I will have a chance to be with Jonathan again to try to start our own family. We've no privacy on board this ship and no likelihood of homes before spring, so sadly it won't be soon.

Chapter Two
Plimouth Plantation

Fear and sickness are spreading through the ship. Men, women, and children have all departed this earth at the hand of God, nearly twenty-five in number since the first of December. It begins like the winter sickness which we had in England and in Leiden, but it ravages the body so quickly that few have been able to recover once they become ill. My days are spent in a haze of tending the sweat-soaked brows of the ill, the bodies of the dead, and the few bare linens soaked with blood, sweat, and vomit. Unlike the sickness we have known before, those who become infected bleed profusely as they become more ill, and at that point there is no turning back.

Jonathan lies on the floor next to me as we both try to get a few precious hours of sleep while other members of the congregation take their turn with the sick and dying. "Who has gone?" asks Jonathan wearily. "I'm starting to forget."

It's a long list and I recite the names slowly as I try hard to picture their faces, some of which are already fading from view.

Edward and Mrs. Fuller

John Allerton

Edward and Mrs. Tinker, who lost their boy in December

Richard Clarke

John Crackstone the elder

John and Alice Rigsdale

John Langmore

Margaret Richards, Mary's mother

Edmund Margesson

Christopher and Mary Martin

Degory Priest

Mary and Elinor More, whose brother Jasper died in December

Rose Standish

Edward and Agnes Tilley

Names, faces, friends, Mrs. Fuller. I had cherished her so dearly as a second mother to me during our voyage. She reassured me and comforted me, and now she lies cold and dead on the shore in a small shallow grave. The men agreed it would be best not to let the Indians know how many of our number have gone. They have seen them skulking around the stores building and watching us from behind the trees. Afraid that they may try to attack us if they feel they have an advantage, we bury our dead as quickly and quietly as we can. No prayers on deck as we did before, only the plaintive plea for God's mercy on their souls as we wrap them in the barest of cloth to be taken to their final rest.

Mary has not been the same since her mother's passing, and while I do my best to console her, I know it is a wound beyond any salve I may have for it. Her faith is strong, and she turns to God for her comfort, but she seems to find less of it than she had hoped. Her father sits quietly all day, holding the babe and mourning his wife. As I turn over to sleep, that sluggish and achy feeling that has been in my head for the last few days stabs me like a poke from a sharp stick. I wince in pain and use my hands to push back against the assault. My forehead is hot to the touch, and I can feel a bead of sweat trickling down my temple. "Jonathan, I'm not well…"

I hear voices but they seem so far away, as if I am underwater and they are on the shore. Muffled and undiscernible, just a jumble of sounds. The wood beneath my hands feels cool to the touch, and I'm aware that I am wrapped in some linen, but little else seems to penetrate the fog that I am in. Mary brings me some broth to drink but I can't make myself sit up to take it. "Please Sarah, please try, you must try to eat something." I hear Mary pleading but the pain is too much, and I only want to sleep. I do not know if it is day or night or how many of each may have passed, I only know that I do not want to live.

I pray quietly in my mind. *Dear God, please end my suffering and take me to be with you in heaven*, I plead.

But I am still here.

A shaft of light lies across my face; I can feel its warmth. Slowly I open my eyes to see Daniel, Mary's son, peering closely at my face. "Mother," he cries out, "I think she is awake."

Instantly, Mary is at my side, and I feel her warm hand in mine. "My dearest Sarah, you are still with us by the grace of God, and we thank him most sincerely," she prays aloud.

"Clearly God only listens to you, Mary, and not to me," I say bitterly. Every bone in my body aches and I feel as if I have been in the same spot, in the same place, forever. "How long have I been sick?"

Mary sighs. "Nearly two weeks. I did not think that you were going to survive."

I struggle to clear my head and pull myself up on my elbows to try and see beyond the curtain next to us. "Where is Jonathan, is he ashore? Can you bring him to me?"

Holding even more tightly to my hand, Mary motions across the room to Elder Brewster, who is quickly at my side. "Sarah, I'm sorry to say that Jonathan got the sickness and has gone to be with the Lord some four days ago." His voice is calm and low, and my mind works hard to process what he has said, but it is all so confusing. Jonathan is dead? Somewhere in the cabin I can hear the wailing scream of a woman who is clearly in pain. An animal sound, wounded, afraid. In my mind I know this woman is in desperate need and someone should go to her, but I can't get up.

"Sarah, you mustn't exhaust yourself, please stop," pleads Mary.

It is me; I am screaming.

Sleep is my escape. To wake is to confront the reality that Jonathan is gone, and this is a reality I simply cannot face. Abraham is a constant at my side, as is Mary, and while they do their best, I cannot be consoled. My life has been destroyed. The man that I loved, the man that I followed here to this place, is gone. God has taken from me the one thing that I most dearly loved and needed, and I cannot understand. I am angry at the world, at God. But I am also angry at my father for saying we should come, even at Jonathan for bringing us here. If we had stayed in Leiden, he would be alive. The sorrow and anguish that fills the air has only grown more and more oppressive. My own grief is like an open wound which oozes daily, reminding me that it is my ever-present companion. I should have died; Jonathan should not have. I was promised God's protection and mercy, yet I have neither.

The days are growing longer now and lighter for the men's work on shore. More light by which to bury our dead. We are all going to die I am sure; just like the Indians before us, there will be nothing left of us but bones. As the month wears on the list of the dead continues to grow, and now, Jonathan is on it:

Jonathan Bailey, dear husband of Sarah

Thomas Rogers

Elias Story

Edward Thompson

Elizabeth Winslow

John and Joan Tilley

Mary Allerton, wife of Issacs

Sarah Eaton

John Turner

William White

Roger Wilder

Alice Mullins

Thomas Williams

Solomon Prower, only fourteen

There are only a handful of women left now to cook, clean, and care for the remaining children. My bones ache and my head hurts, but I know I must get up and help. "How are we ever going to manage?" I look at Mary, her face haggard and gaunt.

"God will get us through this, we must be faithful to him and continue to trust that our plight is God's will and not for us to question."

"Mary, how can you say that when it is clear that God has forsaken us here, and left us all to die," I say bluntly.

"Stop," Mary cries out as she grabs my shoulders and shakes me as if to shake the bones from my body, "you cannot say those things Sarah, you cannot." She begins to sob, her arms suddenly around me, holding me tightly. I can feel the force with which her crying racks her now small and frail body, and I think for a moment that she might simply collapse into a pool of wet, salty tears.

My own sobs come quickly, and we cling to each other, sharing our pain and our grief, two souls in anguish as one. I have lost my husband, Mary has lost her mother, and we have both lost the vision we had for the future ahead. But Mary still has Edward and her children, and her father. I only have Abraham, who now needs me to be mother, father, and friend, and I have no comfort to offer him. I cannot even comfort myself. But I must try. I smooth the front of my dress and hold Mary at arm's length, looking into her eyes, and broker a faint smile. I straighten her cap and wipe the last tear from her cheek. "You are right, God will see us through our trials," I say with as much conviction as I can muster. I have to be stronger, I have to believe in the future, for Mary, for myself, for Jonathan. I stand taller and push my shoulders back, my hands neatly folded in front of me, my eyes dry and clear. "Tell me Mary, what can I do?"

We begin in earnest to clean the cabin from top to bottom, removing all the curtains and taking them out to wash. A few of the deck hands help us remove all the straw so that we can clean the floors, scrubbing on our hands and knees from end to end. While the work is difficult, the hardest part is gathering up all the remaining belongings from those who have passed. I save Jonathan's vest and wear it under my dress; the rest of his things I give to Abraham. Clothing from all the others is once again dispersed among the remaining group, no longer Saints and Strangers but simply survivors. Mary and I and the remaining five women each get one or two additional dresses and coats and caps, which are most appreciated and sorely needed. With needle and thread, we are able to resize some of the men's clothes for the children, and to use the scraps to make bags for gathering nuts and seeds on shore.

Rearranging the cabin and rehanging the fresh curtains to create larger sleeping areas provides a constant visual reminder of how many people have gone. Two whole families have been wiped out with not one survivor. Children have been left orphaned, and widows and widowers share alike in their sorrow. Abraham and I move to the other side of the cabin, away from the spot where I had lain with Jonathan. I can no longer bear to be in that place without him beside me. The nights are the worst, when the cabin is mostly quiet and I have only my mind for company. My thoughts whirl about like dry leaves on a windy fall day, swirling in circles going ever faster and faster. What am I to do? Should Abraham and I try to go back with Captain Jones when he returns to England? I don't know what we would find if we did. We would still then need to get passage to Amsterdam, and I do not know if my parents are alive or if my sister is still there.

We could stay, I suppose, and try to make our lives here. Surely more people will come. I know there are other Separatists who wanted to leave, some who could not afford to come and some with business ventures that needed to be concluded. A large town will spring up here, surely, more women, a future wife for Abraham, and for me… I dare not think of life with another man, but I know it will have to come to pass if I am to survive here. While widows are allowed to own property and I could live on my own with Abraham, it would simply be too difficult, and I still hope to one day have children of my own. I shall likely marry again, and there are certainly plenty of widowers in the congregation now.

Each night the men talk quietly of the day's efforts; the common house now done, they are completing the canon placements on the hill opposite the settlement, which they call Fort Hill. They chose to build on this spot in large part because of these two hills, one to build our homes on and one for our protection. Encounters with the Indians are becoming more common, and one of the sailors has even killed an Indian, he said for fear of being killed himself. Before moving everyone on shore, we have to know that we can protect ourselves from an attack. Captain Myles Standish, our military leader, has organized the men into two groups that take turns with watches to ensure our safety both day and night. He has even taken the women out to show us each how to properly use a musket. While the noise was deafening, and the blast drove the gun into my shoulder in a most painful way, I am glad to know that if need be, I could defend myself and others.

Every day the men venture into the forest to cut down trees, as work on homes has now begun in earnest. The sound of axes chopping wood carries all the way to the shore, where we spend more and more of our time cooking and washing. It is a relief to spend less time on the ship and to be on dry land. "Abraham, mind your feet don't get wet," I remind him as he walks along the sand gathering driftwood for our fires. The winter is fading, and the sounds of birds calling out to one another floats on the air. The trees have not yet started to bud but the snow has all but melted, even though in some places it had been up to our knees. The men drag the logs up to the top of the hill, where they fit them together to form the frames of the houses. The wood will keep the buildings strong against the wind and snow, and the daub made from mud and clay will hold everything together. The children help gather reeds from the marshes, and Mary and I cut grasses and bundle them to make thatch for the roofs.

This morning is remarkable for its warmth, and we are all working diligently in the settlement when suddenly and without warning, an Indian approaches. The men jump down from their ladders, dropping their hammers and grabbing their muskets, but the Indian does not seem to have any weapons. He pauses for a moment, taking in the scene, and then says confidently, "Welcome, Englishmen!"

There is stunned silence and Captain Standish steps forward, his musket held loosely in his hands. "You speak English?" he asks cautiously.

"I do," the Indian replies. "My name is Samoset, and I am a sagamore, as you say, a leader, of the Abenaki."

We all stare in disbelief. His English is a bit broken, with a strange accent but understandable, and he is neither afraid nor threatening. This is certainly not how I had imagined my first encounter with a savage, and I feel none of the fear I had expected.

I am fascinated by his dress, the bright colors and skins that he wears as a cape, the feathers adorning a hat band of some type. Beyond that he wears very little, and I am careful not to look at him too closely. His skin is the same color as the wood on the Mayflower, a dark brown with a hint of red where the sun hits his bare arms. The edge of his cloak is lined with what appear to be beads of some sort that glint red and blue in the light of the sun. He certainly isn't going to be able to hide in the forest in those clothes! I wonder if this is how he dresses all the time or if these are his special occasion clothes. I hope the women are not sent back to the ship—I want to learn more about this strange man who has so confidently presented himself to us.

We gather on the floor of the common building, Mary and I and the children staying to one side while the men sit with Samoset on the other. "I am from a tribe in the north where the English men have a fishing camp, and that is where I learned to speak your English," he says in a rich, deep voice that commands attention. "I am proud to say I know the names of all the sea Captains who come to this camp." He smiles widely, revealing a few missing teeth. He has come to visit the sachem, or chief, of this region—an Indian by the name of Massasoit who leads the Wampanoag tribe. These are the Indians the men have seen in the forest.

"I am most sorry for our actions against your people " says Elder Brewster sincerely. "We did not know if they meant us harm, and one of our men did kill one of their tribe."

"For this is a great land," Samoset says, "and we live here peacefully, and it is our hope you will as well."

The men nod in agreement, although I can't help but think of the cannon sitting on Fort Hill. Do the Indians think we came to harm them? You certainly couldn't blame them if so.

"I will stay nearby this night and return to your camp tomorrow," Samoset announces, "and I will bring with me the Indian named Tisquantum, he is from the Patuxent. His tribe lived upon this land for many moons, but they live no more," Samoset says sadly.

"Sarah, Mary, you and the children should go back to the ship while the light is good, we will stay a bit longer with Samoset," says Mr. Bradford, interrupting my rapt attention on all the Indian had to say.

Reluctantly we gather up our things and make our way back to the ship. Mary bustles quickly down the path as if the devil himself were in pursuit. "Slow down Mary, the children can barely keep up," I exclaim. "Why are you in such a hurry?"

"I don't like the Indian man, he frightens me, and he is a heathen. I did not want to spend any more time in his presence, I am glad to get away," she says breathlessly, continuing her rapid pace. I laugh inwardly, thinking of how afraid I had been of the idea of the savages, what they would be like, what they might do to us. Mary had been the one who thought there was nothing to be afraid of, but now she is the one who is afraid. I found the Indian fascinating, while Mary couldn't get away fast enough.

The next day, true to his word, Samoset comes back to Plimouth Plantation with the Indian called Tisquantum. His English is also quite good, and he speaks it with the same tone as Samoset—a melodic kind of rhythm to the words, almost on the verge of singing, which I like very much. Tisquantum had been taken some years ago as a slave by an Englishman who had come to these shores. The Englishmen brought with them a sickness that wiped out Tisquantum's whole tribe after he had been taken to Spain. When he was finally able to return, everyone and everything he knew was gone. The last of the Patuxent tribe, Tisquantum stayed with the other tribes who still lived in the area and become part of the Wampanoag tribe.

I feel a tightness in my throat like I did the day Jonathan told me we were lost, a feeling like I'm going to be sick. Did we know that our coming to these shores might harm the people already here? Are we risking the lives of the Wampanoag? I'd been so caught up in how the Indians here might hurt us that I never thought about all the ways in which we might hurt them.

I get up from the spot on the floor where I've been grinding flour, walk over to where the men are sitting, and stand in front of Tisquantum. "I am sorry that we brought to your people the English sickness," I say softly. I feel the eyes of all the men upon me, but no one speaks.

"Squanto is how I am called," he says as he stands, his face just a few inches from mine.

"I am Mrs. Bailey, but you may call me Sarah," I find myself saying unexpectedly.

"Your husband is here," Squanto says, looking expectantly at the faces in the room.

"No, my husband took the English sickness and went to God a few weeks ago," I say haltingly.

"I am sorry too for your sadness, Mrs. Sarah," he says with a little bow, and in that moment, I know we are not so different after all.

Spring has finally bloomed, and it is glorious indeed, with many of the trees in flower and leaves of green on every previously empty branch. The air smells sweet with the warmth of clover and so many new scents that I have never known. The land here is verdant beyond my wildest dreams; if only Jonathan could see it now. The sea is calm, a deep blue rimmed with white frothy waves that lap the shore. The men, with the help of Samoset and Squanto, have brokered a peace with the Wampanoag tribe, and an uneasy quiet has fallen upon us, each still somewhat unsure of the other. The Indians are helping us to plant and have given us corn to turn into the fields as well as squash, wheat, and beans. We are grateful for their help, for any help, as these last few months have been most difficult and have certainly taken their toll, even on the living.

The pigs and chickens we brought with us are enjoying the warm sunshine, pecking the ground, and rolling in the dirt. Seven houses are done, and we are all now living onshore, Abraham and I with Mary and Edward. The house is not large, just one room with a hearth at one end. Salvaging the curtains we used on the ship, we've created a small area for Abraham and Daniel to share, one for Mr. Richards, one for Mary and Edward and Mehitable, and one for me. It leaves just enough space left over for us to gather over meals. While not grand, it is a relief to finally spend every night within its four walls and away from the *Mayflower.*

The men set about making furniture, first a table and chairs and then a cradle for the baby, and finally beds for the adults. The boys, who will not be boys much longer, will have to endure the floor a bit longer, as our attention has turned to preparing the fields for planting. Everyone in the colony works every day in the fields, preparing the furrows and the seed. From atop a rise in the field I can see all the way to the bay, the deck hands on board the *Mayflower* working to prepare for departure, heading back to England. It has been a comfort having the ship there. As awful as those months onboard were, once it is gone there will be no way for us to leave this place. Only a small boat for fishing will be left behind. But I no longer have moments when I think of returning to England, and as I stand here surveying the beautiful hills rolling out as far as the eye can see, I know this is where I belong. Jonathan was right, this is the place God intended for us to be. I only wish he were here to see it now in its finest hour. My heart is still heavy, and each day I wear my grief just as I do his vest. Hidden under my clothes so that others won't see it, but there, a reminder of what I have lost and what might have been.

All of us that remain, fifty-one of the one hundred and two who came to this place, are now gathered upon the shore to say goodbye to Captain Jones and his crew. He also lost several of his men during the sickness, and he leaves knowing that our hold upon this land is tenuous. If he returns in one year, will he find us still here? No one can say for certain. "Captain Jones, we wish you and your crew God's speed in returning to England. I wish we could do more to provide you with provisions," says Captain Standish apologetically.

"No need to worry, with the seas in our favor we will be back in England in just a month, and we have enough to meet our needs." Captain Jones takes Elder Brewster's hand in both of his. "You and your congregation have endured unspeakable difficulties and loss, and yet, your devotion to God and conviction to this effort has never wavered. I am proud to have known you, all of you, and I wish you God's continued blessing," he says as he shakes hands with each one of the men in turn.

"God Bless you, and thank you," echoes across the crowd as Captain Jones boards the shallop for the last time so the men can row him out to the *Mayflower*.

Before the men have even returned to shore, the anchor is hauled on board and the sails unfurled, huge expanses of white against the bluest of skies. The ship slowly begins to turn into the wind, and in an instant, she is moving away from the shore. A few of the crew stand along the railing, watching as the land fades away, and the children run along the shore waving their goodbyes. The ship quickly becomes just a spec on the horizon as we turn to go back to the fields. One last glance over my shoulder and she is gone. We are on our own. We will survive, or we will die, but there is no going back now.

"Abraham, could you bring me some more wood, please," I ask as Mary and I begin to prepare our evening meal. We clean clams and mussels that we have been gathering along the bay. Mr. Richards has also been able to kill two geese today, and one of those will serve us well for dinner. Small biscuits made with acorn flour and one of several squash that Squanto had brought for the colony round out our meal. It is more food than we have enjoyed at once since leaving England.

"Dear God, please bless this food as it nourishes our bodies, as your word blesses our souls," says Mr. Richards solemnly. I glance up but his eyes are still closed. "And dear Lord, bring your peace and healing to those of us still grieving the loss of our loved ones, especially my dearest Anne and our dear Jonathan. Amen."

His eyes are shining with the threat of a tear, as are mine. Mary's tears have already escaped, rolling down her cheeks, and she reaches out to squeeze his hand. "I miss her too, Father, but I know she is in heaven, they both are," she says, looking at Abraham and me with a smile.

"Will I go to heaven with Jonathan when I die?" says Abraham with a small voice, not yet a man's but more than a boy.

"Of course, you will," I say reassuringly, "but that will not be for many years to come, you have a long life to live, as Jonathan would want you to." He seems reassured.

After supper there is nothing left but a few scraps for the pigs, and it is an odd feeling to leave the table with a pleasantly full stomach.

While our lives have improved considerably in the last few months, life has a way of reminding you that it is fragile and sometimes fleeting. Just last week Governor Carver became ill while working in the field, complaining of a bad pain in his head. Several of the men helped him back to his home where his wife, Katherine, tended to him, but sadly, he died after just a couple of days. He was buried in the ground on Coles Hill with as much ceremony as we could muster, a stark departure from the times when we quietly buried our dead at dusk to hide away our plight. As the Governor of the Colony, it was only right that he receive this recognition, and some of the men even fired off musket volleys to mark his passing. His poor wife seemed so frail I was afraid she would not survive the day.

The men gathered to discuss this turn of events, and now William Bradford is to become the new Governor, with Isaac Allerton continuing in his role as Assistant Governor. Captain Standish will still advise the Governor on military matters, as William is a man of God not so familiar with these things, and we are lucky to have Captain Standish with us. Edward speaks highly of the men leading the Colony during our evening meal, and he feels confident that we will continue to grow and prosper here. Our wish to be in control of our fate has certainly come to pass. The congregation is content to set our own rules according to God's ordinances and to keep our own council on matters of church and family.

Squanto is in the colony every day to instruct us on the right way to plant the corn and to help with the community garden in which we all work. Mary and I brought a few seeds for herbs with us, and we start a small garden behind the house. Squanto has done so much to help us. He has acted as our watchful guardian, allowing us to sleep soundly at night knowing we will not be attacked. He also guided the men around the land, showing them the best hunting and fishing places, in addition to helping with the crops. After some time, he was joined by a son of Samoset who is called Nintisqua. Together they now live with us inside the stockade, which is nearly completed. The men worked for several days to build a small hut for them to live in just across the field behind our house, and I can see them in the evenings outside their hut cooking their meals.

Abraham has befriended Nintisqua and is helping him with his English in the evenings, often sitting outside their hut using a stick to write words in the dirt. I can often hear them laughing over mispronounced and misunderstood words, and it lightens my heart to hear Abraham laugh again.

Tomorrow will be a happy day for us, a wedding, a new beginning. Edward Winslow, who lost his wife, Elizabeth, in the winter sickness, is marrying Susanna White. She also lost her husband to the sickness in December. This will be the first marriage in the new colony, and we are all excited about the opportunity to celebrate God's blessing on this union. The wedding will be at the meeting house on Fort Hill, and Mary and I are trying our best to make the setting a beautiful one, which is easy to do now with so many flowers in bloom.

As Mary comes through the door with Abraham and Daniel, I can see she has an armload of flowers and greens. "Let's see if we can tie some garland together with these vines," she suggests. It is such a nice change to do something with the boys besides hard labor, and we laugh and jostle each other, making light work of our task.

"I think that looks just beautiful," I say, stepping back to admire our work.

"I do too," says Mary. "I know Susanna will be very pleased, she's not expecting much."

It is hard not to think of my own wedding day. Our four-year wedding anniversary would have been coming up soon. A sigh escapes my lips.

"What's the matter, Sarah?" Abraham says, peering at me from underneath his long eyelashes.

"Oh nothing, just…." I don't have to say anything more, he already knows, and he wraps his arms around me, now nearly as tall as I am.

"I miss him too," he says simply, and I am not sure if the crack in his voice is his age or his emotion. I am grateful to have him with me, but I also feel the burden of this young lad under my care. He will be a man soon; will he find enough of a life here? I hope so.

The day of the wedding is warm and sunny, and from the top of Fort Hill the gentle breeze brings in the slightly salty bay air. The evergreens and flowers add their perfume to the event, and you could not ask for a more perfect day. Could it be that just a few months ago our days were black and dark, filled with death and sorrow? In some ways it feels like a long time ago, but in others, like only yesterday. Susanna and Edward look dashing in the best clothes we as a congregation could muster. Governor Bradford preforms the ceremony while the entire congregation watches, our prayers and blessings for their happiness flowing freely. We even allow ourselves a bit of a feast afterwards, a meal of wild turkey and boar as well as some early sweet peas and cabbage. It is a wonderful day and a great distraction from the months of toil that we have endured and must still endure ahead.

Samoset and his son, Nintisqua, join us for the ceremony and feast, and I am surprised at how much their English has improved in such a short time. "I am very much thankful for being allowed to share in this day with the people of my new friends," says Samoset.

"Share this day with my new friends," corrects Abraham.

"Now you stop," I say with a glare, "Samoset is doing very well with his English, probably better than you some days!" Abraham stares at his feet sheepishly, and it is clear he was enjoying being the teacher for a change. "Nintisqua, are you enjoying your English lessons too?" He looks at me with his smiling brown eyes and I can't help but smile back.

"Yes, Mrs. Bailey, and very much appreciate Abraham for his help."

"You can call me Sarah, as your father does," I say encouragingly.

"Ninti is going to take me out to show me how to track animals through the woods," says Abraham excitedly.

"Ninti?" I look at him quizzically.

"That's what I call Nintisqua, his name is just too hard to say!" he moans.

"That is disrespectful, and you should be ashamed of your laziness and apologize," I say rather sternly. I sometimes feel like I am not doing a very good job of parenting.

"It is fine with me; I don't mind if Mr. Abraham wants to call me Ninti."

"Well, that's fine between you two, but he certainly doesn't warrant *mister* in response to that behavior," I say, chastising Abraham. "So, is it safe to be out in these woods tracking animals?" I address my question to Samoset rather than his son.

"Oh yes, I have learned from my father and he from his father before him. I have taught my son, and now Nintisqua can teach Abraham. You will find that rabbits and turkeys and many other small animals are very nice to have for your meal," he says with a big grin.

"Well fine, Abraham, if Samoset says it is safe, but you mind Nintisqua and do as you are told, understand?"

It is clear that he does and that he is truly looking forward to the adventure.

The crops are doing very well in the fields and the men seem pleased with the progress we are making. Early spring harvest is well behind us, and Susanna, Mary, Elizabeth, and I are busy preparing foods for the root cellars to sustain us during the winter. We work from sunup to sundown without stopping, as we know the days will soon begin to draw short. Squanto, Nintisqua, and many of the other Indians work with the men daily to ensure a good harvest in the fall, which is rapidly approaching. There have already been a few days when I felt the need to wrap myself in my cloak early in the morning. I love the early mornings before the world begins to stir; I walk the village, which is slowly but surely emerging here along the street we have named Leiden.

I wonder what Jonathan would think about how far we have come. We are such a small group, but we have created so much from nothing. I hear a wolf baying in the distance, calling for his pack to join him on the morning hunt. "Good morning, Mrs. Bailey," says Mr. Winslow as he passes by on his way to the field.

"Good morning." I nod in his direction. The sun is just coming up over the horizon, and its pink and gold hues fill the sky with a blaze of colors, the heralding of a new day. I breathe deeply and the air fills my lungs with life and hope.

"Sarah, come and sit by me a moment," says Mary, smiling, as I come back to the house. "I have news."

"Is it your father?" He has not been well, and I worry that this would be another blow she could not bear.

"No, I have missed my course now for two months, I believe I am with child," she says cautiously.

"Oh Mary, I'm so happy for you and Edward," I say, hugging her tightly.

"I know how much you want children Sarah, and I didn't know how you would react."

I smile. "You need not worry on me; this is God's blessing for you and hopefully someday he will bless me as well."

"We have to find you a husband first," Mary says with a tone that tells me she is both teasing and serious.

"I know, but it is too soon for me to think of that, as my heart still lies on Coles Hill with Jonathan," I say, looking down at my hands in my lap. My hand that held his as we ran through the forest just nine months ago.

I look up at Mary, who is gazing at me intently. "I know you loved him dearly, as he did you, but there will be love again. I just know that God has someone for you," she says.

"I hope you are right, my dearest friend, but for now we must celebrate this new life, a new beginning."

The harvest time has begun, and we all work very hard every day cutting corn, beans, and squash and digging root vegetables. The apples too have been a delight, and we gather as many of those as we can, ripe and red on the trees. We are looking forward to making cider, which will ferment in the root cellars during the winter. The work is backbreaking, and I fall into my bed each night exhausted, as do we all. In addition to the harvest, the wash needs to be done each day, as under linens must be changed daily to keep our bodies and souls clean. Mrs. Carver passed away this week, just a few weeks after her husband, some say of a broken heart. That now leaves just six women for the day-to-day keeping of the Colony. I don't know how we will manage, but we must.

Squanto and some others of the Wampanoag tribe have gone into the wilderness to trap otter and beaver along the rivers for the furs that must be collected. While some of these furs are for clothes for both the Indians and for us, most of the pelts will be saved and sent back to England as part payment for the funding of our trip to the new world. Edward is taking Abraham with him, and he is very excited to explore more of the area outside the stockade. "You obey Mr. Crippen, and keep dry and warm," I implore Abraham as I tuck an extra biscuit in his pocket.

He kisses my forehead. "I will, do not worry about me," he says, smiling the way young men do at the start of an adventure, their hearts wide open to the world and all its possibilities. About half of the men will go along on this trip, the others staying behind to watch over the plantation. We are planning a feast when they return to celebrate the harvest, a day of thanksgiving to God for his blessings on us, a holy day of prayer and celebration.

Massasoit and some of his tribe have been coming to the Plantation for the last few days, bringing food in preparation for the feast, as he has learned the men are returning soon. He has brought deer and birds of many kinds as well as greens, corn, and some fruits, some of which I have never seen before. The Indians have created a small, temporary village just outside the stockade in which to stay for the next few days, but I have not seen any women or children with them, only men. To my surprise, nearly ninety men are now camped outside our walls and the air is filled with the clamor of voices and singing, which sounds beautiful although I do not understand the words. The Indians are skinning and preparing most of the meat, and it is up to the women to make some bread from corn and to cook the greens and squash in large pots to serve for our feast. By the time the men arrive, our day of thanksgiving preparations will be nearly complete, and tomorrow we will begin our feast.

"Abraham," I call out, waving excitedly. The men are returning, and I can see him near the front of the pack. My goodness, I think he has grown two inches since he left just a few days ago, and is that the hint of a whisker I see on his chin!

"Sarah, it was so amazing, the land, the animals we saw, we even saw a bear." Abraham cannot contain his excitement.

"What is this bear you talk of?"

"A very large wooly creature with huge claws that can kill a man with just one swipe," he says with eyes as wide as saucers.

"And you came near to this creature?" I ask, fearing the answer.

"No, not very near, the Indians kept it away with loud shouts and they threw some rocks, but I did get to see it. Ninti says a few of his tribe have killed 'em with traps and they skin them and wear their fur as a cloak."

Edward kisses Mary a few times, and it is a happy moment as we gather up the treasures the men brought back to include with our feast. Outside I can hear the voices of Squanto and Samoset in song as they accompany Massasoit and the other men of the Wampanoag to the area we have set aside for games and celebration. In this moment life feels good, it feels right for the first time in many months, and I am happy. God has so blessed us with this bounty, and it is good to celebrate.

Men being men, there is always a bit of competition whenever they get together, and this is no different. The Indians show their skill with the bow and arrow, and Captain Standish, Mr. Winslow, and a few of the other men shoot their muskets at targets the men had set up. There are foot races and other games and laughter, lots of laughter. As Mary, Susanna, Elizabeth, and I work to put the finishing touches on our feast, Nintisqua works alongside us butchering and cooking the variety of meats the Indians had brought. It is unusual to have a man working with us preparing food, but very welcome given how few women we are to cook for so many men. I'm sure deep in my bones that none of us would be standing here today if it were not for Samoset, Squanto, and Nintisqua. Their help with planting and teaching and giving us seed saved us in ways we could have never saved ourselves.

"Nintisqua, I don't know if we have properly thanked you for all that you and Squanto and the others have done for us. This day of rejoicing is not just for us to thank God but also to thank you for all that you have done, for without you we surely would have perished."

He looks at me with those brown eyes, so kind and thoughtful, his eyes rimmed with small lines like a sunburst. I realize we have been simply staring at each other for what feels like a long time, and I avert my gaze.

"Mrs. Sarah, you are kind, and do you say, pleasant to thank us on this beautiful day of feasting," he says in that warm sing-song voice.

For some reason I feel myself blush. "May I ask why there are no women of your tribe who have come to the feast?" I say shyly.

"Our women and children must stay in our camp to watch over our fires and to protect our crops from animals while the men are away," Nintisqua says.

"Oh, I hadn't thought of that," I respond, somewhat embarrassed that I had not considered that the women might be capable of taking care of their homes while the men were away. Perhaps the Wampanoag see their women more as equals than we do.

"We must all work together for the good of the tribe, our men, women, and children, just as you do here. I see how very hard you work to help with Mrs. Mary and the children. You are a strong warrior."

It was all I could do not to cry from trying so hard to contain my laughter. "Me, a strong warrior?" I say incredulously.

"In our tribe, women are strong like men, and you are strong, but what you say, more pretty?"

Now I really was giggling like a schoolgirl, hiding my face behind my apron. "Well thank you Nintisqua, I am very heartened and thank you for the compliment." I smile. No one had called me pretty in a long time, and no one had ever called me strong.

A few days later as I walk up to the top of Coles Hill, the dying sun casts long shadows through the trees and the breeze begins to turn cool. The shadows move like dancers twirling across the ground, arms intertwined. The winter is coming, and this may be my last chance to visit the place where Jonathan lies in the soil. I sit down on the hard, slightly damp ground and pull the stray grasses from around the simple cross that marks his grave. It has been over a year since we left England, and this place has become my home. The fear that I felt when we left, and even after we arrived has gone. The heartache, not yet. "I do miss you so," I whisper to the wind. But even I can tell it is time to turn my attention to the future and away from the past. It's time to live again, not just survive. Nintisqua was right; I am strong.

As I walk slowly back to the plantation, I gaze out to see the last of the sun's rays shining off the water, but there is also something else. A ship. I run as quickly as I can down the hill, the brambles and bushes grabbing and tearing at my skirt as I go. A loose rock, and I suddenly find myself half falling, half sliding down the path. As I reach out my hand to steady myself, the stones tear at my flesh. Almost there, my heart is beating nearly out of my chest, and it is all I can do to catch my breath. It is possible? A ship in the harbor—but is it friend or foe?

The stockade gate is only a few yards ahead, and I can see one of the older boys, John Cooke, standing guard. "John, run, run, get Captain Standish, run!" I yell out, my voice barely carrying over the wind, but I see him turn and sprint off. It's all I can do to make it inside the stockade, and I work quickly to close the gate behind me. It's heavy but my fear has given me strength, and as I drop the latch in place, my legs finally give out and I sit and lean against the rough wood.

The men are all running toward me now; they must have been together in the meeting house. "Sarah, Sarah, what's the matter?" I hear their voices swirling through the air. Edward helps me to my feet.

"A ship, there is a ship on the horizon," I say, still gasping for breath.

I see the disbelief on their faces. "Sarah, are you certain?"

"Yes, I'm certain."

Governor Bradford and Captain Standish quickly take control and organize a small group of men up to Fort Hill to survey what they can in the fading light. "Sarah, here, have some cider," Edward says as he hands me a cup one of the men has fetched for me.

I gulp it in huge swallows, thankful for the flush of warmth it gives me, and realize I am shivering and without my cloak. "My cloak!" I cry.

"We will find it and bring it back to you, now let's get you to the house," says Edward, already guiding me down the street between the houses. Everyone is now outside with their torches, and I can see the unease in their faces, the light flickering across the shadows of their eyes. Children standing a little closer to their mothers, babes held a bit more closely. You can almost feel the fear hanging across the street as I walk slowly toward our home. The question on all our minds goes unanswered.

They sit there, unmoving, as if frozen in place. For several weeks now the ship has remained off the tip of the Cape, and the militia have positioned and loaded a cannon on Coles Hill. The French are known to pirate along the coast and the English are no friend to them. The stress of this daily watching has become nearly unbearable. Thinking at any moment we may be attacked, everyone sleeps lightly, listening for the sounds of the cannon. At last, after nearly two weeks, the ship turns and comes into Plimouth harbor, and we can see that it is an English ship. Great relief washes over us all. We can see many people standing along the railing waiting to take the shallop to shore. It will be strange to have new people in the plantation—our group is so small, and we have become very close, almost as one family living in multiple houses.

I know that young men dream of far-off distant shores where they can go and make their fortunes—men who are not first born, who have no land and title to inherit and who must make their own way in a world that's not always kind to those who start with little. Surely that was in the back of the minds of many of the Strangers who came here with us. A chance to make their own way, in a new place without the constraints of who they were, or more importantly, were not. The *Fortune* is full of such men, roughly thirty-five of them, most unmarried. Only a few women and even fewer children. One of the wives, Martha Ford, gives birth to a son just a few days after coming ashore. The passage from England seems to have been an easy one, but their arrival an altogether different story.

To my great surprise and delight, a man on the *Fortune* who knew my family has brought a letter from my sister Margaret. Father has passed away and is buried with Richard in the churchyard. Margaret has married Richard Anglesey, as father had foretold, and is with child. Mother is still unwell and lives with them but takes no part in daily living, sadly. I am most pleased to know that my sister is well, but my heart grieves for my mother, and I pray for God's mercy on my father's soul.

"Edward, do you know why the ship stayed offshore for so long?" says Mary, a question that has been on all our minds.

"Like us when we first arrived, they questioned the barren nature of the land and the bleak shoreline. Thinking surely they had made a mistake, they were going to turn back. But after several weeks and with no provisions, they realized they must try to make landfall. Once they came into the mouth of the river, they could see some of the plantation, and so they decided to drop anchor," explains Edward, which seems quite understandable. "We did not know that they were coming, and more critically, they are very ill prepared. No provisions to spare, no pots or pans, and frankly, not even enough clothes for the winter that is to come," he adds with a tone that does not hide some contempt.

"So, what will we do? We barely have enough for ourselves," cries Mary.

Edward shakes his head. "I know my dear, but God has called on us to be merciful to our brethren, and we will make do as best we can, as we always do."

To make room for everyone in the few buildings we have erected, families are shifted around to make some of the homes into barracks of a sort for the many single young men. William Tench and his son, Phillip, would join us in our home as we all work to make space for the newcomers. We are now nine and Mary pregnant with another baby due in the spring.

Phillip would sleep with Abraham and Daniel. Mr. Tench would sleep with Mr. Richards. "We had no idea you had so little here when we left England, or we would have come better prepared," says Mr. Tench over a meager meal of venison stew.

"So many of our numbers have perished in the last year, leaving only twenty-two men for the purpose of construction and farming, it has been a challenge. Without the help of the Indians, we would not have survived," replies Edward.

Mr. Tench looks quite surprised. "I would have never imagined the savages would be responsible for your survival. I'm sure the people in England would be most shocked, as, I must say, am I."

"We owe them a great debt," I say quietly.

"You lost your husband, Mrs. Bailey?" says Mr. Tench.

"Yes, to the winter sickness."

"It is remarkable to me that any of you survived at all, praise be to God for your safety," says Mr. Tench, looking at me intently. I lower my gaze, but I can feel my cheeks flushing from his attention. "We have many young and able-bodied men with us, and we will be able to build and plant at a much greater capacity than before," observes Mr. Tench, surveying the table.

"I'm sure that is true," I say with a tinge of criticism in my voice, "but first we must survive the winter on provisions that were meant for far less people than are here today."

Mr. Tench clears his throat and shifts in his chair, clearly uncomfortable with my observation. "Yes, indeed, Phillip and I will do our best not to be a burden," he says.

I realize I was being harsh; they could not have fully understood what they would be coming to. "I'm sorry, Mr. Tench, I didn't mean that you and your son were not welcome here, you most certainly are, and we thank God for your safe passage," I say, trying to sound more welcoming.

He is staring at me again, and this time I am sure Mary and Edward have both noticed—how could they not? "William, Mrs. Bailey, please call me William," he says as he lightly squeezes my hand resting on the table.

"Sarah," I reply, "just Sarah."

William and Phillip quickly become part of our household, and despite the winter cold, the men from the *Fortune* do in fact begin building new houses right away. The going is slow, but they're making progress. Once darkness settles in, we gather around the fire and William and Edward exchange stories to entertain the boys while Mary and I clean up after the evening meal. Abraham and Phillip are becoming fast friends, and soon they are begging to take a day off from building to do some trapping with Nintisqua. Phillip has not yet been outside the stockade and can't wait to see for himself this vast land he hears about each night. Edward, William, and I agree to let the boys go for just one day with our blessing, and Abraham is beyond excited to show Phillip his prowess at tracking and setting traps.

It is not a terribly cold morning when Nintisqua calls at the house to collect Phillip and Abraham, but nonetheless the boys are well bundled up and provisioned for their day's adventure. I trust they will behave, and I am reassured by the fact that Nintisqua knows his way around these woods better than anyone. I have no doubt they will have a joyous and hopefully productive day, perhaps bringing home a rabbit or two to add to our evening meal.

But by mid-morning the sky has begun to darken, and the clouds appear angry as they roil across the gray sky. By the time we sit for our mid-day meal it has begun to snow. At first the flakes are small and barely stick to the ground, but within hours, the snow is coming at a furious pace and the winds have picked up considerably. I can't help but check outside the door every few minutes for a sign of the group's return, but I can no longer even see the end of the street. The snow, which had been fine earlier in the day, now comes down with flakes the size of a dog's paw and clings to every surface. The wind whips the snow wildly so that it appears to be coming from every direction.

"It will be fine Sarah, you know Nintisqua will take good care of the boys," says Mary reassuringly, just as Edward and William come through the front door.

They are covered in white just from their short walk from the end of the street, and I rush to them, hoping they bring word. "Have you seen the boys?"

"No, we were hoping they were here," says William, tension evident in his voice.

"We've not seen them since they left this morning." I feel a tightness in my chest that I haven't felt for some time.

"Not to worry just yet, I'm sure they are fine," says Edward as he shakes off his coat and hat.

"No need to panic," agrees William, although panicking is exactly what I am doing.

"We should go and look for them," I say as I set about gathering up my cloak and scarf.

"No, not now, Sarah," says William, gently guiding me toward a chair by the fire. "It's certainly not safe for you and not even for Edward and me. We will have to trust Nintisqua's wisdom and God's grace to keep the boys safe and to return them to us." He lays a blanket across my lap. "I promise you as soon as we can, we will go and look for the boys, but for now, we all just need to be patient and to trust in God." I can see the concern in his eyes. I also see something else, his genuine care for me, for Abraham and Phillip, and I am a bit comforted.

"William, I'm going to alert the others to be watchful in case the boys arrive at one of the other homes first," Edward says, putting his coat back on.

"Yes, I think that is wise," William replies. "I'll stay here in case they return."

As the snow continues, a hush falls over the plantation and not a sound can be heard outside; it's as if the world has come to a stop. Only the crackling fire and an occasional cry from Mehitable break the stillness. I sit quietly and stare at the fire, thinking of the first time I saw Abraham. He was such a handsome little boy, full of excitement and wonder. Laughing at everything, constantly muddy and dirty, and with a smile nearly as endearing as Jonathan's. He is growing into a fine young man with a whole future ahead of him. Or so I hope; it would be most unkind if his life were also to be cut short like his brother's.

I have come to love him as my own child, and although he is a child no more, the thought of losing him is more than I can bear. I lost my own brother when he was about this age, then Jonathan…no, I couldn't lose Abraham too. I feel a tear begin to slide down my face and then the gentle tip of William's finger as he wipes it away. "They're going to make it home, Sarah, please don't cry," he says softly. I want to believe him, I want to trust that God will protect them, but sadly God has disappointed me so many times before that I just can't be sure.

I hear voices outside the door, and William and I leap nearly in unison to open it, but it is only Edward. "No sign of them yet, I'm afraid," he says. "Now that it's dark I have to believe they will settle in somewhere for the night and try to wait this out, as I would."

William nods in agreement.

"They are going to be out there all night?" I feel the words catching in my throat and turn quickly away to hide the flood of tears that I can now no longer contain. Mary wraps her arms around me, holding my head to hers, my wet tears splashing onto her cheeks. Mr. Richards brings in more wood for the fire, and Daniel helps Mary with the evening meal, but I cannot bring myself to eat. Is Abraham eating? Is he cold? I can't help but think we were wrong not to go look for them. William pulls a chair up next to mine. "You should get some rest," I say as I look at him, the firelight reflecting the tension on his face.

"I'll stay up with you," he says softly.

We talk for a while, and William tells me all about his upbringing in Hamptonshire, not far from where my own parents were raised. His father was a dairy farmer with a large parcel of land on which to feed his cows. William was the sixth boy, born to his parents in 1588, and one of eleven children in his family. By 1606 he had married a girl from his village, Anne, and she gave birth to Philip just a year later. It was a difficult birth, and sadly she did not survive. William lived with his brother and his family for nearly twelve years helping on the farm, but the family grew to such proportions that the dairy could no longer provide for them all. After some time, he decided to take Phillip to Plimouth, where he worked on the docks. He was there when the *Mayflower* left for the new world, and he decided that he too wanted to see what this grand new adventure could provide. He and Phillip left on the next ship headed for the Plimouth Plantation.

I think about my own coming to the new world, driven by very different needs than his. We had been escaping something rather than seeking something, and yet here William and I both are, in the same place, feeling the same fear.

At some point I must have drifted off to sleep, as I am startled by a sudden rush of cold air and snow blowing in from the door. There in the darkness, barely visible in the remaining firelight, stands a very wet and snow-covered Nintisqua and, behind him, Phillip. But where is Abraham? In an instant William is up, his arms wrapped around Phillip, but I stand frozen in place, afraid to speak, to even breathe.

"Mrs. Sarah," Nintisqua says slowly, coming toward me, his hair frozen with snow, his furs matted and wet. "I am sorry to say that during the night on our way back to the stockade, Abraham became lost from us. We tried our best to find him, but in this very heavy snow and the darkness, we could not."

I sit back down on the chair. "Is he dead?"

"I do hope that he is not," says Nintisqua cautiously. "I have taught him how to survive in the woods and he will do what needs to be done. I returned with Mr. Phillip to see he is safe, but I am going back out for Abraham and I will not return until I find him." He holds his clenched fist against his chest. "It is my promise to you, Mrs. Sarah."

"I'm going with you," says William quickly, gathering up his coat.

My heart leaps into my throat. "William, are you sure…" I say, feeling both grateful and terribly frightened.

"We will find him," he says as he wraps his arm around my shoulder, holding me close to him, close enough to feel his breath on my skin.

I should pull away from such familiarity from a man not my husband, but it is all I can do not to wrap both my arms around him and pull him even closer. "Thank you, please be careful. Phillip and I will be waiting for you and praying fervently that God will keep you all safe."

"When I return, dear Sarah, we will talk about the future, our future," whispers William softly.

My eyes brim with tears. "Yes, we will," I whisper as I watch him go quickly out the door.

I do not know what the day will bring, but I am afraid, very afraid.

By morning the snow has stopped, and the ground is blanketed with a cover of white undisturbed by either man or beast. The sun glistens off the wintery covering, magnifying the crystals in the air, and the wind is still and calm. Edward and several of the other men make their way to the stockade gate to clear enough snow for it to be opened and to determine if it would be possible to send out a search party. In some places the snow hits a man's knees, making it very difficult to move about, and it seems unlikely that anyone could manage it. I stand outside shivering in the cold, leaning against the house, my eyes fixed on the end of the street. Nothing, no movement of any kind. "Sarah, come in, you're going to catch your death of cold," begs Mary, who has come to the door with Mehitable perched on her burgeoning belly. "Go, you mustn't get chilled, I'll be fine," I insist as I push them back inside and close the door against the cold.

The sun is just beginning to drop behind the trees, their shadows growing long across the white landscape. It is growing colder in the fading light of the day, and it chills me to the bone. I am starting to face the realization that they are not going to return today, perhaps not at all. Phillip without his father, and me without my last tie to Jonathan, my dear Abraham. I reluctantly turn to go inside when a motion in the distance catches my eye. I stop; my breath freezes in my chest. I see something, but what is it? Or…who is it?

All the men have long since returned to their homes, deciding the snow was too deep for a search party, and I have seen no one all day except for the occasional wood-gathering trip. I wait, and slowly but surely the movement in the distance comes closer and closer. It is a man, I think, but he looks odd. There is another man, too. Suddenly I am wading through the snow, moving as quickly as I can. It is Nintisqua and William, who has Abraham slung over his shoulders as he carries him to me through the snow.

"William, William!" I scream, my voice a mix of fear and relief. Doors fly open around me as people come out to see what is happening. The snow feels more like mud as I struggle to lift my legs and move myself forward. William's face finally comes into focus, red from his effort, icicles on his eyebrows and in his beard. Nintisqua looks exhausted and spent. Abraham seems limp, and I am sure he must be dead.

Finally, the gap closes, and I am able to see for myself that Abraham is very much alive, moving slightly and groaning with each step that William takes. "Quickly Sarah, go and stoke the fire and prepare a place for Abraham near it, and draw some fresh cider and a cloth with some water, hurry now," grunts William, sweating from his efforts.

I retrace my steps, more quickly now, using the path I had already created, and I burst into the house, startling everyone inside. "Edward, please come and help," I plead urgently as I relay to Mary what we need. I follow Edward back out to the street, where he relieves William of his burden. It is all William and Nintisqua can do to make it to the house, and Elder Brewster and Mr. Winslow have come out from their homes to help them along. Soon the house is full of men working to revive the rescuers, while Mary and I tend to Abraham on the floor.

"What happened?" I ask urgently.

"After he was lost from us, he did as he should and found a place to stay the night where he could cover himself with limbs from the tree and use the snow to make a cave," says Nintisqua, barely able to speak as he lowers himself into a chair. "I was able to track him this morning, but he had left his den. We finally found him; he was lying next to the river. It looked that he had gone for water but somehow fell in and barely saved himself from the rushing river." I gasp, for surely, he feels as cold as ice even though he is now lying next to the roaring fire. His lips are blue and his skin ashen, the color of the gray sky when no sun can get through. It seems like no blood runs through his body at all.

We hurriedly remove all his wet clothes and wrap him in warm blankets. On his forehead, a large raw and painful-looking gash, one whole side of his face covered in blood. "I think he must have hit his head on a rock when he fell in the river," William says over my shoulder. In an instant I am on my feet. My reticence gone, I throw my arms around him and hold him tightly. I know everyone in the room is staring at us, but at this moment, I do not care. No one chastises me; in fact, no one speaks at all.

"Are you well?" I whisper.

"Yes, Nintisqua and I took turns carrying him. I'm cold and tired but I will be fine now that I am back with you and Phillip," William whispers back.

I reluctantly release him and kneel next to Nintisqua, now sitting next to Abraham on the floor. "I cannot thank you enough for what you have done. God has blessed our family by bringing you to us for this moment, and I am truly thankful to him and to you," I say, holding his hand in mine.

He smiles at me through his weariness. "I made a promise to you, Mrs. Sarah, and I would not, what you say, fix my promise to you."

"Break, you wouldn't break your promise," I hear faintly. It is Abraham.

Right there in front of the fire, Abraham lying on the floor, William asks me to be his wife, and I say yes. I never could have imagined the turn this day would take. This day of waiting, watching, and fearfulness has ended in the most magical and wonderful of moments. A wife again, a new life when I thought many times that my life had died along with Jonathan. We celebrate this night for all that God has wrought in our lives, and William and I stay up all night talking about our future. Where to build our home—a home of my own finally, my dream is going to come true.

CHAPTER THREE
A NEW BEGINNING

With the warmer weather now fully upon us, the men have been working on our home for the last month. We could not marry till it was complete, and while it has seemed as though that day would never arrive, it is now done, and the day is here. The house is very nice, and William and the men have done a wonderful job of building it—my own home, our home, at last. I would never have thought that this is how my life would be here, but now I cannot imagine it any other way.

We stand hand in hand in front of Governor Bradford, the Crippens, a few of those who traveled here with me on the *Mayflower*, and of course Abraham and Phillip. For a moment my mind wanders back to the day I wed Jonathan, a happy day indeed. This, the day of my second wedding, is no less happy, to be sure. I have a new husband, a new son, and a future where there once was none. The women have been busy helping to prepare the inside of our home as a wedding gift, and Edward, Phillip, and Mr. Richards have been busy making furniture. A table and chairs at which to eat, a bed for William and me, and one for each of the boys. Two chairs to sit by the fire and two chests, one for our clothes and linens and one for pots and other cooking things.

Our house is just like the one Edward built for Mary, one room with a hearth at one end, except that we added a wall separating the two sleeping areas, the boys on one side, William and I on the other. I have not lain with a man in nearly two years now, and I am both nervous and excited. I have grown to love William dearly these last few months and remember each day the gift of Abraham he has given me. But he has also given me more. I was not sure I would feel this love for another again. I knew I would marry, but marry for love? I did not think it would be so. My heart is warm and full, and I cannot now imagine my life without him.

I've been working every night to embroider our linen and passing the time by helping Mary with the babe, a boy born a few months ago, whom they have named Samuel. "I imagine you will be very happy to finally have your home to yourself," I say to Mary as I gather up the last of our things to move to our home at the other end of Leiden Street.

"No, my dear Sarah, I will miss your company and your help, but I am so very happy for you and William to be on to your own life, and hopefully you will have a babe soon to be a friend to my Mehitable and Samuel," she says with a glint in her eye. I have to admit that vision of the future occupies a lot of my own thoughts of late, and I surely hope that Mary is right. But I also know not every woman is blessed with a child, and even after several years Jonathan and I did not have a babe. Perhaps this time will be different, God will decide. I walk down the street. Now, with nearly twelve houses completed, the men are starting on a street to cross this one where the common meeting house lies. An additional store house has also been completed at our end of the street to make the distribution of seed and provisions easier, especially in the winter months, which can make the street a sea of mud. A real town is springing up from the dirt, and my new life lies just ahead on the right.

William is waiting for me at our door, a broad smile on his face. "Mrs. Tench, welcome to your home," he says, making a broad sweeping bow as he opens the door. The smell of the house is so inviting. The wood smells crisp and clean, mixed with the grass and reeds in the thatch that blend with the fragrance of the wildflowers arranged on the table. A beautiful pewter pitcher filled with cider, a gift from Mary, also sits on the table next to some biscuits and fruit. The furniture is broad and sturdy with solid legs and arms, and two rockers are next to the fire, which already crackles in the hearth, its flames spreading a warm glow throughout the room. The one window's shutters are open, letting in the slightly damp breeze and allowing the sun's rays to splay along the floor.

"It's perfect," I say as I kiss William softly.

He pulls me closer to him, kissing me more deeply, and I feel myself relaxing in his arms. Deep within me a stirring, a longing so intense it takes my breath away. He smells of soap, tobacco, love, and life. My life, my husband, my home.

"You're leaving," I say with surprise as he heads for the door.

"Not right now, no," he says with a smile as he lowers the bar on the door.

I smile at him. "What about the boys?" I say with the giggle of a schoolgirl.

"They can come back later," he says huskily as he gathers me up and carries me to our bed in the corner.

Abraham and Phillip never did come home last night, another gift from Mary, I'm sure. I look at William lying quietly next to me, his arm across his face shading his eyes. He is a handsome man to be sure, strong and wise, and oh, I am so lucky to have him. A wonderful father to Phillip and now to Abraham, I know he would be wonderful with our children too. I need to get up to stoke the fire and prepare a morning meal for him, but I want just one more minute to feel this peace and happiness in my soul. *Thank you, God, you have not abandoned me after all*, I say to myself. William stirs and I slide closer to him, laying my body the whole length of him, entwining my feet with his. He pulls me close and kisses me on the forehead. "Good morning, my dearest," he says with his eyes still closed.

"Good morning, husband," I reply. He smiles, and I truly have never been happier.

The planting now in, Governor Bradford has organized a mission to see Massasoit at the village of Pokatoket. We need to ensure our continued peace with the Indians, and it was decided to give Massasoit a chain of copper as a show of our desire to continue to maintain our good relationship. While the Indians are always welcome visitors, their frequent trips are a strain on our food stores, and we are unsure how the fall crop will come in. Any friend of Massasoit will always be welcome, however, and we will know that he has blessed a visit from anyone who arrives bearing this chain. Mr. Winslow and Mr. Hopkins join Governor Bradford on this trip, leaving Captain Standish in charge while they are gone. I am grateful that William is not going, happy to keep him home and out of harm's way.

I need not have worried though, as the men return in just a few days with a good report.

A shallop has arrived in the harbor, with ten men from the *Sparrow*, a fishing vessel. They have anchored at a place called Damaris Cove Island in the north, and they have sent this small boat to explore along the coast. It is odd now to have visitors from time to time, as we were so much alone during our first year, except for the Wampanoags, who were of so much help to us. While the fishermen brought no provisions, it is good to hear their news of the world and to see new faces. They seem impressed with what we have been able to accomplish with so few men and such limited supplies. Little do they know how very close we all came to perishing during those first few months.

It is not long before more men arrive, a ship every few months now, it seems. Some men from the *Charity* and *Swan* have scouted the area and have decided to settle just north of here. Their ships and men will spend the late summer here while plans are laid out for the new settlement. Sixty more men have now joined our plantation, and not one woman.

"I am spent," I say wearily as I wipe the sweat from my forehead on my apron.

"Me too," Mary says, stirring a pot with one hand and holding Samuel with the other. The full heat of the summer is now upon us, and its warm and welcome sunshine has turned into a sweltering and nearly unbearable heat. "We simply can't continue cooking for this many men with so little help," she continues firmly.

"Agreed, but what shall we do?"

"Let's go speak to Governor Bradford," she says with an assertiveness I've not heard in her voice before.

Something is going to change, that is certain. Mary strides down the street with a gait bordering on a march as we make our way over to Governor Bradford's home. Mary knocks on the door rather harshly, and we are both startled when the door quickly swings open to a rather flummoxed governor standing on the other side. "Why do you knock on my door so loudly and so early," he asks, not bothering to hide his irritation.

I look at Mary, who does not back down. "My apologies for the disturbance, but this could not wait. Something must be done and done now," she says firmly.

Suddenly and without warning, my breakfast reappears and I empty the contents of my stomach onto Governor Bradford's doorway and his shoes. I am mortified.

Mary, however, takes it all in stride. "See, this is what I mean, we are working so hard we are making ourselves sick," she says as she uses a cloth the Governor gives her to wipe up me, the stoop, and the governor's shoes.

"Sarah, come in and sit down, I will get you some water."

I feel less queasy in the cooler air of the house and the comfort of the chair. "I'm so sorry Governor, I don't know what came over me," I say, taking small sips of the water he offers.

"We need help. We cannot do so much of the cooking for this group of now over one hundred men," blurts out Mary.

"I agree," says the governor, nodding as he looks back at us both with consternation on his face. "Between the work of the children and caring for your own men and cooking for the entire settlement, it is more than you should bear." He seems thoughtful for a moment. "Starting tomorrow, we will give to your service the boys who are not breeched, and also I will ask Nintisqua if he will assist you. He is very skilled at cooking and I'm sure he will gladly help."

"Thank you," I say rising to go, "and I am so sorry for my earlier indiscretion."

As soon as we are out the door Mary grabs both my arms, turning me to look square into her eyes. "Sarah, have you missed your course?" she says, her mouth turning up ever so slightly at the corners.

I think for a moment. What day is this? Have I? "Yes, I think I did, yes." The realization suddenly hits me like a rogue wave on the shore. "Mary, I have to tell William," I practically scream as I grab her hand and begin running toward my house.

"You go," she says, laughing as I run all the way home.

I fling the door open. "William, William," I call out, tears of joy beginning to run down my face. No one, the house is empty, he must be in field. I turn and head to the gate, slower now but still with purpose. I am with child; I am with child? The words keep running through my head. Could it be after all this time, I am going to have a child of my own? I love Abraham and Phillip to be sure, but a babe, truly a blessing of my own, would make my life complete. I walk with purpose, and it only takes a few minutes to reach the rise at the edge of the field.

At the field, I see Arthur Smith, a friend of William's who had come with him on the *Fortune*. Arthur often sups with us, and he is a true friend to us both. "Sarah, what are doing here, is all well? Are you hurt?"

"No, why would you say that?" I reply.

"I can see that you have been crying."

"Oh, yes." I wipe my eyes on my apron. "No, I'm fine, do you know where William is?" I am barely able to keep from sharing my news, but surely the father should know before his friend!

"Just there, beyond that cluster of trees," Arthur points to the field in the north. "Do you want me accompany you?" he asks with a look of concern.

"No, no, I'm fine, thank you Arthur," I say with a huge smile on my face, giving his arm a squeeze as I head toward the other field to find William.

"I'm very happy for you both," he yells after me. I can only laugh as I pick up my pace. At the bottom of the hill, I see William just a wee distance on the other side of a small creek that runs through the field next to the trees.

"William!" He glances up from his hoeing, shading his eyes against the sun. He is so handsome standing there, his shirt slightly damp from the heat of the day, his face tan except for the small lines around his eyes.

"Sarah?" He drops his hoe and splashes through the creek, heading for me as quickly as he can. "Sarah, what's happened, you never come to the field," he says, scanning my face for clues.

"I was sick this morning, at Governor Bradford's," I say quickly.

"If you are ill, why are you here? You could have sent someone to fetch me."

"I'm not ill, I'm with child…" The words hang there in the air between us, and I can't believe I have said them out loud. His eyes soften as he takes me in his arms and holds me tightly. The world seems to quiet around us.

A few birds sing out their song from the trees in the grove, and the wind barely rustles the leaves. In this moment,

I feel a peace and happiness I thought I would never feel. "Are you sure, my dearest?" William says finally.

"Yes, I'm sure."

"You are going to be the most wonderful of mothers, and I am so thankful to God for this blessing."

As I look at his face, I know that all my trials in this life have brought me to this moment. "God has indeed blessed us, and we are going to have a babe." I smile at him. Life is good.

But all is not well in the colony. Disputes have been born between the men who came most recently to our shore and the rest of the plantation. While their help with the harvest has been most welcome, several of the new men have been charged with stealing from the general stores. The Indians have also complained to Governor Bradford that they are stealing their corn as well. Ill prepared for this new life, they have disregarded their honor and are acting obstreperously. They have moved on now to their own settlement, called Wessagusset, but more troubles have of late transpired, and it does not bode well for Plimouth or for them.

Winter will be here soon, and they are consuming their stores so quickly they will have little left to sustain them during the harsh cold months and have asked for our help. The leadership of the plantation, William now among them, met today to determine how to address this circumstance. "So, what are we to do?" I implore William, my hands resting on the small mound of my stomach now protruding through my dress. "We can barely manage for ourselves, how can we possibly take on the burden of another sixty men for the winter?"

"It has been decided we will engage in a joint trading mission to the Indians with a few of the trinkets and goods that the men of Wessagusset have brought with them. While I wish these foolish men had brought provisions instead, perhaps we can make the best of it in this way," William says pragmatically.

"Are you going?" I ask, hoping my voice does not hint at the trepidation I feel.

"No, in your condition we decided it was best if I stayed behind. We don't think there will be trouble, but no need to tempt fate."

I sigh, more loudly than I intended.

"You would be worried for me," William says with a smile.

I lean over and kiss him softly on the lips. "I would be lost without you, my dear."

"I will always be here for you," he says as he kisses my hand. For a moment I can't help but remember that Jonathan had said those very words to me when we left England.

The trading mission was somewhat helpful, but by November Governor Greene of Wessagussett has died and John Sanders has taken charge. Winter has now arrived in its full glory, with wind and snow swirling across the landscape. It reminds us we are still at God's mercy in this place, no matter how far we have come. I spend my days cooking and cleaning as the four of us huddle in our house, keeping warm by the fire. Phillip and Abraham have undertaken the task of building a cradle for the baby, with supervision from William of course.

They have grown into fine young men, and Phillip, now nearly fifteen, is beginning to talk of his future. With so few women here, it is no surprise he might be thinking of leaving. "What about the young Miss Remembrance Wilton, the niece of John Howland?" I ask Phillip and immediately notice the redness increase in his cheeks.

"I don't think she likes me," he mutters.

"She told him she thought he was a cockscomb," snorts Abraham.

"She did not," retorts Phillip, slapping Abraham on the arm.

I try hard not to laugh at Phillip, but the movement of my now rather rotund belly gives me away and he glares at me as if I had slapped him in the face.

"I'm sorry Phillip, I wasn't laughing at you but rather Miss Wilton's choice of words," I assure him. "Have you done something to make her think you are an arrogant young man?"

"No, I don't think so," he says, glaring at the floor.

"Well, I suggest you consider making amends with Miss Wilton for any perceived slight and see where that gets you," I say, trying to sound wiser than I should at not quite twenty-three years of age. It would have been so much easier to be a mother to Phillip if I'd had an opportunity to grow into the role with him rather than starting with him at such an advanced age.

"The cradle is looking very good, you two," says William. "Phillip, you seem to have a real knack for woodworking. Why don't I inquire with Francis Eaton and see if he will take you on as an apprentice? You are a bit old to start, but you are a quick learner and already possess some skills from what I can see."

Phillip looks up from his work, his eyes aglow at the prospect. "Really, Father?"

"Yes, I will speak with him when I see him at the assembly tonight."

"There is an assembly tonight," I say, tilting my head to indicate this is more question than statement.

"Yes, we need to talk about what is happening in Wessagusset," says William, clearly concerned. "They are still trading with the Indians for food and now in much distress as they have almost nothing left. Seeing their consternation, the Indians have increased the price, and so they are now trading their clothes and other things which they need."

I stare at him in horror, my hand immediately going to my stomach. "That is awful William, what will happen?"

William shakes his head, clearly having no answer to offer.

I return to my knitting—the babe will be here before I know it, and it feels like there is still so much to prepare. I lay my head against the back of the chair and close my eyes as I feel those little kicks, which have been steady now for a few weeks. It is a comfort to me to know the babe is strong and growing, and I daily ask God's blessing on us both. I am nervous of the labor to come, but Mary and Susanna will be here with me, both experienced, and I will trust myself to their care.

February has come cold and bitter, the winds howling around the house like a wolf looking for its mate. My dearest has tried his best to seal any cracks, but we still must keep the fire burning brightly to stay warm. My time is almost here, and just getting up from my chair has become an effort and one I seldom attempt without help. I can feel the babe has shifted down, and I must use the chamber pot now every hour it seems. William is brewing birthing ale at the hearth in preparation for my lying in. The days are so short and the nights long and cold. Tonight, I cannot find a way to be comfortable—it reminds me of sleeping on the ship, the hard wood floor digging into my hip and shoulder.

But I am here in my bed, which William has stuffed with extra wool on my side for my comfort, so I do not know why I cannot rest. In my belly, I feel a new a tightness, and it is becoming more persistent. Beads of sweat form on my forehead even though the air is cool, and the ache in my back has become like a hot poker. My mind drifts between the pain and the anticipation of the birth to come. "William, I think you need to fetch Mary and Susanna, it is time," I say finally.

The sun comes up after a very long night, which I would not have survived if not for God's grace. The pain is more than I have ever experienced and more than I thought I could ever endure, but the babe is now almost here. "Sarah, drink some of this," Mary says, offering me another mug of birthing ale. It warms my throat and comforts my mind. "Now when the next pain comes, you must push to move the babe out." Push…I am exhausted, and the thought of pushing seems overwhelming, but I know I must.

I nod, grabbing the cloth straps attached to the bed as the pain courses through me again like the weight of the world on my body. "Push, push my dear, you are almost there," encourages Susanna. I bear down with everything I have and let out a howl like that of a wounded animal. In the sudden rush of blood coming from between my legs, a head is now visible, and I watch as slowly Mary coaxes the rest of the babe out. I lie back on the bed, exhausted, and Mary cleans the child, whose cry now fills the room. I can feel hot tears sliding onto the bedding below my head.

"William, this is your daughter," says Susanna as she hands the babe, now wrapped in swaddling, to him. I watch as he unwraps her just enough to get a better look.

"A girl, my dearest, a sweet, beautiful girl, just like her mother," he says, sitting down beside me and handing her to me. I take her in my arms, and in that moment, the agony of the night passes away and there is only joy. As I hold this little bundle in my arms, I cannot believe she is my own. A daughter and a mother have both been born this day by the grace of God, and I am truly blessed.

"We will be going now," says Mary, "and we will keep the boys at our house for a few days while you get settled in."

"So, what shall we call this beautiful gift from God?" asks William, smiling. "We could name her Elizabeth, after your mother?" My mother, was she even still alive? Would she ever know she had a granddaughter? "Sarah?"

"No, I don't think so. I think we will call her Patience."

He kisses me on the cheek. "It is indeed a most perfect name."

Chapter Four
Trials and Tribulations

The chill in the air is starting to wane and the snow has turned to rain as the days begin to warm and the shadows grow a bit longer. Patience is suckling well and growing fat and happy. She is already a great source of fascination for her father and her brothers, who do their best to entertain her in the evenings while I prepare our meal. The warmer air has not, sadly, brought with it better news from the north, and now, I truly fear that our peaceful life may be disturbed.

Some of the tribes near the Wessagusset settlement have moved their huts closer to the colony, which some there have seen as a threat. A messenger arrived yesterday to talk with Governor Bradford and the councilmen. Edward Winslow has said he has also heard from Massasoit that several of the tribes, especially the Massachusetts, Nauset, Paomet, and Capawack, are banding together, perhaps to attack the settlement. Edward had saved the life of Massasoit during a hunt, and Massasoit now feels kindred spirit with us, especially since the death of Squanto some months ago.

William comes late to our evening meal, and I can see concern in his eyes. "Abraham, would you and Phillip take Patience outside for a few minutes to give her some fresh air before it gets dark?" I ask, not wanting the boys to hear too much until I know more. William eats quickly and I allow him to finish his ale before I ask any questions. As it turns out I don't need to ask; William is quick to tell me all that is happening, including that Captain Standish is taking a small force to Wessagusset to see what needs to be done. "You are not going, I hope?"

William takes my hand in his. "You are shaking my dear, are you well?"

I want to lie, to say I am unwell, if that will keep him here. "No, I am fine. You are going, then?"

"Yes, I need to go, I have more fighting experience than many of the men here—which isn't to say much—and Standish trusts me, which will be critical on this trip."

I rise to clear the dishes from the table.

"Sit down, leave that, it can wait." I do as he asks but can barely bring myself to meet his gaze. "You will be fine; I'll only be gone a few days, and you have Phillip and Abraham here to help you with Patience."

I know it will likely be so, but still. Sometimes God does not see things in the way we would like them to be seen.

Would it be fine? I sleep fitfully that night knowing William will leave in the morning, and the sun rises much too soon.

"I want to go too, Father," begs Phillip.

"No son, not this time. I need you here to look after the house, Sarah, and the babe. You will be the man of this house until I return," he says, his hand on Phillips's shoulder.

"Yes Father, I will take care of everything," Phillip replies, and I can see him stand a bit straighter and taller.

"Thank you, my son. Abraham, you will help him and mind him," reminds William as he pats Phillip on the shoulder, kisses Patience on the forehead, and gathers up his things. I am standing in the doorway as he makes his way down the street, when suddenly he turns and sprints back to me.

"Did you forget something?"

"Yes, yes I did," he says, taking me in his arms, kissing me, and enveloping me in his embrace. "I love you my dear Sarah, and I will return as soon as I can," he whispers.

"I love you my dearest, God's speed."

In an instant, he is gone.

The house has been quiet. Phillip and Abraham spend most of their time preparing the fields, and we have a small garden of our own now, which also needs tending. I take Patience out in her basket while I work to continue clearing the patch of dirt behind the house so we can plant squash and beans and some herbs. The day is clear and the sky is blue, the ground fragrant and soft from the spring rains. I see Mr.

Wright walking past and stop him to see if he has any word. "No, I'm afraid not Mrs. Tench, we have no word from Wessagussett. But I'm sure your husband is well," he says as he tips his hat. If he has no word, how could he know that William is well? I return to my hoeing, but my mind is far, far away until Patience's cry of hunger brings me back to earth.

Three days have turned into four and now five, and the men have not yet returned. Moments with Patience are blissful and calm my mind, even if only briefly. I think I'm starting to see the whisp of a smile, one I hope her father will be back to see soon. Patience is changing before my eyes, and I hope for him that he does not miss too much of her.

Mary and Edward come with Daniel, Mehitable, and Samuel to share our evening meal. Mr. Richardson passed away last month, and I thought it would cheer Mary to see Patience. Mehitable is on her feet and into everything, and Daniel chases her in the grass behind the house while Edward shows Phillip and Abraham how to sharpen their knives, a recent gift from William.

"It's just a simple stew," I say as I put the trenchers on the table.

"It smells wonderful," Mary says as she coos at Patience on her lap, Samuel sitting up now on the floor next to her.

"I can't believe he is sitting up already," I exclaim as I scoop him up from the floor. His peals of laughter could be heard to the heavens.

"He is in a hurry to grow up, that one," says Mary as she makes room for him on her lap. "They will be home soon," she answers the question on my mind I dare not ask.

"Yes, I'm sure you are right, everyone says so," I say as I gather up Edward and the boys from the back of the house. "Edward, will you say the prayer?"

It has been a week and still no sign of William or the other men who have gone with Captain Standish, but I have heard that Nintisqua has come to see Governor Bradford, so perhaps there is some news. "Phillip, can you stay with Patience for a few minutes while I go and speak to the Governor? I won't be long," I promise as I set out along the street. As I turn the corner, I see Nintisqua coming my way and I hurry toward him. "Is there any news?" I ask, trying to keep my voice from cracking.

"Yes, Mrs. Sarah, I have heard that the men will be returning very soon. There was a very rough fight, and some men were killed from Wessagusset. Also, the Chiefs from two of the tribes were killed, very bad I say, very bad." He shakes his head in disbelief.

"Oh no, that is awful," I cry out, covering my face with my hands. "But the men from here, how are they?"

"I have not heard news to say they were harmed, but it was a bad fight so who can say. I do not know, as I have not seen it with my own eyes," he says, looking at me somberly. I stand in the street staring at him, not sure what to say or do. I hear every beat of my heart resounding in my ears as though it will surely explode. "I am with great hope that Mr. Tench is not hurt, Mrs. Sarah." Nintisqua startles me out of my own thoughts.

"Thank you Nintisqua, I so appreciate your telling me," I say softly.

I don't think I will mention this to Phillip just yet. I don't want to worry him; one of us worrying is certainly more than enough. Instead, we will focus on getting the house clean and the garden planted so that we can show William how we have kept faith in his absence. "Thank you, Phillip," I say as I take Patience back into my arms. Can he see how tightly I hold her, the lines of worry on my face? I hope not. "Abraham, would you and Phillip help with our evening meal by killing and cleaning a chicken for me?"

"Of course, we can do that," says Abraham, excited to do something useful. Chasing after a chicken will certainly keep them busy for an hour or so. As I sit and rock Patience for a few minutes, I think about the last year, such a happy time for us—our own home, our own babe, the boys nearly grown, and everyone healthy. Would it last, or would God remind me again just how fleeting happiness can be?

The sun is warm on my back, but the breeze is pleasant, and it is a good day for working in the garden. I have nearly all the herbs in, and the boys are working on a small fence to keep the rabbits and deer from eating the new growth. "So, how are my girls this morning?" I hear from over my shoulder, a voice I have heard in my dreams for many nights now. I am in his arms in an instant. "Not so tight, my dear," he says with a grimace, and I realize he has been wounded.

"William, you are hurt, what has happened to you?"

"It is a small cut. I will tell you about everything tonight but for now, I need to kiss my dearest Patience," he says as he gingerly lifts her from the basket where she is sleeping. As if on cue, she lets out a yawn followed by a slight smile, and her father just beams. "She has grown an inch while I was gone," he chuckles, kissing her on the forehead. "She is well? You are well?"

"We are now that you have returned," I say with a smile and a sigh that reveals just how tense the last few weeks have been.

William shakes hands with the boys, and they beam with pride, feeling more like men than boys, but I can see that a warm embrace would have been just as welcome.

Now that everyone is in bed, I have a chance to redress the wound on William's shoulder, where it seems he was stabbed with a knife by one of the Indians. I make a poultice of sphagnum moss as my mother taught me and place it under the dressing. It is clean and without pus and should heal well, but I can tell that it is the source of some pain and apply a warm compress to soothe it. "So, can you tell me what happened to you? Nintisqua told me that some Wessagusset men and Indians were both killed."

"Indeed," says William, "it was the most difficult of situations…

"When we arrived at Wessagusset, Captain Standish assembled all the colonists into the stockade so that we would be at our best defense. The next day a group of the natives came to meet with us in the Common House, including Chief Pecksuot, the leader of the Massachusetts. The captain had told us to be on our guard, and in case of trouble we had agreed on a signal. Our talks seemed fruitful and an understanding of the need for peace was emerging, but suddenly Standish gave the signal to attack.

"I don't know if he saw something, we did not know why he signaled, but it became a fight in just a few seconds. Standish killed Pecksuot with his own knife, and we each battled one of the Indians. I was wounded in a struggle with one of them and managed to kill him but not before he stabbed me. All but one of the Indians in the room were killed, and he got away to tell the village of what had happened. The captain then decided to attack the natives in the village—I am sure because he thought that they would now attack us in retaliation for the killing of their Chief.

"During that battle in the village, we killed many more Indians, but four of the men from Wessagusset were also killed. We brought back the head of one of the Indians to put on a pike by the main gate as a warning to other tribes that we will attack if we are provoked.

"Sadly, now the settlement at Wessagusset is no longer viable, as the colonists had been relying on the Indians for help and even bartering their labor in exchange for food. Clearly, they can no longer do that, so those men will be coming here to live in the Plimouth Plantation. I'm sure they are on their way, if not already arrived, with what few possessions they have left."

I look thoughtfully at William, trying to read the expression on his face, but there is nothing that reveals to me his inner thoughts. Had he killed a man before? Is he feeling guilt, or relief? I am not sure what to say at this moment—perhaps saying nothing is the right path. I rise and go to him, wrap my arms around him and hold him close, my cheek resting on the top of his head.

After a few moments I feel him start to cry, and I hold on even tighter until the heaving of his body stops and his breathing becomes regular again. "God's mercy is very great," I say softly, my lips pressed against his ear.

"It surely is," he says as he turns his face up to kiss me gently on the lips. "I love you dearest Sarah, you are my true love."

"My husband, you are my life and my love. You and our family are all I need in this world to be happy," I whisper back.

William rises and leads me to our bed.

Phillip is moving today to live at the shop of Francis Eaton and begin his apprenticeship to the woodworker. While I am excited for him to take this next step in his future, it will be sad not to have him around the house every day, as he is of great help to be sure. As we walk with Phillip down the street to Eaton's shop, the cry goes up in town that a ship is coming into the harbor—an English ship! Most of the town begins gathering at the dock, many of the men of the *Fortune* and some from the *Mayflower* anticipating that onboard this ship might be some of their wives and children.

The *Anne* maneuvers slowly in the harbor, turning to dock against the wharf we had completed just some months ago. We can see many women and children waving from the deck while the men handle the sails and rigging. I recognize the daughters of Elder Brewster, Patience and Fear, although they have certainly grown since I saw them last in Leiden. Next to them Elizabeth Warren, the wife of Richard, who had come on the *Mayflower*, and their five daughters, as well as the Cooke and Godbertson families. So many familiar faces —it is a joyous day indeed.

Though sadly, not everyone gets the happy reunion they were expecting, as Sarah Priest arrives to reunite with her husband Degory only to learn that he died in the first winter sickness. For now, we will take her in to our home, as I can surely understand and perhaps soothe her grief. I am almost giddy to see so many familiar faces and more importantly, so many women and girls. I'm sure Phillip, Abraham, and every young man is excited to see this sudden change in the community too. It is a day we shall not soon forget, and the arrival of many chickens, several pigs, and two dogs makes it even more exciting. The *Anne* is well equipped with much needed supplies, plate ware and ale, seed, cloth, so many things of which we are in sorely short supply.

To our astonishment, just a week later the *Little James* also arrives in the colony—a pinnace that will stay in port to support fishing and for military defense. All together an additional ninety people have joined our plantation, which is becoming a real city now.

The men start immediately to build additional houses to accommodate the new families, while many continue to sleep onboard the ships as we had done until homes can be raised. With the recent arrival of the men from Wessagusset as well as the new arrivals, there are many hands to put to work. Just two weeks after the arrival of the *Anne,* Governor Bradford marries the widow Mrs. Southworth, who had been a dear friend to the governor and his family while we were in Leiden. It is only a small ceremony, as the entire town is intent on getting homes built quickly before the winter sets in.

"Sarah, look, she's trying to stand," exclaims Abraham, holding Patience by the hands, her feet firmly on the floor, her body wiggling in delight, lifting each foot in turn and patting them on the floor.

"So she is," I reply, smiling. I love to see Abraham with her; he is so patient and loving, a good older brother. I wonder what Jonathan would think of him being the sibling to a child that was not his.

"Abraham, we need to think about what you are going to apprentice to," William says as he walks past him, stopping to ruffle his hair.

I stop stirring the cornmeal I'm preparing for our evening meal to look at Abraham. Already? He seems like just a small boy at times, not my true son but nearly so, and I can't bear to think about him leaving home.

"I think I would like to be a sailor," Abraham says assuredly.

"My boy, where did you get that idea?" I do not try to hide my surprise.

"When we were coming here Jonathan would take me up deck, and I loved watching the sea. The waves, the sky, the sound of the wind in the sails, I thought it was all just wonderful," he says, looking dreamily into the distance.

"Well, clearly you've given this some thought," I say, smiling at William and trying not to show my apprehension.

"Since the *Little James* is staying here in Plimouth, I could speak to Captain Emanuel Altham to see if he might have need of a young apprentice onboard?" William looks at me questioningly and I nod my approval.

Before I can even speak, Abraham is already off the floor and out the door to tell Phillip his news. I cannot help but laugh and Patience heartily joins in. "It is a good solution," I say to William. "He can follow his desire but stay close to us, I think it is good."

"I thought you might. He will have to understand that this is real work, not just for his pleasure, but I think he can do a fine job," William says, and I couldn't agree more.

By the time the harvest is over it is just the three of us in our home. Sarah Priest has married a fellow passenger from the *Anne*, and Abraham is living on the *Little James* and seems very happy with his decision to apprentice there. Our garden has provided us with a wonderful harvest in addition to that from the colony's fields, and we have been blessed to receive a new chicken and a piglet. William has been busy making protection for them from the winter cold out behind the garden. The wood is stacked, the larders are sufficiently prepared, and for the first time in a long time, things feel safe and secure. Within the town there is now a butcher, a miller, and a shop that makes barrels, and the common house has been enlarged to accommodate our growing community.

However, some of those who arrived most recently are struggling to adapt to life here and seem to prefer living under their own rules rather than those already established by our colony. To that end, some twenty or so of those arrived on the *Anne* and *Little James* have moved to an area south of our settlement that we are now calling Hobs Hole. It is our wish that these people thrive under their own efforts, and perhaps it is for the best. Many of those who have come of late seem ill prepared for the difficulties of this life, and some talk about going back to England on the next ship. As for us, we are settled here in our home and prepared to enjoy a quiet winter. The snow has already begun to fall, earlier it seems than last year, and I'm afraid it will be a very cold winter.

"I think it best I do some hunting tomorrow," says William as we crawl between the covers, trying to stay warm. "With the snow coming so soon it will become more difficult, and I think we could use some more game to sustain us through the winter, would you agree?"

"Yes, of course, if you think that best, I will be fine here with Patience," I say confidently. "If I need anything, Mary and Edward are just up the street."

It is still dark when William gathers up his things and heads out the door, and I bring Patience into bed with me and feed her, enjoying these last few moments before the sun rises fully to begin a new day.

Just as I am putting her back in the cradle, I hear a noise from the back of the house. "William, did you forget something?" I open the door, and the cold air swirls against my warm cheeks. No sign of William, but at the back of the garden I see the morning light glinting off the eyes of a wild and angry creature staring at me. It is a large bear, trying to get into the area where we keep the piglet. It is hard to make it out entirely in the dawning light, but I can see that it's a massive creature, grunting and snorting as it paws at the wood. Its breath makes billowing clouds of steam as it roots around the makeshift pen.

The poor piglet cries and squeals as it tries to move as far away as it can from the beast's thick and wooly paws. Fierce looking claws, nearly the length of my own hand, extended out five or six inches past the flesh with ominous intent. The animal lifts its head and sniffs the air, looking in my direction. We can ill afford to lose the piglet, but what can I do? A glint of light catches my eye and I realize William left one of the muskets near the door. I know he would have left it loaded, and without a second thought, I grab it, level it… and fire. The sound of the blast reverberates through the house with a fiendish force, rattling the plate ware and causing Patience to scream out from her cradle.

The bear roars, baring its teeth as it rises up on its hind legs and staggers back, paws thrashing at the air. I'm not sure if I hit it; either way I had expected it to run away. I grab the shot bag and powder and load the gun as quickly as I can, preparing to shoot once more, when the animal, without warning, simply falls over, still. I raise the musket and fire again; this time I am sure I hit it. I lean against the doorway to catch my breath for just a moment before I drop the musket and hurry to Patience, who is still crying most loudly in her cradle. "It's fine, my dearest, it's fine," I whisper as I hold her tightly and rock her from side to side.

"William, Sarah, are you safe?" calls out Edward Winslow, our neighbor, now banging at the front door, and I quickly open it to let him in.

"In the back," I point with one hand, still clutching Patience with the other.

Edward runs out the back door and sees the bear lying there on the ground. "Where is William?" he cries out, fear crackling through his voice.

"He's not here, he has gone hunting," I say, still a bit breathless.

"I don't understand?"

"I shot it, the bear."

He looks at me with a shocked expression. "Did it hurt you?"

"No, it was after the piglet, is it dead?"

"Yes, quite dead," Edward says. The piglet! Edward goes in search of him and finds the frightened animal hiding under some planks of wood that had fallen when the bear collapsed. "He is here and unharmed it seems." I let out a sigh of relief. "Sarah, you are a most strong and capable woman," Edward says with admiration in his voice.

"I know," I say, as the corners of my mouth turn up just a bit.

By the time William returns later that evening, the whole town is talking about the woman who killed the bear. Before he even made it back to the house, he had heard the story several times, and I'm sure it became more elaborate with each retelling. "So, I go hunting, and it is you who kill an animal right in our own yard," says William, smiling as he hugs me close to him. He inspects the dead animal, still lying in the yard where it had fallen. "You should have just shut the door and let the creature have the piglet, it could have attacked you and even Patience," he says.

"I was not going to let that animal take our piglet, William, we need it for the future meat it will provide," I say, somewhat stubbornly. "Besides, I knew exactly what to do. Captain Standish taught the women how to use a musket when we first arrived, and it is a lesson I have not forgotten."

"I thank God you and Patience were not harmed, and thankfully, we'll have the meat from the bear, which is most welcome since I found only one small turkey," says William, laughing at the irony.

The winter is indeed a harsh one, the snow so deep at times that we can barely get out of the door for firewood. I spend many days mending and making new clothes for Patience and for the new babe, as I am with child again, a true blessing from God. Phillip has come for our evening meal, but he eats little and seems anxious and distant. "Is all well with your apprenticeship?" I inquire.

"Yes, it is quite well, but…" he trails off. William and I look at each other and then at Phillip expectantly. "Father, I would like for you to help me, as I want to become betrothed to Remembrance Wilton," Phillip says with more authority than I think he feels in the moment.

William looks at Phillip thoughtfully, trying to read his face before responding. "My son, you love this girl?" he says, looking Phillip squarely in the eye.

"Yes, yes I do Father, very much," he replies, meeting William's gaze.

"But Phillip, I thought you said Miss Wilton didn't like you?" I venture.

"I was wrong." He blushes two shades of red. "She is also in love with me and wants to marry," he assures us.

"Phillip, you have just started your apprenticeship. I think it would be best if you waited another year or two before you think of entering into a marriage contract," William says. It is clearly not what Phillip was hoping to hear.

I see the heartbreak in his eyes, but I don't want to undermine William. They are both so young, Phillip barely seventeen and I am guessing Miss Wilton is roughly the same age. I was only seventeen when I married Jonathan, but he was twenty and working with his father. "Phillip, where would you and Miss Wilton live?" I ask, thinking I already know the answer.

"We were hoping we could live here, with you?"

William shakes his head. "We do not have enough room for you and Miss Wilton here, as we are expecting another babe in the fall ourselves," says William matter-of-factly.

"Oh," says Phillip, crestfallen.

"William, perhaps there is an answer we could consider." I touch him lightly on the sleeve. "If Phillip will help build an additional room onto our home, then we might be inclined to help him with his contract, providing that he and Miss Wilton understand that they must wait until next year to be married," I offer.

William looks from me to Phillip, who now, hands clasped almost as if in prayer, looks expectantly at his father. I hope I have not overstepped. "I think that is a fine idea, Sarah," says William finally, patting my hand. "If you two are very much in love then waiting another year or so will not be of consequence to you, and you can continue to court with our blessing."

Phillip leaps from his seat to throw his arms around William. "Ah hum," he says, clearing his throat before stepping back to shake his father's hand and trying to put on his best grown up face. "Yes, that will be most acceptable."

"Come here, my boy," William says, grabbing Phillip and hugging him with a force that makes him squeal just a bit. We enjoy the rest of our meal, laughing and planning how to add on to the house and thinking about the future, our future as a family.

There is much conversation in the Plantation about the unhappiness of some who came on the last ship, and some have determined to return to England, which is unfortunate. We need, however, only those strong backs and sound minds who are committed to the congregation, although there are nearly as many who are not part of the group as who are. Those tradesmen and their families who came to pursue a new life here have been necessary and welcome. Sometimes they can be found among us in the common house during worship, but often they keep to themselves. Governor Bradford has decided that we will no longer farm together as just a community, and families will now be allowed to sow and harvest their own larger plots of land. To that end, land has been divided among the families for this purpose, and so it is good that Phillip will be back with us, as we will need his labor for our harvest.

As the weather has warmed and with the planting done, William and Phillip have begun to work on adding a new room to the house. Miss Wilton, dear Remembrance, our Rem, has become a regular visitor at our home and table. She and Phillip are very infatuated with each other, and she is a lovely young woman who will make a good wife. She has also become a great help to me around the house as my growing belly makes some chores more challenging. "Mrs. Tench, look, Patience has a new tooth," says Rem as she hoists Patience in the air, peals of laughter mixed with drool emanating from her mouth.

"My goodness you are in a hurry to grow up, are you not my dear babe," I say as Rem holds her up to me for a kiss on the cheek. She is plump and happy, with her father's nose and my eyes, clear and blue with a twinkle that warns me she will be a mischievous child before long.

I hope the next child is a boy, for William would surely like more sons, although there is clearly a great affection between him and his dear daughter. I look down from my cooking to see what is tugging on my skirt, and I realize our dearest Patience is now walking on her own! I clap my hands in delight and she joins right in, unclear about what we are celebrating but not wanting to be left out. We must make some time now to sew leading strings into her gowns to help her walk.

Another ship arrived a couple of months ago and we now have our first cattle, which is a welcome addition to the colony, and we are hopeful that we will be able to get one of our own soon. Phillip and William have become proficient hunters in the woods outside the stockade, and Rem and I spend many days butchering and salting meat for our winter stores. The summer has been warm and hazy with few storms, but already the wind is beginning to change and you can feel the slightest sting on your cheek first thing in the morning. The cradle is ready for the babe, and I've sewed as many things as I dare and am hoping to use some of Patience's things, which she is quickly outgrowing.

My lying in is much easier this time, and Mary has little work to do, which is good as she is also with child herself. As I hoped it is a boy. We name him William after his father, but we will call him Wills. He is red faced and healthy and seems a contented child. My arms and heart are full, and I marvel at how much my life has changed in just four short years. As I rock Wills my eyes close, and I think of my sister Margaret. I wonder what life is like for her now. Is she too rocking a babe by a warm fire while one sleeps in a cradle? I miss her. I wish we were all here, together in this place that has become my home. William and Phillip, Abraham and the babies are a wonderful family to be sure and I thank God for them and his blessings on us, but my sister it seems it now lost to me.

Phillip is now living with us again, and he and William work a little each night to make furniture for the new room. Phillip has become quite skilled, and his apprenticeship continues to go well. He will be able in another few years to start his own place of work, with some help from his father of course. Tools and supplies with which to get started will be of some cost, but the monies generated will be of great value. We have limited ways to generate our own income since all fur trading is handled by the Governor for the repayment of the debt the congregation incurred when we commissioned the *Mayflower* to bring us here. This arrangement will continue for some years, as we are not close to paying our notes.

Just as I am about to put Wills down for the night, I hear an urgent knock at the door. William opens it to find Edward standing in the dark, a light mist of snow in the air, with only a small lantern to light his way. "Sarah, can you come, it's Mary, it is her time, and she is having some trouble," he says urgently.

"Of course, I will come, but isn't Susannah more experienced with this than I?"

"She is with sickness and cannot come, please Sarah, we must hurry," says Edward, and he turns and starts back to the house before I can even grab my cloak as I hurry after him. The street is dark, and it is rapidly getting colder. My breath fills the night air with white streaks that reflect the lantern's light. Edward says nothing as we move quickly through the darkness.

We are still two houses away from the Crippens', but I can hear Mary's screams rising from the chimney with the smoke and ash. I grab up my skirt and run the rest of way. "Mary, I am here, Mary, look at me," I say, throwing my bag on the floor and grabbing her hand with both of mine. The bed is covered in blood and Mary's face is red and soaked with sweat. "How long have you been pushing?" I ask, trying to wipe away the blood so that I can see what is happening.

"For what seems like hours now, and I cannot seem to move the child out," Mary says, panting with exhaustion.

As I look between Mary's legs, I see... the babe's foot. "Edward, you need to get one of the older women, I don't know what to do, please Edward, now, you must get help now," I whisper urgently but softly, not wanting to scare Mary any further. "Mary, everything is going to be fine." I hope I sound more confident than I feel. "Lie back now and try to catch your breath."

"Oh, Sarah, the pain is so unbearable," cries Mary, her head in her hands, and I hear her words of prayer, barely a whisper above the tears. "Dear God, please deliver me safely of this child and hold us in your grace and mercy."

"Amen," I add as I place a warm wet towel across the child's foot, which is no longer moving. I can't bear the thought of losing Mary, or of Mary losing the babe, and I am so afraid.

Mary is breathing hard, and her face contorts in pain. "Now, Sarah, the babe is coming now," she screams, her hands knotted in the linen, her eyes focused on the sky.

Another foot appears, and I grasp both feet in my hands and tug gently and the child slides out in a sea of blood. The poor little girl isn't breathing, and I take her gently in my arms and rub her chest, her arms, her legs, willing her to cry. But there is no sound. The air is still, so still. There is no sound except for the whispers of a moan from Mary and the crackling of the fire. I stare into this sweet face as tears spill out over my cheeks, dropping on the babe's chest. She still does not stir, and I know now that there is no life in her. "Dear God, please take the soul of this precious child into your care," I whisper softly, holding the little girl's cheek next to mine.

Sarah Priest has arrived with Edward, and she takes the babe from my arms as Edward does his best to comfort Mary, who does not seem aware of what is happening. Perhaps that is for the best.

"There is nothing you could have done," says Sarah as she wraps the wee girl in a linen and lays her on the bed next to Mary. Edward begins to weep ever so softly as he collapses on the floor next to the bed, holding Mary's hand, but Mary does not stir. I dare not think it, I dare not look at her, but my heart already feels her absence, and I know that this place will never be the same.

The days have gone by in a whirl of sorrow and guilt. I sit here holding my precious Wills while my dearest friend lies in the cold hard ground on Coles Hill. Her little girl is with her, the babe that Edward has named Elizabeth. Daniel is helping as best he can for a boy of only eight who has just lost his mother. Mehitable and Samuel are staying with other families to give Edward time to adjust to this new life. A life without Mary. The woman who was always so sure life would be good, that God was gracious and kind, is no more. Why would God do this to Edward? To her children? Mary was the most devoted of believers, and her reward was to leave her babes without their mother. How was this the work of the kind and loving God that Mary so trusted?

We see little of Edward this winter; I feel he blames me for Mary's death, and I cannot bring myself to speak to him. Each time we gather in the common house for worship I see him. He sits with Daniel, his eyes cast down to the floor, never looking up, speaking to no one. I don't know what I would see in those eyes were he to look at me. Hatred or sorrow or anger, I don't know, I just want to know that he does not feel that this is my fault. Sarah Priest has come to call several times and reassures me that I did what was right, but I can't help but think I should have done more. It is God's providence surely, but still. When I lie down to sleep at night, Mary's face is often the last thing I see. I will never forget her.

As the dark days shorten, the spring brings with it news from England. King James I has died and his son Charles I has been crowned King of England, Scotland, and Ireland. While our lives were difficult in England at times, we are still English and loyal to the crown. The King's passing is noted with prayers and toasting to the health of Charles I. The men gather at night to discuss how these changes may affect us, but there seems to be little concern and William expects no impact on us. We focus instead on filling our days with planting and preparing for the wedding of Phillip and Remembrance, which is to take place in just a few months. The addition to the house is done, and Phillip is living there now, preparing for his future. He is a great help with the children and will be a very good father himself, I believe.

In addition to news from England, this latest ship brings with it the arrival of several new families under the leadership of a man named Thomas Morton, and they have not been a welcome addition to our colony. Boisterous and pagan in their behavior, they insist on celebrating May Day in the old

English tradition. Governor Bradford and Elder Brewster agree that this celebration is not to be a part of our settlement, but as more and more comers do not follow our religious traditions, keeping out unwanted elements becomes harder and harder.

"I don't understand why the May Day celebration is so bad," says Phillip, decidedly unhappy that he is not permitted to participate. William looks to me for a response, as he does not always himself fully appreciate the Puritan way.

"Well, Phillip, we believe there is only one God, and he is divine in his right to guide us. May Day celebrations, while they may seem to be just fun, honor the old gods, which we do not believe in," I explain.

"If you say it is so," grumbles Phillip as he makes his way to his room.

William smiles. "You are a very good mother to him," he says, hugging me close. "To all the children, you are a fine mother indeed."

"I do my very best for you, and for them," I say matter-of-factly. "I hope it is enough."

"It is indeed my dearest, more than enough," says William with a smile that truly warms my heart.

After much debate, Thomas Morton and his followers decided to make their own settlement to the north, and they have been gone now several months. We will prepare for the winter as we were. Phillip and Remembrance are happily married now and living with us, and so it is a large family that gathers each night around the table as we share our evening meal and prayer. Abraham has been able to come and stay for a few days to celebrate with the newly married, and it has been a joy to have everyone here. He has grown into a fine young man, and I hope he continues to stay near to us.

I can't help but smile at Phillip and Rem, they are so young and so very much in love. Phillip dotes on her, and it is enjoyable to see them together. Rem is as always great help with the babes, Patience keeping her busy as she runs to and fro in the house now that it is too cold to be outside. I feel it will not be long before a child of their own comes along.

Nintisqua has come to the house, as he will be going with William and Phillip tomorrow for the last hunt before the deep winter is upon us.

"We have not seen you much in the colony of late, Nintisqua, is all well with you and your family?" I ask as I lay out the pewter for our meal.

"I am sorry to say, Mrs. Sarah, that my wife has died some small time ago," he says solemnly.

"I am genuinely sad for your loss," I say as I squeeze his hand.

"She has not gone far, Mrs. Sarah, and the hawk comes to see me, to say that she is with me."

"I do not understand?"

"Her spirt is in the place of our ancestors, but she stays close to me to guide me, along with others from my family who have gone before. When the hawk comes to me it is her way of, what you say, comforting me?"

"Ah, I see," I say, although I'm not sure I do. "It must be nice to know she is watching over you." I wonder if our loved ones could do the same from heaven. Was Jonathan to be found in the mist in the air? Could Mary see her babies to know that they are well and cared for? It is a nice thought, although I'm not sure Elder Brewster would share my enthusiasm.

"Please try not to have any encounters with bears while I am gone," William says as he kisses me goodbye, settling Wills into bed with me on his way out the door.

"I promise," I whisper back so as not to stir the babe. These moments when the house is quiet are so precious, but it is fleeting, as just a minute later Patience has crawled in beside us as well.

"Mama," she gurgles as she snuggles up close to me. It is one of her few words and one which she repeats many times throughout the day. Phillip has been trying to get her to say his name, but it's just too much for her and only a "ffip" results from her repeated attempts. "Rem" has been mostly mastered, which simply serves to frustrate Phillip even more! We spend the days mending and sewing more gowns for Patience, whose swaddling gowns have all now gone to Wills. She is walking well now and so we remove the leading strings and set them aside, as we will surely need them later for Wills.

William and the others return in just a few days, without incident, and they have brought many furs to give for our debt and meat to last us the winter. They were able to kill two deer and to bring all the meat on a litter, so we shall be well stocked for the cold months to come. "There is something going on between our Mr. Morton and the Indians, I believe. I shall have to speak to the Governor about it," William reports as he settles in front of the fire, rocking Wills to sleep.

"What do you mean?" I say, surprised at this revelation.

"Nintisqua was talking with some natives we encountered on our hunt, and they say that Morton has worked out a rival fur trade with them. Our colony is the only one permitted to make such arrangements, as we must have furs to provide to Thomas Weston to repay our debt to him." William is clearly irritated by Mr. Morton's behavior.

Weston had funded our venture, and our repayment depends on our ability to provide furs that he can then sell across Europe to erase our debt. If Morton is providing an alternative source of furs, then it will drive down the price, making it harder for us to pay off our debt. "Why would he do such a thing, William, clearly he must know of our situation?" I feel my own irritation growing.

"Greed. Money is the master of many men and the opportunity to acquire more of it is more than most men can resist."

"You should speak to the Governor right away. If this is happening it cannot stand," I say, my hands on my hips.

"Yes dearest, now take Wills to his cradle and then join me in our bed. I have missed you these many days and the sight of you standing there looking so indignant is very endearing," William says, grinning from ear to ear.

"My pleasure, dear husband, for I have sorely missed you too," I smile as I kiss him on the top of his head and whisk Wills off to sleep.

William was right about Mr. Morton, and there was a tremendous uproar in the colony as the depth of the betrayal became more widely known. William and the other men of the leadership have been meeting every day to determine how to respond. Finally, it has been decided that, as a breach of our law, this cannot stand, and Captain Standish will be sent to arrest Mr. Morton. I am grateful that this time, William will not accompany him. His arm still suffers from the knife attack some months ago when he last went with Standish, and he need not put himself at more peril. Morton will be held in our stockade until the next ship comes from England, and then he will be set on it to return and face charges—for it seems furs were not all that Mr. Morton was trading, but arms as well.

Life is becoming more hectic here; our small world becomes larger and more crowded day by day. A real town has arisen where once there stood nothing. Our labors, although hard, have born unto us this place to call home. I cherish this time, the quiet nights, the familiar faces, and the safety and security I feel. Surely this is God's blessing on us, but will it last?

CHAPTER FIVE
HOW THE WORLD HAS CHANGED

A letter is only a piece of paper until you read what it contains, then it can change your whole life. Yet, it is still just a piece of paper. I rock slowly, Henry nursing quietly at my breast. The letter from the Captain of the *Little James* tells me that Abraham took ill and died while off the coast of Maine. He was barely twenty-one in age. I will not be able to bury him with Jonathan on Coles Hill, as he has been buried at sea, as is the tradition. I would have liked for him to be here with his brother and our son James, who died some years ago at just a few days old. And Mary, my dearest friend Mary, gone now nearly five years. We have only seen Abraham from time to time for some years, but it is a great sadness to me to know that we will not see him again in this life and that he dies leaving no children to continue his family's name.

Our family has grown, and we have been much blessed. Patience is now nearly nine, Wills seven, Elizabeth is five, Mary almost three, and Henry a few weeks. The house is nearly bursting at the seams, but it is a happy home and blessed with the laughter of children and grandchildren. Rem and Phillip have a babe of their own now too. Things have not been easy for them as their first child was born without the breath of life, but Rem has fully recovered with the birth two years ago of a healthy boy they named Isaac William Tench. William was bursting with pride at his grandson and proud to have the boy bear his name. We have built on to the house again, a room for the children, and each now has their own bed, except for Henry who is in a cradle.

Phillip has now opened his own furniture-making business down near the new market, and he is doing very well. William helps him some days, but as we all now plant and harvest our own food, much must be done on our own land too. Between the shop and the fields, the men are busy from sunup to sundown. Rem is helping me to expand the herb garden, and I have begun making a few simple potions, those which my mother taught me, to ease the upsets of day to day living. Mary struggles with her food, often unable to keep anything down, and she is small and frail. I'm hoping that something will ease her unpleasantness and help her grow. "Sarah, are you sure we should be making these potions?" says Rem, a hint of hesitation in her voice.

"Of course, why not?" I say, furrowing my brow.

"Elder Brewster has said that potions are of the devil and that healing comes from God and only God."

I stop, wiping my hands on my apron as I think carefully on what I want to say. "Rem, these are things my mother taught me, and her mother taught them to her. My mother was a fine God-fearing woman with much respect for Elder Brewster and the leaders of the Congregation. I do not believe she would have taught me these things if she thought they were unclean. Besides, Samuel Fuller is a doctor and a deacon in the church, and he uses many things to help heal others," I say with both conviction and a clear conscience.

"Yes, I suppose you are right," Rem says at last, "and if it helps Mary, I'm sure it will be God's doing."

"It will be indeed, as all things come from God," I reassure her, hugging her close to me.

"Mother, am I unclean?" says Wills behind me. Before I can even turn to look at him, Rem is beside herself with laughter. Covered in mud from nearly head to toe, this little boy I call my son is barely recognizable as a human child.

"Wills, whatever have you been doing?" I respond, trying to conceal my own desire to laugh.

"I was catching frogs by the stream, and I fell," he replies, his eyes downcast, the toes on his bare feet twitching to and fro the only part of him that moves.

"Well yes, my son, you are unclean to be sure but not in the way in which Rem and I were talking. Now go to the well and do your best to clean up the mess you are in before you come back to this house," I say sternly but with a hint of a smile.

As Wills walks away, his shoulders slumped and his arms swinging loosely at his sides, my laughter bubbles up like a spring on a hot summer's day.

Wills, now realizing I am not terribly mad at him, stands a bit taller and waves back at me as he runs off to the well.

"Patience," I call out toward the house.

"Yes Mother," she replies, her smiling face at the back door.

"Please go and help your brother. I've sent him to the well to wash up."

"Why the well, Mama?" she replies, clearly confused.

"Oh, you will see," says Rem, her eyes watery from laughing so hard. "Go quickly, Patience, or you will miss the spectacle!"

These children bring me such joy, I simply cannot imagine my life without them.

But there is work as well. It takes me and Rem a whole day just to wash and clean clothes for the family, and there is always cooking and mending to be done. Each night it seems there is some garment to fix or a hem to let out as the children grow bigger by the day. Rem is quite the accomplished seamstress, and her needlework is beautiful. She has taken to making beautiful collars for Patience and Elizabeth as simple adornments for their dresses. Isaac and Wills are still in short breeches, but it will be no time at all before they'll need long pants, and so the work must start soon.

Several ships have come in the last few months, offloading hundreds and hundreds of settlers bound for the new plantations north of here known as Salem and Charleston. Even our own little plantation of Plimouth has become a bustling town of over three hundred. The settlers are here under Governor John Winthrop, who leads the new towns with a charter from King Charles I. The newly formed Massachusetts Bay Company is paying for the establishment of the colonies to ensure that the now very lucrative fur trade will continue. Men will not come without women, and women will not come without houses. Still, things here are not as they are in England, and anyone must be prepared to work hard to survive in this place.

Elder Brewster and his family have left Plimouth to work land he has been granted along the islands, one of which has now been named Great Brewster. Ralph Smith, who arrived last year, has now taken on the role of Elder for the congregation along with Roger Williams, and I find him to be most agreeable. Edward Crippen took the children and moved to Salem, and I have heard that he has married again and has a new child. Mary would be glad, I think, to know that he has found happiness and that the children are being cared for. I no longer see Mary's face every night, but I see her smile when I look at my own Mary, named in her memory. I never could have imagined this life when I left England, and yet now it seems as if my life was never meant for anything other than this.

William is a fine husband and a wonderful father. I am starting to see signs that he is growing old, and I know I must face life without him someday, but I hope God takes mercy on me and it is not soon. It is the great pleasure of my life to care for him and the children, and I would suffer greatly without him in my life.

"Mother, can I help you in the garden?" Patience says, tugging on my sleeve.

"Of course, my dearest," I say, stopping to kiss her on the top of her head, which seems to be coming ever closer to my own. "We are going to have to do something about putting some length on your dresses soon, I can see your ankles." I watch her walk the length of the garden gathering up fresh corn for dinner.

"Can we?" Patience replies with excitement only a young girl could muster for such a mundane task. We work quietly, enjoying the warm spring day, and the sun grows close to the horizon before we know it.

William comes through the gate without a word and scoops Patience up in his arms, her laughter echoing through the air. "My dear young lady, what are you and your mother doing in this garden?" he asks with a serious adult air.

"We are planting and pinching the plants, Father, can't you see?" Patience gestures to the neat rows of green.

"Yes, I can, I can see that. Do you think it hurts when you pinch them?" he replies, trying not to smile.

"Oh, I don't know Father, do you think so?" she says, the sudden concern now obvious in her little voice.

"Your father is teasing you little one, do not give in to his efforts," I say, ushering Patience into the house in front of me. "Wills, you come along as well." I kiss William on the cheek, immediately sensing his tension. "What is it my dear, is everything well?"

William shakes his head, "No, there have been some heated discussions today in the council. We shall talk after the children are in bed, I want Phillip to hear also as this impacts us all."

I can barely focus on our evening meal and bedtime for the children cannot come soon enough, as my mind is racing with thoughts of what William's concern must be. Elder Brewster has left, and I hear Captain Standish is also leaving to start his own colony. Perhaps it is just that, but I can't help but think it must be more. As we have grown there have been more challenges but nothing we have not been able to overcome, and I hope that will not change now. Phillip adds one smaller log to the fire while Rem takes Henry and Isaac to their room so that we may talk. She has little interest in what goes on in the colony, preferring to focus on Phillip and the children. William stands gazing at the fire as if unsure as to how to start. I know not to hasten him when he is thinking, and I wait expectantly.

"Father, you said we needed to talk. Is there something happening in the colony, is it Captain Standish?" says Phillip, clearly unable to wait on William any longer.

"No, it's not that, we have known about that for some time, and we are prepared to make new arrangements for the leadership of our defenses. It is Roger Williams and his teachings, which are becoming more of a concern."

"I don't understand," I say, knitting my brows together, "I thought that everyone found Mr. Williams quite acceptable, and they were happy to have him here to support our congregation. What has changed?"

William paces back and forth in front of the fire, his hands behind his back, his eyes focused on the floor in front of him. Again, we wait. "Mr. Williams has decided that we are not conducting ourselves properly, and he has become very vocal about the changes he thinks need to occur," says William finally. Phillip and I can only exchange glances, since neither of us seems to know what behavior had offended Mr. Williams. Was it something we had done? "He thinks we should be more mindful of being separate from the Church of England, and..." William pauses, "that the colony has no standing when it comes to enforcing The First Table."

I stare at William, almost unable to speak. The First Table is the first four commandments handed down by God. That thou shall have no other God before me, or make images of other Gods to worship; that thou shall not take the name of the Lord God in vain; and finally, that the sabbath is a holy day to be respected and preserved. These concepts are the very fundamentals of our religious teachings. How could he possibly think that the colony has no say in the enforcement of these teachings? "William, I am at a loss for words. I do not understand why Mr. Williams would say these things. What does it mean?"

"It is more than just this alone, although this is certainly concern enough, but he also does not feel we are treating the Indians fairly," he says.

"We are most kind to them, whatever does he mean?" I protest loudly, thinking of all the times we have repaid the kindness and help we received.

"He believes we should pay them for this land, this land that was theirs before we arrived," says William, shaking his head from side to side. "It would be financial ruin for the colony and for us." Indeed, had we been in England, we would never have presumed to simply take another man's land without payment. But that is exactly what we did to the Indians, so are we saying they are somehow less than we are? That they do not deserve the same consideration we would show to people who look like us? I rock slowly back and forth, the slight squeak of the chair and the crackling of the fire the only sounds in the room. "Son, what do you think?" William says finally, breaking the silence.

I can see Phillip is struggling with a response, as I would be if William had called on me. "Father, I cannot see a simple answer to that question. To say we do not need to pay them for this land is to say they are not the same as other men and that we are not breaking the law. I am not sure if it is God's law or man's that must dictate here, and I do not know if it is wrong to not make payment to them. But I for one do not see an Indian man as any less than any other man..." His thoughts trail off as William slowly strokes his beard, nodding in agreement. I think back to when Ninti and William went out in the woods the snowy night that Abraham was missing. Had Ninti not risked his life for us the same as any other man would have done? Would his death not have been a death, just the same as if William or Abraham had died?

My mind swirls with the implications of what we must consider now that Mr. Williams has made his concern public, but I still do not know what the solution is. "We surely cannot say that the Indian man is less than the white man, can we?" I say, looking at William earnestly, unsure what I want the answer to be.

"No," says William with a tone of resignation, "I don't think we can. No one would have survived that first winter without them, and you my dearest, and our babes, would not be here if not for them. Phillip and I would have arrived to find a very different world."

"So how will we resolve this?" I wonder out loud.

"Father, I do not know how I could afford to pay for this land. Does that mean we will have to leave the Colony and go somewhere else?" says Phillip with a pained expression.

"No!" I shout with a force that surprises even me. "I am not leaving this place; this place is my home."

William looks at me with a wide stare, clearly taken aback at the fervor of my protest, but I am firm on this. I have worked too hard to make this place my home to leave it. The walls of the room suddenly seem to be coming closer; I need some fresh air, and I grab my shawl as I head out to the street. The sun is now gone behind the hills, and only the light from the houses casts its glow across the ground, lighting my surroundings. Candlelight flickers in dancing shadows like lovers in a slow dance. My lungs celebrate the feeling of the cool evening air and my heart stops trying to leap from my chest. The air is still, and the smoke rising from chimneys makes small swirls in the sky as it disappears into the darkness. The song of distant crickets floats across the air, mixed with the muffled sound of voices and the clanging of pots.

I have come to love this place, to love my life here. I have endured pain to be sure, but the joys, oh the joys have been so much greater. This is the land of my children, and their children to come. But have we done wrong? I hear the door open, and I feel William behind me, saying nothing. His arms wrap around me and I lean against his chest, feeling his strength and comfort. "Whatever shall we do?" I whisper into the darkness.

"I do not know, my dearest," William whispers back. "We will do our best to do what is right, in God's eyes, and in our own, whatever that may mean."

I nod in agreement, feeling both relief and dread for the unknown that surely awaits us.

The leaves have begun to fall from the trees, and our days are spent preparing for the cold that is to come. Patience helps grind flour and Elizabeth helps keep Henry occupied. Wills spends much time with his father gathering and chopping wood for the cold to come. He echoes William's every move, and it warms my heart to see them together. Mary, small and frail still, spends much of her time in her cradle, sleeping more than is right, Henry already beginning to equal her in size. I can only hope that she makes it through this winter. I don't mind the winter cold as much as I once did. The children all gathered around us in the house, we sing and play games to pass the time, and laughter and love fill the air. Phillip, Rem, and Isaac join us most evenings, and the fellowship of their company is much appreciated. As William grows older Phillip is a great help to him, and he and Wills have grown close as well. This is good, as Phillip will be nearly like a father to Wills someday, although I hope not too soon.

Oh, so quickly another winter has come and gone, and after much distress, Roger Williams has left the colony and gone to Salem. While this has made the congregation more settled, it has not resolved the question of whether we should pay the Indians for this land, and it hangs in the air like smoke from a fire. But there is no time to think on it now, for the pox has come to the colony. Now, all we can think about is survival. The sachem of the Wampanoag has died as have so very many of the Indians, many we call our friends, including Nintisqua. This sickness is so vile and to those who suffer its impact a horrible death, their skin covered in painful sores that ooze blood and horrible pus. Some covered with so many sores you cannot separate one from the other, the sight and smell of rotting flesh is more than most can bear.

It is not safe to be near others and so we keep to ourselves inside our house, and we venture out only to take wood or water to those who are sick. Our stores are good but having just come from winter not as ample as we would like. I fear William going into the woods to hunt as he may encounter those with the pox, so we ration as best we can. Rem and I venture out a little each day to tend to the garden while William or Phillip keeps watch, armed with a musket to make sure no one comes near.

We will need to plant very soon or there will be no harvest, and so it is agreed that William, Phillip, and Wills will work the field and I will go with them to keep watch as Rem stays with the little ones. Patience is big enough to be of help and to fetch for Rem. Dear Mary is still so small and pale and having to stay inside all day is no good I fear, but it is safer than being outside where the sickness can travel on the wind. The days are warm and wet and good for planting, and the time goes quickly and easily, but it is not enough to protect us, for trouble finds us despite our attempts to hide from it. Rem has the pox.

Phillip paces the floor in front of the fire as Isaac plays quietly nearby, his brow deeply lined with worry and with fear. "All will be well Phillip; we will keep Rem in your room, and you and Isaac will stay in here with us. I can tend to her as needed," I say, my hand resting on his shoulders, revealing his quaking.

"Sarah, I can't ask you to do that, you have children of your own who need you. I will take care of Rem, if you can take care of Isaac."

I look at William's face, his nearly blank expression telling me nothing of what he is thinking. Risk his wife or his son, there is no good solution to our problem. As so many are facing, so shall we, and lives must be risked for lives to be saved. "Yes, I think that is best," says William finally, "but I'm afraid it will be more difficult than we imagine."

"Why is that, my dear?" I say cautiously. I follow William's gaze across the room to see Mary lying on her side next to Henry's cradle, her face red and her hair wet, with the smallest of dark spots beginning to form on her cheeks.

"No, don't touch her," cries William, grabbing my hand just as I am about to reach for her. "Phillip, can you take Mary into the room with Rem?"

"No, no, I need to be with her, I'm her mother, I must stay with her!"

But William is holding both my hands now tightly in his and it is impossible for me to get away. I watch as Phillip picks Mary up and goes through the door, and I feel as if my heart will tear in two. I bury my head in William's chest as the sobs shake me nearly to my knees.

"My darling Sarah, I know this is most hard, but you must think of the other children. Henry is not even weaned, and Patience, Wills, and Elizabeth need you too."

"But Mary needs me!" I cry out like an animal caught in a trap from which it cannot be freed. I hear my heartbeat echoing in my ears.

"This is in God's hands now, we must trust that he will guide and help Phillip, Rem, and Mary and that his mercy will be on us," says William, holding me tightly against his chest. My sobs have slowed to a trickle, and I force myself to focus on the task of getting the children all settled into their beds.

William puts water on to boil so that I can begin scrubbing the floors, the walls, everything in our rooms to remove any traces of this vile sickness. Wills, Patience, and Elizabeth each grab a rag and help to ensure we get every corner. "I'm going to need to make a poultice for Rem and for Mary, can you get me some rosemary and sage from the garden?" I ask, looking up from my efforts.

"Of course, I'll get a torch and go out now unless you think it can wait until morning," replies William.

"No, it can't wait, there is no time to spare, if we are going to have any chance of saving them, we must act now," I say, my mind jumbled with the thoughts of all that must be done.

"I can get it, Father," says Patience, already on her way out the door.

The nights and days blend as if there is no sun and no moon; only the smell of sickness and death are constant and predictable. I have heard that the Brewster's lost their two daughters, Fear and Patience, who had survived the first winter sickness. Their husbands, Isaac Allerton and Thomas Prence, now without their wives and the mothers of their children. Governor Bradford has told the council that nearly all the Wampanoag tribe of one thousand has died; fewer than one hundred of them remain. Nearly twenty others in the town have died, but Phillip is doing a good job caring for the girls and has not shown any signs of the pox, and we continue to hope for the best. But as is often the case, God seems deaf to my nightly pleas begging for his mercy.

"Sarah, it's Mary," says William, shaking me gently from my sleep. He doesn't need to say anything more; I already know. I felt it earlier in the day. There was a change in the wind, in the sky, in the breeze, as if the world already knew it was going to be different, changed, a lesser place. I climb out of bed onto the cool wood to see a small bundle wrapped in cloth lying on the floor in front of the fire. Unable to even stand, I crawl on my hands and knees to where Mary lies on the floor, picking her up in my arms and holding her tightly to me. Her little body is stiff and cool, and only the smallest part of her eyes is visible through the cocoon that envelopes her. I hold her tightly in my arms. As I kneel with her in front of the fire my mind is flooded with the sharp pins and needles of loss. Jonathan, Mary and her babe, our James, Abraham, and now our own Mary. And more, so many more.

Some of the names I have forgotten but I remember the faces. I see them often in my dreams, the faces of those who came to this place for a better life, only to lose what little life they had. "We will bury her next to James," I say, the tears staining my cheeks.

"Yes of course, my dear, I will see to it first thing in the morning," says William, kneeling next to me. "Now let us pray to God here on our knees for his grace and mercy over the soul of our dear Mary and his continued grace for Phillip and Rem."

I want to say amen, but the words are only in my mind, for once again I wonder, if God is merciful, why does he make us suffer so? Why, oh why take another child from me? I do not know. My faith is shaken once again, and my heart is broken. I'm not sure I can go on, and yet the sun is already rising on another day and despite it all, life finds a way to begin again.

I sit quietly on the banks of the stream watching the children splash about on this beautiful summer day. Patience all of fourteen and as tall as I am, Wills taller than her, and Elizabeth, Isaac, and Henry would be like steps on a stair if it were not for our missing Mary. I dreamt of my dearest Mary Crippen last night—she came to me, and I saw her holding my little Mary and rocking her in her arms as she cooed and laughed. It was a most pleasant dream. Rem, after several barren years, is now with child again. She lies on her back next to me, staring at the clouds as they slide across the blue, her rotund belly pointing up to the sky. The pox seems like a distant memory, even if Mary still comes to me from time to time in my dreams. I think about how big she would be now, running and playing with her brothers and sisters. Her little laugh seems to come to me on the breeze, but I know it is only the rustling of the leaves…or is it? Nintisqua said that after his wife died, he would know she was near because she would send the hawk to comfort him. Was the rustling of the leaves really Mary's way of saying she was near and watching us? My heart feels no relief, so it must only be the wind in the trees; my dearest child is not here.

This year of 1637 has already been a difficult one, and tensions are high in our town and in villages all around as turmoil with the Pequot Indians has been stirred up again. William and the men of the council are truly concerned. The Pequot have taken over many of the other, smaller tribes to control trade between English and Dutch settlers and the Indians. They have married their women against their will to men of other tribes, waged war on other Indian peoples, and tried every manner of trickery to control their fate. They have also managed to amass a great many weapons, which makes us all very uneasy. This alliance they have with so many other Indians extends over many, many miles and seems to be swelling to a level that threatens our peace with the Narragansetts and Mohegans, which was already hard won.

It seems the Pequot have also not been forthright in their dealings, having given both Captain Standish and other leaders from the Dutch East India Company rights to the same land. Now, not only are we in a dispute with the Pequot, we are at odds with other Europeans looking to settle in this area. "William, I don't understand how it is that the Pequot sachem has sold the same land to different colonies at the same time, how is that within the law?"

William tries to stifle a laugh. "My dearest, it is clear you are naïve about the ways of the world. Whatever would you do if I were not here to look out for you?"

"I shall manage somehow," I reply, hands on my hips, quite irritated, for his laughter feels like a reproach.

"I am sorry, I did not mean to slight you," he says, pulling me close to him and burying his face in my hair. He smells of hay and sweat and the day's work, and I can't help but inhale as if it were a fine perfume.

I kiss him, feeling his lips soft against my own. What I wouldn't give for just one afternoon as it was when we first married. Just the two of us alone in our house, our bed. But with four of our own children and Phillip, Rem, and their child, privacy is a luxury we cannot afford very often. "So, I still don't understand," I repeat softly.

"Did the Indians do something wrong?" Patience chimes in.

"Ah, yes, well, it was not lawful and certainly not of good moral character for the Pequot sachem to do what he did, but I'm sure he had no such cares at the time. There are so many people here now that land is becoming a much sought-after prize, and the Pequot clearly could not restrain themselves from using that to their advantage."

It is true, every few months a new settlement seems to arise either as new people arrive or as members of the

Plimouth Plantation leave to start their own villages and towns. I have never felt the urge to leave; this is my home and I feel safe behind its walls. But there are so many other towns and villages now around us and to the north that I can no longer name them all. There must be nearly twenty thousand of us here now, by my reckoning. Ships full of hopeful young faces looking to make their way in the new world. Was it only seventeen years ago I was one of them?

"The Indians cannot be trusted," says Wills as he comes through the back door with an armload of wood for the fire.

"My son, why would you say that?" I reply, thinking of all the times that Nintisqua, Samoset, and so many others were our only hope when things were so bleak.

"I've heard some of the men say so, even you, Father."

I look at William in disbelief.

"Wills, not all Indians can be trusted, just as not all men who look like us can be trusted. It is important to judge each man on his own merits and decide for yourself if you can or cannot trust their word. There are some Indians I have not trusted, and there are some I have trusted with my life."

Wills looks skeptical but seems to understand what his father is trying to say.

"So, what will happen now?" I ask, fearing I might know the answer.

"We will do our best to negotiate with the Dutch and reach some agreeable terms," says William, but his tone makes it clear he is doubtful at best.

As is often the case when we think things are within our control, we quickly learn they are not. Perhaps they never were, and control was simply an illusion all along. Within days the news comes that changes so much for all of us. At a village to the north a boat had been seized off Block Island, and its captain, an Englishmen by the name of Oldham, and a local trader were murdered by some Indians there. Those Indians then ran away and took refuge with the Pequot. In retaliation, Governor Vane, the head of the Massachusetts Bay Company, who was settled nearby, sent John Endecott and a force of some ninety men to Block Island to kill all the Indian men there and to take their women and children captive.

While many of the Indians from Block Island did not resist or managed to escape, Endecott burned the village to the ground anyway. Then, he chased the Indians to the mouth of the Connecticut River, to a settlement there led by Lion Gardiner. Reluctant to join in the fight against the Indians, Gardiner blamed Endecott for poking the nest of the hornet, which he felt would only bring further death and fighting between the Indians and the settlers. He was right; there were far more than the stings of hornets to worry about. I can only watch as William packs his belongings, gathering up the things he needs into a small satchel as he moves quickly around the room. Phillip, I'm sure, is doing the same thing in his room as Rem watches.

"William, I know you must go, but Phillip? Rem is heavy with child, and she will want Phillip to be with her."

"Sadly, my dear, sometimes we must do what must be done, whether we want to or not," he says, his voice echoing with regret and a tone I have not heard before.

Is it fear? I know I am afraid, so deeply afraid my legs tremble beneath my skirt. Phillip emerges from their room, Isaac holding tightly to his hand. Rem's face is red, her eyes swollen and hollow, the streaks from her tears dried now but still visible on her face. "I'm ready, Father," says Phillip, his voice waking me from my stupor. It is a voice I have not fully heard from him before, a husband, a father, a son, now truly a man who is leaving to fight his first war.

"My dearest Sarah," says William, holding my face in his hands. I look into his eyes as he smiles softly. "I love you with all my heart, and I so dearly love our children. Know this my love, I will do my very best to return to you, but if I do not, it is not for want, for all my heart desires is to be here with you."

I choke back my fear and my tears. "I will pray each and every day for your safe return, and for Phillip as well, and all the men. God's speed, my love."

Rem nods her head in agreement, unable to even speak.

I hold him close, tightly. Maybe if I simply do not let go, he will not leave.

"I must go," says William as he sits me down in the chair by the fire. "Wills, look after your mother and the other children, you are the man of this house now and I trust you to take care of things." William hands one of the muskets to

Wills. My heart misses a beat, thinking of my boy as the man of this house.

"I will Father, as you would do," says Wills, shaking his father's hand.

All the children are in bed except for Wills, who has decided to make camp outside of the house to keep an eye out, even though I've assured him that we are safe inside the stockade.

I lean back in my chair, rocking slowly in front of the fire. My mind wanders back to my childhood when we were in Leiden. My mother cooking in the kitchen, Margaret and Richard and I running through the house as my father chastises us in a voice that says he's not really being stern with us. We laughed, we played, we lived. As a child you can't wait to grow up, to do the things that are forbidden to you when you are small. You feel like the world isn't big enough for you and that you can't possibly be satisfied in it until it's as big as it can be. You don't think about what comes with living in a bigger world. The pain, the uncertainty, the things you would rather life did not bring to you.

But there is also the joy of finding love, of motherhood, of living a life that you would want to live again and again despite its trials. I hear Henry muttering in his sleep, and I tuck the blanket around his little legs, which always seem to be uncovered by morning. I look around at these precious gifts from God and smile. I have suffered much in this life, and I have been blessed. It is fair, I think. God has taken and he has given to me both. But I can't help but wonder how much more will be taken from me before my life is over.

What little news comes to us is not good, and this war between us and the Indians will end only when one of us is utterly destroyed. The Indians raid small towns and villages, burning homes and killing settlers, and we respond in kind, wiping whole villages off the map. I hear the men talk in the common house when they think the women and children are not listening, but I always sit near them even if my back is turned. My eyes are cast down on my needlework, but my ears strain for the sound of the names William or Phillip. I am continually disappointed. They say nearly three hundred Pequot were killed in one village alone, but no news on the lives of our men.

I watch the other wives whose husbands have also gone to fight. They seem so calm and serene, as if their husbands have simply gone out to plant the field. My face, I fear, is not so calm. My skin feels tight around my mouth and eyes, as if the stress of smiling would make it crack and bleed. "Mother, am I doing this right?" says Patience, holding out her sampler for my inspection.

"That's very lovely, you are doing a wonderful job," I say, nodding in approval.

"Are you sure Mama? You look so sad I thought maybe I was doing it wrong."

Staring into her face I see the reflection of my own fear and sadness in her young eyes, and the pain of it cuts me to the core. "Oh, my dearest," I say, pulling her close to me and hugging her tightly. "My sadness is never of your making; you bring me only the greatest of joy."

"Is it Papa and Phillip? Is that what is making you sad?"

"Yes, I miss them very much, as I'm sure you do too, but we will keep praying for their health and return with faith that God will bring them back to us safely."

Patience leans against my shoulder as I force myself to sit quietly on the floor and focus on my work. I want to run. I want to go as fast as I can to where William is and throw my arms around him and see for myself that he is safe. It is all I can do to stay still. I look down at Patience's hands carefully and slowly tracing out with her thread the tiny letters on the ivory cloth. A, B, C, the entire alphabet taking shape before her. Along the edge of her cloth the words *God is my strength, God is my light, God is my hope* appearing over and over. And as God is her strength, so I must be as well. I straighten up and wipe my eyes. My children see me as their strength, their light, their hope, and so I must be. I cannot let my own fears overcome me. No matter what God has in store for me, I must be here for Patience, Wills, Elizabeth, and Henry. They need me, and I need them, more than they will ever know.

"I think we should gather up your brothers and sister and go home, can you fetch Henry from outside."

"Yes Mother," replies Patience, always eager to lend a hand and likely relieved that the needlepoint is done, at least for now.

"Wills, can you help me with these?" I say, handing off our parcels.

"Of course, Mama, I can manage it," he says with a twinkle in his eye. It seems he has grown a hand's width in the last few months since his father left. William will be very proud of him. He has taken on all of William's normal chores without complaint or fuss. Patience is also now preparing the morning meal, and the family works well together to ensure all is done. Phillip will be relieved to know that Rem has been safely delivered a few weeks ago of a little girl she has named Grace Elizabeth, as they had agreed.

The days are getting longer, and the house is getting very crowded. I shall have to talk with William and Philip when they return about adding on again. We shall need another space for Patience, who is now too old to be in a room with Wills. She and Elizabeth should have a bit more privacy. Wills, Isaac, and Henry can share a room, and Grace can stay with Phillip and Rem until she is old enough to join the other girls. By then, Patience will probably be married and in a house of her own. The thought of it sets me back on my heels. My daughter, my firstborn, married and hopefully a mother of her own. There are many men in town still without wives, and I have seen several of them watching Patience as she goes to the butcher or to the mill. She has grown into a beauty, her long brown hair shining golden in the sun, and she is tall and lean like her father. At times I see the face of my own mother in hers.

The ticking of the clock seems to go faster and faster, my children growing up, my husband growing old, nearing his fiftieth year. My own father with our Lord now these many years. I wonder often what became of their lives. Did they stay in Leiden, or did my mother return to England? I shall never know. My life here has become so rich and full, but it has not been without its want for the family I once had. As we walk toward the common house for our holy day prayers I look around at the familiar faces. So many have been through so much, we are in most nearly every way a family. It is true there are people here now that I barely know, but at its core, this town is my family. Wills walks a bit ahead of us talking to his friend Richard, their ever-deepening voices carrying across the morning breeze. Patience carries Grace while Rem and Elizabeth walk alongside her arm in arm. Behind me, Henry and Isaac use sticks to make lines in the dirt.

I nod at Susanna, the Fullers, the Edwards, the Howland's, the Winslow's, and the Whites as we all make our way down the street. The warm sun at our backs and the cool breeze in our faces, it is a glorious day. Nearly to the common house a murmur begins to spread through the crowd; I can't quite hear what is being said, but suddenly I see some of the women begin to run toward the gate. It can only mean one thing. The men have returned. "Wills, stay with the children," I shout, grabbing Rem by the hand as we join the other women and now a few men running toward the gate, which is now open. On the other side, I can see some men moving toward us in the distance. They are too far away to see who is there, but I can see the group is small. Much smaller than the group of men who left. My heart is in my throat and Rem is holding my hand so tightly I fear it will break, but I dare not let go.

I feel Rem release her grip as she outpaces me, heading toward one of the men who I now see is Phillip. A sense of relief washes over me—if Phillip is here, surely William is too. I scan the faces of the group as they come closer and closer. In a moment it seems that all the men are surrounded by loved ones, and cries of joy and celebration echo through the air. He must be here somewhere, but in the crowd, I cannot find him. I search every face until I finally find Phillip again and he turns toward me, his eyes so much like his father's. Those eyes, so familiar and so dear, are filled with pain and sorrow, and I stop moving, I stop breathing. I know in that instant that my love, my dearest husband, is gone.

Chapter Six
The Tides of Fortune

William. He is my first thought each day and my last thought each night, even after nearly three years have passed. Every day I still feel the pain of the moment that I realized he was gone, although the pain no longer makes it hard to breathe. As I tend the garden, I need only glance around me to see how much has changed in such a short time. Phillip did add on to the house, and now it's nearly the largest house on the street, save Governor William Bradford's. The garden too has grown to meet the needs of our ever-growing family, and it takes me nearly all day each day to tend to it. My hands till the dark, cool soil, making way for the rows and rows of lush plants that will sustain us through the winter.

After William died, I insisted that Phillip and Rem take over the larger room of the house, as was right with Phillip the new head of our household. I removed myself to the smaller room Phillip and William had built so that Rem could join our family. It is fine for me, and I've taken Patience and Elizabeth into this room as well. Wills, Henry, and Isaac are in the children's room (although Wills is certainly no longer a child), and Phillip has added another nursery room where his babes Grace, Josiah, nearly two, and his just born brother, Samuel, sleep. Josiah, like my Mary, is somewhat sickly, and I spend much of my evenings making poultices and tonics for him to try and revive him. It seems to be working, and his cheeks are rosier and his legs a bit fatter.

"Phillip, do you think that you could build for me a small lean-to behind the house?" I say as we sit down for our evening meal.

"Whatever for, Mother?" says Wills, as he stuffs a biscuit into his mouth.

"I need some more room to make my tonics and dry my herbs, I've nearly taken over this table many days now, leaving us no place to eat," I reply.

"Mrs. McClure asked me today what we were giving Josiah. Her little girl Mercy is struggling as Josiah was, and I told her you would make her up something for the babe, I hope it's not too much trouble," says Rem optimistically.

"Of course, my dear, anything to help." I smile as I squeeze her hand.

"I can do it," says Wills, wiping his face on his sleeve.

I smile as I look upon this grown man, my son, nearing his seventeenth birthday. His father would be so proud of him. Since William died, Wills has been working with Phillip at the shop, and he's become a fine woodworker in his own right, but his mind still wanders like a boy from time to time. The shop is doing so well we have even hired a man to help with the planting and harvest so that Phillip and Wills can spend more of their time making furniture for the never-ending flood of new immigrants. "I would like that, son, if Phillip agrees."

"Of course, but it will have to be in the evenings. There are too many orders at the shop for me to spare you during the day," replies Phillip, looking quite pleased that Wills had shown some initiative. Wills too looks proud of himself, and so it is agreed that the lean-to will be built.

"Rem, can you take me to see Mrs. McClure so that I can better decide what tonic the child needs?"

"Yes, I'm happy to, would you like to go today?"

I nod in agreement. If a child is sick, there is no time to waste.

Josiah and the McClure babe both continue to improve, and I make more tonic nearly every day from the bark of the willow tree along with sage and chamomile, as my mother taught me. Wills makes me a few small wooden bowls for mixing and keeping my preparations, and they line the shelves of the new lean-to. Friends and neighbors come to call every few days for the things I make, looking for some help and relief from our physical woes. With Patience and Elizabeth now tending to the younger children and doing more work in the garden, I find I spend a great deal of time here in my new little room. The smell of the herbs and the freshly hewn wood mixes together to invigorate me, and I look forward to coming in here each day.

I've been teaching Henry how to gather herbs, and he's become very good at it after just a few weeks, although he did once bring me rosemary instead of sage, but never the mind, he is still a little boy and will learn it soon enough. The hyssop, lavender, comfrey, and fennel are all growing well in between the rows of peas, corn, and squash that now fill our garden.

"Mother?" Patience's voice pulls me from my thoughts. As she stands in the doorway of the lean-to, I am amazed to see what a young woman she has become. She is a beauty with the best of her father in her face, and when she smiles, I see so much of William in her.

"Yes, my dearest child," I respond, wiping my dirty hands on my apron.

"I'm not a child anymore, Mother," I get in reply.

"You will always be my child," I say, kissing her on the forehead, which I can only accomplish now by leaning up on my toes.

Patience plops herself on the stool next to my worktable and meticulously smooths her apron while avoiding my gaze. I know this means an important conversation is coming, so I take the other stool and sit across from her, taking her hands in mine. "What is it? Are you ill?"

She shakes her head slowly. "Oh no, Mother, no, nothing like that," she replies, still avoiding my gaze. I gently raise her chin until she can avoid me no more, and the hesitation in her eyes is unmistakable. I wait. "It's just that… it's…" her voice trails off.

"What is his name?"

Patience throws her head back, her laughter ringing across the shed as she puts her arms around me. "I should have known that of all people, I could not hide myself from you," she replies, her eyes now shining with excitement.

James, it seems, is his name. He is the son of John and Jane Hopkins, who came to the colony in 1634 abroad the *Avalon* with James, his two brothers, and a sister. He is employed by the tailor across the street from Phillip's furniture shop. A tailor, like my Jonathan.

"Tell me more, my dear." I lean back against the leg of the table as Patience regales me with tales of their chance meetings at the well, his lyrical voice and hearty laugh. And of course, his robust but neatly trimmed beard and lovely blue eyes. It is clear she is smitten.

Suddenly, a small, round, and very dirty face peers around the edge of the lean-to. "Yes, Henry, what do you need?" I ask of the small urchin, reluctant to think of him as my son in this moment when he looks more like a lost waif who wandered into the yard.

"I'm looking for my ball, Mother, the one that Wills made for me, I can't find it anywhere," he replies with a more serious nature than any ten-year-old boy should be able to muster.

"Where have you searched?" I try not to look at Patience, who is having a great deal of difficulty keeping a straight face.

"I believe I have looked everywhere, including in with the pigs, but I still cannot find it," he wails, stomping his foot for emphasis. Well, that explains his appearance.

"Have you asked Josiah if he might have it?"

"He can barely walk, Mother, I don't think he would have my ball," Henry replies with a bit more sourness in his voice than is appropriate.

But before I can respond, his sister is on her feet, no longer smiling. "Enough, Henry," she says, grabbing her brother by the corner of his collar. "You will not speak to our mother in this way. Although you are upset, being unpleasant is not acceptable. Please offer her your sincere apology, and you should also ask God for his forgiveness for your behavior." I lean back against the table leg again and smile. Patience would be a wonderful mother.

It was agreed that Phillip would speak with James Hopkins, and a formal period of courtship has begun. The Hopkins are both very kind to Patience, and James is clearly as smitten as she is, so it is a good match. We're planning for a wedding in the winter when all the harvesting is done. Patience and her sister Elizabeth can talk of nothing else, and each evening the two of them endlessly compare stitches for the decoration of the dress that Patience will wear to exchange her vows.

My children are barely children now, with Henry in full breeches for over a year already. There will be no more children in my life save my grandchildren, and grandparent is a role I will relish. James and his father have been working on a house for him and Patience, and Phillip is making a bed as a wedding token for them. It is hard not to drift back to the time when a house was being prepared for William and me. The memories now bring me more joy than pain, but the pain is still there. Like the misty fog in the morning, it seeps into my bones until the sun drives it away each day, only to return on the morrow.

As the day of the wedding draws near, I have decided to gift Patience the pewter pitcher that Mary had given me as a wedding token when I married William. I wonder if Daniel, Mehitable, and Samuel have married. Would Mary be a nan by now? The thought makes me smile. I could very much imagine Mary in the form of Mrs. Fuller, who shepherded us all during the months of our crossing, the task mistress to her herd of grandchildren.

"Mother, why are you laughing?" says Henry from across the room. "If setting the table for evening meal is fun, I will gladly help you," he offers.

"Your help is very much welcome my boy, but it's a fond memory of a friend that brings me to laughter," I reply.

"I wish I had a friend who could make me laugh so," responds the serious-faced Henry.

"I hope that someday you have so many friends and so much laughter that you will simply not be able to contain yourself," I say, ruffling his hair as his playful laughter joins my own.

The day of the wedding dawns beautiful but cold, with a light mist of frozen crystals hanging in the air and sparkling in the morning light. The common house has been decorated with boughs of evergreens and small paper flowers that Patience and Elizabeth have toiled over for many months. Governor Bellingham will perform the ceremony, and everyone is resplendent in their finest clothes. Phillip and Rem with Isaac, Grace, Josiah, and Samuel in his father's arms walk ahead of us across a light dusting of snow from last night. I can see the Hopkins's coming from the other end of the street, James taller than all the rest, trying to catch a glimpse of Patience. Henry takes the lead as Elizabeth, and I do our best to ensure that Patience does not find any holes of mud along the way.

As I sit and listen to the Governor and Elders from the church offer their blessings to the newly married couple, I cannot help but thank God for all that he has brought to my life. To see my first-born beaming with happiness has done my heart so much good, and I am grateful for it. The house will be quieter without her in it, but I know she will be just a short walk away, and I'm sure it is a walk I will make often. "Mrs. Tench, I want to thank you for all that you have done for this day," says James. Patience was right, his voice is deep but lyrical and most pleasant to hear. We must get him to speak at congregation.

"James, it is my humble honor to have you as husband to my dearest Patience, and I offer my blessing and my hope that God will bless your union and bring you both his grace. But for me, my desire is that God brings me a grandchild."

"Mother!" Patience says, the redness in her cheeks rising to the corners of her eyes.

"Yes, Mrs. Hopkins?" I reply, which makes her smile.

As I had hoped, in just a few months' time Patience was with child, but this morning her appearance on the front porch is not about that child but another, in urgent need. "Mother, would you be able to come to Mrs. Howland? She needs help and she has asked me to come for you regarding her son Jabez. He seems to have a fever which they cannot break."

The Howland's live in the very large house a few doors down from Patience and James. My brow furrows as I think about what I have that may help this boy. Comfrey with some willow bark, perhaps? "Yes, yes of course. Patience, grab the small satchel by the back door so that I can take a few things with me." In a matter of moments, we are on our way, just a dozen or so homes north of ours along the main road. It is a beautiful house and every time I pass by, I marvel at the sight, given that John Howland should not be here.

While crossing from England during a rough storm, John fell overboard and by the grace of God grabbed on to a trailing rope as he was falling. He was rescued by a deck hand using a fishing hook at the last moment before the sea would have taken him to its inky depths. His daughter Elizabeth responds to our knock upon the door. "Oh Mrs. Tench, thank you so for coming. Please, my mother is just here in this room with Jabez," she says, her voice barely above a whisper. She ushers us into the room just to the right of the door, and it is dimly lit, the only window covered in heavy cloth. It takes my eyes a moment to adjust to the darkness before I see a small boy lying on a bed, Mrs. Howland on her knees beside him with a basin of water, bathing the boy's feverish brow. He is flushed and yet pale at the same time, his eyes sunken hollows, his skin as white as the belly of a fish, and the bedclothes soaking wet.

"Mrs. Howland?" I say quietly. As she turns her face up to me, I can see the tears in her eyes glinting in the light of the single candle on the bedside table.

"Can you help him? I have tried everything, but still, he burns as if his very soul is on fire," she replies, and I hear the fear in her voice. A fear I know all too well.

"I will do my very best. Patience, why don't you and Elizabeth take Mrs. Howland to the other room and get her something to eat," I say as I help her to her feet. She squeezes my hand tightly, and I hold it for just a moment to reassure her. I hope, I pray, I will be able to help. "I will come for you when it is time," I say quietly.

I pull back the curtain and open the window, letting fresh air and light into the room. Jabez takes a deep breath as if he can sense the change in the air, but his eyes stay closed, and he seems to be in a deep sleep. Laying a few things on the small table, I find the small glass vial of the potion I had made just that morning. Mixing a generous amount with water from the basin, I climb onto the bed so that I can rest Jabez's head in my lap. Cradling his small face in my hands, I gently raise the cup to his lips, parting them slightly so that I can pour small amounts of the liquid into his mouth. At first, much of it seems to seep out, but after a few attempts, he begins to swallow some.

Every few hours I give Jabez another sip of potion and refresh the damp cloth on his forehead. I can see the sun is gone behind the horizon, and the breeze coming through the window has cooled. My back and legs ache and my body is tired, but I don't want to disturb the boy any more than I must. I lean back against the corner of the wall, resting my cheek against the cool wood. It reminds me of being on the ship, Jonathan lying next to me, asleep, as we tossed and turned on the waves. I almost feel as if I am with him, his voice whispering to me from across the sea. "Mama," I hear him call out. But it is not Jonathan, it is Jabez.

"My dearest boy, it's Mrs. Tench," I say as I gently slide him to one side of the bed. The candle has gone out, but the moon shines brightly through the window.

I open the door to find Patience lying on a small pallet that Mrs. Howland has made for her outside the door. "My daughter, get Mrs. Howland," I whisper, gently shaking Patience from her slumber, and she stumbles to her feet.

"Is he dead?" she asks.

"No, he's very much alive, now go and try not to wake the other children." I turn back into the room and from the corner of my eye see a shadow on the wall as Patience slips away into the darkness. I am surprised to see Jabez with his eyes open as I relight the candle. I brush the dark hair from his eyes, his forehead feeling cool and dry to my touch. "Thank you, God," I whisper to myself. Behind me, several sets of footsteps echo down the hall, and the glow of more candles quickly illuminates the room.

"Jabez, my dearest Jabez," cries Mrs. Howland as she takes the boy in her arms and holds him tightly, rocking him against her chest.

"Mama, I am hungry," he replies in a voice barely above a whisper.

"Of course, my dear, I will warm some broth for you," she says, her voice tinged with relief as happy tears stream down her face. "Sarah, oh Sarah, how can I thank you?" Mrs. Howland smiles up at me with such gratitude that I can't help but shed a few tears of joy myself.

"He is still very weak," I caution, "but I am hopeful that the fever has now broken. I will leave you some of the potion, he must have it for a few more days every few hours."

"You saved his life, Mother," I hear Patience say with a note of pride from the doorway.

"Through the grace of God, let us hope that is true."

As we step out onto the front porch the breeze feels cool, and as usual, a slight mist of fog hangs in the air. The sun is just starting to come up, but it is mostly hidden by the white mist swirling around us. "Mrs. Tench?" I hear John Howland's voice as he follows us out onto the porch, quietly closing the door behind him. "I can't begin to thank you for what you have done, but I hope you will accept this as a token of our appreciation for your labors," he says, putting a small leather purse into my hand. I can feel it is heavy with coins.

"Oh, Mr. Howland, I could not," I say as I try to hand the purse back to him.

"No, I insist," he says, closing my hand around the purse. "My blessings to you and your family."

"Thank you," I say finally, dropping the purse into my pocket.

As Patience and I walk silently back to the house, my hand closes around the purse in my pocket, the leather soft and smooth to the touch. Suddenly, and somewhat to my own surprise, I speak my thoughts out loud. "I'd like to open a small apothecary."

Patience stops abruptly. She turns to look at me as I continue gazing out toward the bay, as if there were something to see there. Perhaps it is the future I am looking for, my future. "Mother, do you think that you could?"

"Perhaps, if I took a small corner in the furniture shop with Phillip…" I say more as a question than an answer. I turn to look at her and see the twinkle in her eyes. "Yes, I think I could," I say, smiling back at her as we pick up the pace toward home.

Phillip paces slowly back and forth in front of the fire, his head bowed slightly, his hands clasped behind his back. Rem sits quietly feeding Samuel nearby as I wait expectantly, my hands neatly folded in my lap. My hands still show signs of the day's labors underneath my fingernails. What would he say? We have been talking all day of my thought to open a small shop within the furniture store, but I've finally pressed him for an answer—a simple yes or no will do.

"Mother, you know that I am most grateful for your efforts, as your potions probably saved Rem from the pox and you have certainly helped Josiah to thrive," says Phillip finally. I glance over at Josiah playing on the floor, with the ball finally found by Henry. The boys are rolling it back and forth, which Josiah finds quite amusing.

I see Phillip's eyes flicker to the purse of coins, still lying on the table where I had set it this morning. "I know that others who are grateful for your efforts have given tokens of their appreciation with eggs or vegetables or even small pigs, but I had given no thought to the idea that people would be willing to pay you with coins for this service," he muses.

"Nor did I, my son, I simply thought of it as my way of giving to others, of carrying on the traditions that my own mother taught me. But it is very clear that some are willing to pay and pay handsomely, I must say." I cannot help but feel a sense of accomplishment that the purse, heavy with colonial coins that Phillip said are nearly what he would make at the store in a month's time, is my doing. I could contribute more than just my labor in the house and garden, helping our family to be prosperous—I could be a merchant of sorts. Couldn't I?

As a widow, I have some liberties that other women do not have. There are several women working at the tailor shop, albeit behind the curtain that separates them from the front of the store, but even so. I would be with Phillip and Wills; it's not as if I would be a woman all alone in a place of business.

"I think you should let her do it," says Rem. I am somewhat surprised by her response. I recall not so long ago Rem's concern that my work with the herbs might be unclean. "If it were not for Sarah, we would probably not have Josiah, and the Howland's would not have Jabez, and the McClure babe, and so many others. It is a gift from God that she is able to spare so many from such grief as comes with losing a child. I don't see how we cannot help her to share this gift with others."

I look expectantly at Phillip.

"Fine then, but I want to speak with the Governor first. If he has no objection, then I think we can make a small space for you, Mother, in the corner by the window," Phillip says as he nods in agreement. I cannot contain my excitement and I hug Phillip, Rem, and all the children in turn. My head swirls with thoughts of what must be done but they are happy thoughts, and for the first time since William died, I know that life will be good. That night I carefully craft a list of things I will need and plan how best to spend my coins. New seeds, more bottles, another mortar and pestle.

I was able to find a few things I needed from Salem, but not all. Even after so many years, there are still things we do not have here in the Colonies. I wrote a lengthy letter to Captain Asher, who sailed to England within the week, with a list of things I would need, and he graciously took my request, along with my payment of course, and promised to return with my goods within a few months. While I wait for his return, Wills and I work to build some simple wooden crates with handles and a small cart that I can use to transport my bottles and materials from the lean-to across town to the shop. There is no land near the shop on which to plant, so I will have to continue to use the garden here at the house.

On a bright sunny day in the summer of 1643 a child is born, a son, to be called William after his grandfather. He is a marvel to behold, with wisps of brown hair curling across his forehead, and his perfect pink mouth twitches at the corners as it slowly searches for the hand he waves aimlessly in the air. Finally able to connect it with his mouth, he suckles on his tiny fingers. "Patience, I believe this young man is hungry," I say, smiling from ear to ear.

"So soon!" she exclaims, wiping her brow with the edge of her apron.

"Yes, my dearest, I'm afraid it is a never-ending task for these first few weeks, but it will get better I promise," I say, handing over this precious bundle to his mother.

I rock slowly, watching them. Despite her slight exasperation at the babe's demand for another meal, I can see the happiness in her eyes and the way they soften when she looks at him. "He is perfect, is he not Mother?" she says quietly.

"By the grace of God he is, your father would be so pleased and, as his namesake, so very proud." At that moment, a warm breeze swirls through the window, and on its wings a feather from a small bird, which lands upon Patience's lap. We both laugh, knowing it must be a sign from the heavens that William is watching over us indeed.

My child, my dearest Patience, is now a mother. Oh, how my life has changed. Once I was unsure if I would ever have a child of my own and I never gave much thought to life beyond that. It is such a joy to see the woman she has become, sure of herself and so kind and caring. James is a good husband and a very proud father, and I've no doubt he will be good to his son. I only wish my dearest William could be here to see how much our little family has grown. He would be so proud and so pleased that this little boy bears his name and that the child who made me a mother is now a mother too.

The Governor has approved of my desire to create a small apothecary shop at the furniture store, and Wills and I have been working for a few weeks now on building a workbench and storage shelves along the wall under the window in the front corner of the building. He has also surprised me with a pair of lovely chairs and a stool on which

I can sit while working. Patience has been working on a small sign to hang in the front that simply says "Apothecary," which we will hang below the sign proclaiming "Tench Fine Furniture" already in place. My new treasures have arrived from England, and I carefully lay out my things on the new bench. Jars of herbs line the shelves, and my baskets sit on the floor with many more plants to be dried and parsed into small bowls and jars.

Today, after many months of prayer and preparation, the sign has been hung by the door. I often imagined being the wife of a shopkeeper—Jonathan had wanted to open a tailor shop in the colony. But a shopkeeper myself? I could have never foreseen the twists and turns my life would take to bring me to this point. As I walk along the main street to the shop this beautiful fall morning, I stand a little taller and nod my head at others with more confidence. I am here in this new world, making my own way, making my own coins, making my own happiness. For I am happy indeed to see the children in their glory and the lives they are building. Wills is seeing one of the Smith daughters, Rebecca is her name, and Elizabeth nearly finished with her schooling and Henry right behind her.

It is a life well worth living. Until it isn't.

"Mother, Wills, come, come quickly," shouts Elizabeth as she flings open the door of the shop. Her face is red and drenched with sweat, her white apron dotted with red splashes and streaks where she has wiped her hands.

"Be still child, what has happened?" I say as calmly as I can, while grabbing my bag in case I should need anything.

"It's Henry, he's fallen from the apple tree at the back of the garden and onto one of the stakes that we use to keep out the deer. Mrs. Snow from next door is with him, I came as fast as I could."

My heart leaps into my throat. "Wills, fetch the ship's surgeon from the wharf and come as quickly as you can." I grab onto Elizabeth's arm as we run down the street, my thoughts a whirl of emotions, not the least of which is fear, a fear that seems to find me again and again.

When we arrive home the front door is open, and the Snows have moved Henry into the house. He is lying on his right side on the floor by the back door, his white shirt nearly completely covered in blood as it seeps through the fibers of the linen. Mrs. Snow holds a wad of cloth against the back of his left shoulder, but I can still see the small drip of blood flowing from below it. "I've done what I can, Mrs. Tench, but I'm afraid to push any harder to stop the blood from flowing," she says on her knees next to Henry.

As I move closer, I see the source of her concern. A stake from the fence pierced Henry's shoulder in the front and protrudes two fingers' width out through his back. Henry moans quietly but is quite still. I do not know what to do; should we pull the stake out or leave it in? Thankfully, I do not have to decide, as Wills and Thomas Turner, the ship's surgeon, arrive at that moment.

As I stand in the back of the room watching the men and Elizabeth tending to Henry, I feel as if my very breath might leave me. There is so much blood, I can see it spreading along the cracks of the wood as it seeps across the floor like a crimson river. Thomas has pulled the stake out, and now he and Wills are both pressing cloth as hard as they can to Henry's shoulder, one on each side. Elizabeth rinses cloths in the bucket when they became soaked and hands them back to the men as they desperately try to stem the red tide. "Mother, please come closer, Henry is trying to speak," says Wills, a tear running down his cheek. I hurry to his side and lie on the floor next to him.

"I'm sorry, Mother," he whispers.

"Sorry for what, my dearest son?" I say as I push the hair back from his eyes.

"I should not have climbed the tree to get to the apples at the top; Elizabeth told me not to, but I did not listen."

I glance up at Elizabeth, her eyes focused on the floor as she desperately tries to maintain her composure. "Do not fret, my son, we all do things we should not do from time to time," I say, holding one of his hands and one of Elizabeth's.

Henry looks at me, and I see in his eyes that the end is near. "Mother, even though I did something I should not have, will I still go to heaven?" he says in a voice I have to strain to hear.

"Yes, my son," I say as I squeeze his hand. "You will still be welcome into God's grace, and your father will be waiting for you."

"I want to stay with you," comes his breathy response.

"I will always be with you, my son, and you will always be with me," I whisper back, kissing him on the cheek. His eyes close and he lets out a small sigh before his hand goes limp in mine.

"Dear God, take under your divine providence the soul of our brethren Henry Tench to thy protection and care, and grant your peace to his family, amen," says Thomas.

"Amen."

I lie there for a moment longer, holding Henry's hand. Patience and James, as well as Phillip and Rem, had at some time come into the room, although I do not remember when. Mrs. Snow is apparently outside with the smaller children, although Isaac is here, his face buried in Rem's shoulder as he cannot bring himself to look at Henry lying dead now on the floor. The silence in the room hangs around me like a shroud and I want nothing more than to bury my own face in it to avoid the looks of sorrow and anguish on the faces of my children. Inside my chest I feel the sobs begin to boil up into my throat, and I gasp for air as they come tumbling out of me, but I do not try to stop them. Elizabeth leans over and puts her head on my back, her own cries nearly drowning out my own.

"I should have stopped him, I should have, this is my fault, it's my fault," she cries out as her body shakes from the force of her tears.

I pull her close to me, holding her tightly in my arms. "Elizabeth, hear me now, this is not your fault, nor was it ever. Young boys like Henry will do what they wish and all of us are powerless to stop them. Even if I had been here, if it is God's will, then we would all have been at his mercy," I say firmly.

God's will. Is this God's will or God's punishment? "Mother, come home with me and James," says Patience finally as she helps me from the floor.

"I must see to Henry," I say flatly.

"I will do it, Mother," says Wills. So much a man now, and so much pain he has already endured for such a short life. I nod in agreement and let Patience quietly lead me down the street. William laughs and babbles in James's arms, unaware of the calamity that has befallen us, as it should be.

"He should be buried on Coles Hill, next to his father," I say to no one in particular.

"We shall see that it is so," says James. I am so grateful that Patience has found such a good and kind man, and his assurances are a comfort and his strength a relief.

And it is so. We stand once again on the bluff overlooking the bay as Henry is laid to rest next to William, Mary, and our wee babe James. I look to the heavens for some sign that Henry is safely in the arms of his father, but the grey above me reveals none of its secrets. The clouds hang in the sky as if suspended on strings, not moving at all but simply fixed into place. The air is still but cool, and I pull my wrap around me more tightly. As I look around this sacred place of final rest, I see the names of so many whom I have known. The husbands, wives, daughters, and sons of this place whose dreams ended too quickly. So many, so very many. Our village has outgrown this place, and the newly dead who have no family already in this burial site are being buried in the New Burying Ground on the other side of the colony. I have a place here, next to William; sadly though, the rest of the children will not be with us. But, in heaven we shall all be together again, so it makes no difference where our earthly bones shall lie.

Rem and Elizabeth have spent much time scrubbing the blood from the floor, but as I sit here in front of the fire, I can still see the place where Henry's life seeped out of him. The faint outline of his life still visible on the floor, at least in my mind's eye. And just here on the hearth where William laid our sweet Mary on the floor when she left this world. This home has seen its share of loss, my three children and Rem and Phillip's firstborn. But it has also seen great joy. I close my eyes as I rock slowly, thinking of when William and I first moved into this house, much smaller then, just this one room. I smile. In this house our love brought us six sweet and wonderful children, and I am blessed to have some of my children still with me today. I think of the mothers in this town who have lost them all and who sit alone tonight with none to call their own.

When I came here some twenty years ago it was just the two of us, Jonathan and me. Now my family has grown to eleven. It seems a blessing indeed. Patience, her husband, James, and William; Phillip and Rem with their three boys and Grace; and Wills and Elizabeth. The family will grow again soon I expect, as Wills has spoken to Rebecca Smith's father regarding his intentions. Another wedding, another child, another chance to live a life. While it does not always feel so, we are blessed indeed.

CHAPTER SEVEN
OF GOOD AND EVIL

The shop gets a steady stream of visitors; many come looking to see the fine furniture that Phillip and Wills make, but some now come to see me. A tonic for a cough that will not go away or a fever in a child, and I am busy most days making potions and crushing plants. Phillip was able to obtain fresh whale oil, which has been most helpful for some of the potions mixed with jalap for when one's stomach is in great pain. Often relieving the stomach of its contents can be enough to bring the sufferer relief, and jalap is dependable for this purpose and more effective when mixed with oil.

Phillip now employs a full-time carpenter, and Isaac also spends all his days in the shop, having completed his formal lessons. Wills and Rebecca have been betrothed now some six months, and he is building a house for them just down the street from Patience and James. Rebecca has quickly become part of the household, and she and Elizabeth are fast friends. In fact, I think Elizabeth has taken a liking to Rebecca's brother, Peter, who is a blacksmith working for his father, Tobias, in the town of Boston. I fear that should Elizabeth move forward with this interest she will have to leave the colony, but I have a mule now and a small cart, which I could use to call on her in Boston should it come to pass. We shall see.

Jabez Howland came to see me today. He has grown into a fine young lad, and it does my heart good to see him doing so well. He comes often for tonic for his younger brother, who suffers terribly with a pain in his back. Sadly, his mother passed away last year after a bout of winter sickness, and his oldest sister, Elizabeth, is now the woman of the house, managing as best she can to raise her five younger siblings. She was betrothed to one of the Miller boys but has set that aside to stay with her father at least for now.

I see several other familiar faces this day as potions and tonics go out nearly as quickly as I can make them. The day passes before I know it, and I realize it is nearly dark as I turn out the lamp to leave. I'm startled when I open the door to see a man standing there, his face covered with a cloth and a cloak pulled up over his head, even though it is still warm outside. He avoids my gaze and quickly moves on down the street, but the encounter leaves me a bit shaken although I couldn't really say why. I think nothing more about it that evening, but the next morning upon arriving at the shop, I believe the reason for his visit is clear.

A small crowd of onlookers has gathered around the building, all peering toward the door, but I cannot see what they are looking at. As I approach a murmur runs through the crowd and they part, making way for me to reach the walk. There, in big red letters next to the door, someone has scrawled the word....*witch*. I try not to react as I unlock the door and close it behind me, but my heart pounds so hard I can hear it in my ears. I listen to the voices outside, just whispers through the wood. Would they come in and arrest me? My hands tremble and my mind races back to a time I want so to forget. A time when as a mere girl of twelve, the world around me became a dark and scary place. A place full of witches. I sit down at my bench and look out the window. I can see there are a few still here, but most of the crowd has left.

I hear a noise at the door and hold my breath. "Mother, are you here?" asks Wills as he slips through the door. I realize I have not lit the lantern and in the early morning light it is still quite dark in the room.

"Yes, my son, I'm here," I say, striking a match as I lift the glass globe to light the wick. The yellow light quickly fills the room and Wills is instantly upon me, his arms wrapped around me tightly.

"Do not be afraid Mother, this is the work of a madman, and Phillip and I will quickly see to it that it goes no further," he says firmly. Oh, if it were only that easy. I have seen with my own eyes how words and words alone can drive men and women wild with fear. I've seen the torture and death and destruction wrought by words. Or more correctly by one word —the word *witch*. "I'm going to take you back to the house, and I want you to stay there. Do not leave or go anywhere without Phillip or I, do you understand?"

"Yes," I say meekly, feeling more like the child than the mother in this moment.

As we leave, I see Phillip use one of his tools to scrape down the wood, removing the vile slander that had been put upon the wall. I wonder if it will be so quickly done to remove this stain from my person, this blight now seemingly on my very soul. I look around at the few people remaining but do not see any faces I know well. I search their eyes for some clue as to their thoughts, but they quickly look away and move down the street. We walk to the house in silence and without incident, but I cannot help but feel that behind every window eyes are watching us. How could this have happened? My work has done nothing but bring health and happiness to those I have touched. How could anyone feel that mine is the work of the devil? My hand tightens on Wills's arm. I have endured much in my life: escape from England, travels to this land, and the painful deaths of beloved family and friends. But now, for the first time in my life, I truly feel as though I am facing something I might not survive.

It was a warm summer the year of 1612 in our English village of Pendle. You could see the heat rising off the thatched roofs of our houses, and the clay floor was dry and hard. The thrushes had become little but dust on the floor.

Father was well known throughout the town as the local baker. Along with wheat my mother grew herbs, which she used to flavor some of the breads and to make tonics for the sick and give comfort to the ailing. It was from her and through the few books I could read that I learned my craft. My grandmother was friends with a poor widow, Elizabeth Southerns, although everyone in the village called her "Old Demdike" as she was descended from that family. She had been the local herbalist of Pendel for nearly fifty years. She dealt in potions and tonics and supported her family in this way. My grandmother and mother learned how to use herbs from her. Some believed Old Demdike had special powers, although no one thought that these came from the devil, but simply from her knowledge of herbs and the world around her.

For some years there had been talk of witches in the north who had tried to kill the young King James of Scotland when he was on the throne there. Some said witches had even conjured up the fierce storms that prevented the future Queen Anne of Denmark from sailing to meet her betrothed. Then, as James I of England and Scotland, the King had published a book, *Daemonologie*, to explain how it was that the devil walked among us in the world. Witches made pacts with the devil, who in exchange granted them special powers so that their magic could be used to cause harm. The King commanded that we should do our part to prevent this by protecting our homes and villages against this conspiracy and appealing to God and the King for their protection. For many years, eyes and ears were tuned in watchful wariness toward those who could be in league with the devil.

What started as an innocent encounter on a road outside of town between Old Demdike's granddaughter, Alizon, and an old peddler named John would sadly change the lives of so many, including me. It seems that Alizon was begging upon Trawden Forest, as many poor girls and lads would do, and as she passed John, she asked him for some pins. He would not give them to her, and so she cursed him right then and there, shouting at him as he walked away. After just a short time, John fell upon the ground, the left side of his body becoming stiff and unable to move. His speech was slurred and his vision blurry, but he was able to tell those who came to his aide who was to blame: Alizon.

When questioned by the local justice, Alizon said that the devil in the form of a black dog had told her to lame John and that she was simply doing his bidding. While this was shocking indeed, she did not stop there. She accused her grandmother and members of another clan, the Chattox family, of witchcraft. Nearly twelve in all from those two families were tried as witches who had sold their souls to the devil. The trials lasted several weeks, and each night my mother's tears ran freely as she wrestled with the accusations against her dear friend Old Demdike and her family. Worst of all, it was the testimony of the barely nine-year-old Jennette against her grandmother, mother, sister, and brother that sealed the fate of the accused.

"I have never known her to say an unclean or unkind word," decried my mother, wringing her hands in dismay. "I know that some do not understand the use of herbs and perhaps she has led people to believe she has special powers, but they do not come from the devil any more than mine do."

"Be quiet, my dear wife, do not speak so loudly of your own knowledge of these things," cautioned my father as he made the sign of the cross. "We should pray for the souls of those who stand accused and hope that God will have mercy on them in their judgement."

I had never seen my mother in such anguish, and she became even more disturbed when she learned that Old Demdike and some of the others had confessed to that of which they had been accused. For many nights leading up to the trial we could hear the screams of those behind the prison walls. The thumb screws, the binding of the head, the humiliation of having their bodies searched for marks of the devil. For many, confessions simply became a way to end the torture and suffering. There was no real evidence against anyone, just the word of a young girl and the confused and rambling confessions of tortured bodies and minds. My mother could hardly bear it.

One evening my father stood quietly at the hearth staring into the fire, and I focused on my needlework, no longer knowing what to say to help my mother in her grief. The previous day, Old Demdike had died in prison, alone, in a cold, dark, damp cell, stricken with grief and disease, chained to the floor. Her body was covered with bites from the rats and mice and her skin torn and bruised from the shackles. The next day, the remaining convicted were to be hanged. My mother's tears flowed slowly and silently down her face—she had no words left to say.

"We must attend the punishment tomorrow," said my father flatly.

I looked up at him in horror. "No, Father, please, don't make us go," I cried out, covering my face with my hands.

"The younger children can stay at home as they will not be expected there, but you, your mother, and I must attend. If we do not, some will say that we do not approve of the King's punishment, and we cannot risk any more talk directed at this family, especially given our kinship with the Demdikes. There will be no discussion."

I ran to my bed and buried my face in the blanket for fear my crying would wake Maggie and Richard, who were thankfully too young to understand what was happening. My thoughts turned to Alizon; she was only a few years older than I. Why would she have accused her family, and why oh why had she cursed the man John? Was she really a disciple of the devil, or was this her own mind spinning out of control? I would never know the answers to those questions, because tomorrow Alizon would die along with her mother, brother, and many of the others. A few had been found not guilty, but ten would be hung on the moor above the town at dawn.

I did not draw a moment of sleep that night and was up and dressed before my father had stoked the fire. "You could not sleep, my child?" he said, stroking my hair, which still hung loosely down the back of my dress.

"No Father, I could not. I do not understand how God can let his happen, do you?"

He gazed into the fire as if searching for answers in the glowing embers, but they came to him slowly. "We as mere men cannot presume to know the ways of God. We can only do our best to put our faith in him," he replied finally. Faith in God was one thing, but faith in man was another. Was God taking the lives of these people, or were men?

The day was unexpectedly cool for summer, the sky signaling that a much-needed rain might be on the horizon. The whole village was gathered there on the moor except for the infirm and the young children, save a few in their mothers' arms. The scaffolds rose up against the dawn like children at play with their arms outstretched against the sky. Despite the coolness of the day, I could feel my hair becoming damp underneath my wool cap, and it gave me a chill. I tried not to watch as they led the damned out of the prison, focusing instead on a bird perched high on a tree. He seemed to be watching the gathering from his lofty vantage point, perhaps hoping there would be some scraps on the ground after the crowd dispersed.

I'd never seen so many people gathered in one place at one time. There seemed to be more people even than the village held. Of course, there were a few soldiers sent by the King to make sure that events proceeded as planned, and their uniformed presence on horseback lent an air of majesty to the spectacle. Yet it was anything but majestic. The eight women were led in first, their hands bound together in front of them. Their faces and arms were dirty, with no caps on their heads their hair streamed about them in the breeze, and there were no shoes on their feet. Each was placed at one of the scaffolds, where they waited as the two men, James Device and John Bulcock, were brought in last. The men were less disheveled, and they wore boots but no hats. No one spoke other than the village friar, who was giving a final blessing and prayer to each woman and man in turn.

When he was finished, the magistrates helped the accused up onto small blocks of wood and placed the ropes over their necks. I held tightly to my father's sleeve, inspecting the fabric as if I had never seen it before. My throat was tight, and I felt as though I could not breathe. It was as if I could feel the rope around my own neck, scratching my skin. I put my hands to my throat as if to protect it from the blow to come. Then it began. I heard the thump of the wood as one by one the blocks were pushed out from underneath them. First Alizon, then Anne, Elizabeth, and so on until all of them hung from the ropes, their feet twitching, their bodies writhing. And then they were still. I could not bring myself to look at their faces, only their feet, now hanging loosely from their legs. I heard a woman weeping somewhere in the crowd. Gone was my innocence, as no one can gaze upon what I had and remain a child. "God have mercy on their souls," exclaimed the friar.

"God have mercy on us all," I said quietly.

The memories of those days run through my mind as I sit here in the lean-to. Unable to focus my mind enough to do anything meaningful with my hands, I simply sit and stare at the ground around my feet. What happened in our village was not the end of it. More were accused and more died, most burned at the stake, a death of agony. Many because someone had uttered a word or pointed a finger. Would that be my fate? Worse yet, would it also be the fate of my family? I wish ever so that William were here; he would know what to do, he would know what to say. I cannot even cry in this moment. The fear I feel is mixed with anger too, that my life and the lives of my family should hang in the balance because of another. Not because of what I have done, but because of what someone has said—a coward who writes their vile on a wall rather than speak it to me directly.

I know that I have not always been the most devout of believers, but the Elders know me, and they know my family. The Governor himself approved of my shop. None of us would ever give a passing thought to anything evil or unclean. Even after what happened in Pendle, my mother never gave up using herbs to make potions and tonics for the sick. She was more careful to be sure, and only spoke about it to those she knew she could trust, but she always believed that her knowledge, her skill, was a gift from God and not from the devil. And I believe it too. I will not sit idly by and say and do nothing to defend myself and my family's honor from this slander. I know, however, that it may not be enough.

Many have gone to the gallows professing their innocence till the very last moments of their lives. But there is one thing of which I am sure: I will never confess to a lie.

Phillip has met with the Governor—once again William Bradford, whom I know so well. He was with us on the *Mayflower*, and he married me and William after Jonathan died that first winter. Surely, he knows my heart and mind. I wait until after evening meal when the younger children are in the other room to ask about the outcome of the meeting. "There will be an inquiry," says Phillip solemnly. Isaac looks at me across the table, the glint of a tear in his eye. He is a sensitive young man, and I know he is very upset at these events, as we all are. Rem seems the least concerned and quite confident that nothing will come of this, but I am not so sure. Elizabeth says nothing, so I know not what she thinks. Patience and James have kept their distance at my behest. We've tried to keep our conversation quiet when Grace and Josiah are in the room, and Samuel is too young to understand, thankfully. I see the reflection of my own youthful fear when I look in Isaac and Elizabeth's faces, and it saddens me that I am the cause of this consternation.

"Am I to be arrested?" I ask uneasily.

"No, Mother, no, nothing like that. The Governor himself insisted that you should be allowed to stay here with us until this matter is resolved. There will be a public hearing, and anyone who wishes to come forward to speak on this matter will be permitted to do so, including you."

I walk to the window and peer out into the twilight, quickly enveloping the street in its cloak of darkness. "Perhaps it would be best if I separated myself from you and found other lodgings," I say softly.

Isaac is quickly on his feet and at my side, taking my hands in both of his. "Grandmother, you cannot leave us, if you do, others will think you have done wrong, and since you have not, you should stay," he says with the simple clarity of a young man's mind.

"You are my dearest, but I want no harm to come to you or your family on my account," I say, squeezing his hands in mine.

"But Grandmother, are you not also our family?" he responds, sounding somewhat confused.

"She is indeed," replies Rem without hesitation. I look around the room, and Phillip and Elizabeth nod in agreement. My heart is full at this moment. Whatever may lie ahead, I know that we will face it together, as we always have. Grace chooses this moment to venture from the nursery for a drink of water, and she climbs up in my lap and rests her head upon my chest. I quietly sing her back to sleep. These moments are so precious to me, and I can't help but wonder how many more there will be. Phillip will speak to the Governor again in the coming days to move the hearing forward. I want to get this behind us, and more importantly, I don't want this stain to spread, to taint whatever it touches, especially my children and grandchildren.

I wonder how many times in the past twenty-ought years I have walked this street. It must be hundreds and hundreds of times, going to the well, the common house, and out beyond the gate. I've walked this street alone, with my dearest friend Mary, with my husband William, and with my children. But today, as I walk toward the common house, it feels different. As if somehow my legs are not moving under my command but acting through repetition and habit. I've never felt such a lack of control over myself as I do at this moment.

My mind burns with the many thoughts that have come to me over these past few days. I have no more clarity today than I did when this began about what I will say, if anything, in my own defense. I see a few familiar faces also walking along the road; many are people I have known for my entire time in this place. Others who have come more recently I do not know as well, but I perceive them to be fine and God-fearing people. When I enter the common house, I see that it is set for the hearing with a table on each side and chairs in the middle. One of the Elders motions for me to sit at the table to the right of the Governor's table, which is in the center. Phillip has offered to sit with me, and behind me sit Patience, Rem, Wills, Elizabeth, and Isaac, despite my pleas for them to stay away.

Slowly, people file in and take their seats. Some must stand at the back of the room as there are no more chairs. One of the Elders rises to say a prayer before we begin, but I can hardly bring myself to focus on the words. It sounds to my ears as if he is a far distance away.

"Mrs. Tench?" I suddenly realize the Governor is speaking to me.

"Yes?" I reply.

"Do you understand that you have been asked to come here today in order to address the recent accusation against you?" he says with a solemn tone.

"Yes, yes I understand." The Governor's face is a blank canvas, and I have no sense of what he might be thinking, but he does not avert his eyes when I look at him directly as I respond.

"So, we shall begin," he says, clearing his throat. "Is there anyone here today who wishes to speak against Mrs. Tench in support of the accusation that she is a witch?" That word. As soon as the Governor says it, I hear the room inhale as one. They all know, of course, why we are assembled, but to hear the Governor say it aloud is shocking indeed.

I look out across the room, believing for a moment that no one will speak. Then a man whom I do not recognize rises quietly from his chair at the back of the room. He is tall and thin, his hair, of which there is little, is white, and his shoulders slump as if they were carrying a large weight upon them. He holds his hat in both his hands, and his eyes focus on a spot on the floor just in front of the Governor. A sadness seems to emanate from his person, almost palpable even from the distance at which I sit from him. The crowd ripples as everyone turns to get a glimpse of the person who would name me a witch. "Phillip, do you know this man?" I whisper.

"Yes Mother, he is Jonah Miller. His wife died a few weeks back I believe," responds Phillip. I look at the man again, but his face brings no memory to mind. If I do not even know this man, how could he possibly come to think that I am a witch?

"Mr. Miller, you wish to address this assembly?" asks the Governor.

"Yes sir, I do," replies Mr. Miller. I lean back in my seat, my hands clasped together tightly in my lap. Phillip puts his hand upon my arm to steady me; I hadn't even realized that I was shaking. "Mrs. Tench killed my wife."

The crowd gasps and all eyes turn to me, as behind me, the voices of my children and grandchildren call out in dismay. I can only look back with surprise and fear at this outlandish claim.

"Quiet, please, there will be order during this hearing," says the Governor, banging his gavel on the table. "Mr. Miller, can you explain why you believe that Mrs. Tench killed your wife and how you believe the devil has brought this about?"

Mr. Miller still cannot bring himself to look up at me, instead continuing to stare at the floor. "My wife, you see, she was ill with a pain to her stomach which would not seem to go away. She was suffering so badly she could eat little and drank only bits of broth and beer. One of our neighbors thought that perhaps the herbs which Mrs. Tench offered would be of benefit to her, and so I went to see her and brought some home, which my wife then made into tea."

I search my mind; I simply cannot remember Mr. Miller, but it had become so busy at the shop of late. What could I have given her?

"So, what occurred, Mr. Miller, after your wife made the tea? Did she drink it?" asks the Governor.

"Yes, she did," says Mr. Miller. A murmur ripples through the crowd.

"Quiet," the Governor says again. "Please go on, Mr. Miller."

"After she drank the tea, she lay down on the bed, and after a few minutes she began to shake, and then to thrash about, her arms bent up to her shoulders and her eyes rolled into the back of her head. I tried to stop her from shaking but I could not hold her." Everyone in the room was silent, most now looking down at the floor rather than at Mr. Miller or me. "After some time, it seemed she stopped of her own accord, but then her body was hot to the touch as if she had been put in a fire. Then, she stopped breathing and died." Finally, Mr. Miller looks at me. "I believe Mrs. Tench is a witch and that she poisoned my wife."

Phillip tightens his grip on my arm, and I do my best to steady myself in my chair. It is all I can do not to run—not from this place, but to Mr. Miller, whose grief is evident. I want to comfort him; I want to tell him that the herbs do not always work. I want him to know that I am not a witch, that I am a godly woman who tries only to help those who suffer. But I dare not move.

"Thank you, Mr. Miller, is there anything further you would like to say?" asks the Governor.

"No sir, I have said my piece," says Mr. Miller, sinking slowly to his chair, his chin nearly touching his chest as he weeps quietly.

Governor Bradford looks around the room. "Is there anyone else who would like to speak against Mrs. Tench in support of the claim that Mr. Miller has made here today?" No one moves or makes even the slightest sound. The Governor waits for a moment, and it feels as if time stands still. My chest heaves up and down, the very act of taking in a breath a labor. "Is there anyone who would like to speak in defense of Mrs. Tench as it relates to these claims made by Mr. Miller?" asks the Governor. I look out upon the crowd. For a moment, no one stirs. *This is it then*, I think. I am to be condemned by the word of a man I cannot even remember meeting. I bow my head and say a silent prayer, sure that my fate has been sealed. But then I hear the legs of a chair scraping against the wood floor. Mrs. McClure stands. Then John Howland. Then Mrs. Evers and Mr. Hopkins. Mrs. Smith, Rem, Patience, Wills, and Elizabeth, and now nearly half of those in the room have risen to their feet. I look around in disbelief. I recognize most of the faces, people whom I've helped over the past few years with sick children, husbands, and wives. They all stand silently.

Phillip squeezes my hand. "You are much blessed, Mother," he says, smiling at me.

"Pleased be seated, everyone," says Governor Bradford. "Mr. Howland, may I ask you to speak to represent those who have stood here today?"

Mr. Howland rises to his feet again. "Yes, Governor, I would be most happy to do so." What he says truly shakes me to my very soul. "I will not pretend to know the reasons all who have stood on behalf of Mrs. Tench have for doing so, but I believe that, like me, they are most grateful to her for her gifts. In my case, the gift she gave me was that of healing for my son Jabez. I know that we all agree that God is the giver of life and that only God can heal the sick and dying. I do also believe that he works through his chosen here on earth through his divine providence. Mrs. Tench came to us when my wife, God rest her soul, and I could no longer keep the breath of life in our son Jabez, who was just a small boy. He was sick with a heat in his skin that would nearly burn you to the touch. We could not cool him, and we knew that God would take him soon if nothing were done. Mrs. Tench came and tended to our son through the night with the tonic she made for the fever. We did not know if it would save our son, but we knew that if it did, it would be the work of God, most certainly not the work of the devil. Our family knelt in prayer that whole night, trusting in God to work his miracle through the loving touch of Mrs. Tench. And he did. The fever broke and our boy recovered; he is here today by God's grace. Mrs. Tench asked nothing us of and tended to our boy out of an affection for our family in our time of need.

"I know there are others here who have benefited from the healing that God offers to us mere mortals through Mrs. Tench. I also know there are some, as Mr. Miller has said, for whom the tonics do not work. But Mrs. Tench seeks to heal people with her tonics and herbs, certainly not to poison them, and many here can attest to their healing benefits. I am most sorry for Mr. Miller for the loss of his wife. I know him as a fine, God-fearing man, and I know his grief is most troubling. But he must trust that God has decided who lives and dies, not Mrs. Tench. She is his instrument on this earth, but she is not the arbitrator of life and death. If it were so, she would not have lost her own children to sickness and injury. We should be most grateful that God has placed her among us, and her gifts are to be cherished and appreciated."

"I would ask that if you are in agreement with the words so spoken by Mr. Howland, you show yourself by standing," says the Governor. I watch while each person in the room who was seated, save Mr. Miller and a couple of others, slowly rises to their feet. "You may be seated," says the Governor after counting their numbers.

I look at Phillip. "Surely this is God's grace upon me, but I feel I must say something," I say quietly.

"It surely is, Mother, and no more than you deserve," he says as he rises to his feet. "Governor Bradford?"

"Yes, Mr. Tench?"

"My mother has asked to speak if it be permitted."

The Governor nods in agreement, and Phillip helps me to my feet. My legs feel very weak, but my voice comes out strong and clear, as I hoped it would.

"Mr. Howland, I thank you most kindly for your words and to all of you who have shown your support for me. Those of you here today who know me know that in my heart I have sought only to help those in need as my mother and grandmother taught me. I also know, as many of you do, that one's deeds, no matter how well intended, can sometimes be seen as suspect by those who do not understand what you have done. I have no power over life and death, for as Mr. Howland so surely noted, if I had I could have spared myself and others much sorrow. I have lost two husbands, three children, my husband's brother, and my dearest friend, as well as many others whom I have cared for, in numbers too numerous to mention.

"Mr. Miller, I'm most aggrieved at the loss of your wife, but I must confess I did not know her well nor do I recall your visit to my shop. I sincerely wish that my tonic had been of help to her as they have been to so many others. I do not know why some are healed and some are not, this is only for God to know. But this I know for certain: my gift, if any, comes from his grace and the teachings of other God-fearing women who gave me this knowledge as my birthright. My conscience is clear in this matter, and as I stand here before you today, know that it is without remorse for my actions, for I feel I have acted only out of a desire to help others. I will accept whatever path the Governor decides is my fate. But I will, without hesitation, continue my efforts to give comfort and healing to those in need for as long as God allows me to walk this earth."

When I sit down, I can feel my heart pounding in my chest, and despite the large crowd, there is barely a sound. I wait, holding tightly to Phillip's arm. I feel Patience's hand on my shoulder, and while it's reassuring, I am still in fear. What will the Governor do? "Mr. Miller, as the Governor of this colony, it is within my right to determine the course of action this inquiry requires. It is my belief, and clearly the belief of most gathered here today, that the death of your wife, while most sorrowful indeed, is an act of God," says the Governor firmly. "As no other has spoken against Mrs. Tench and many her in favor, I find this matter to be closed. No further actions will be taken."

And with that, it's over. I feel as if the weight of the world has been lifted from my shoulders. I embrace the children as well as many of our friends and neighbors who showed their support this day. Then I make my way through the crowd to find the one person I must speak with. "Mr. Howland, I cannot adequately express to you my gratitude for your words today," I say. I feel hot tears welling up behind my eyes, but I hold them in, not wanting to appear to be in sorrow.

"I meant what I said, Mrs. Tench, you are a gift to us from God, and our family is most grateful for it, and for you," he replies as he squeezes my hand between both of his. I smile at him, most grateful for his words.

As we walk back home, the mood of the town seems to have changed. Or maybe it is only my outlook that has changed. Faces seem to smile back at us and nod in our direction, as if to signal agreement with what occurred. The sun is starting to fade beyond the trees, only its pink hues reflected in the sky above. The clouds appear to glow from within as they take on colors of gold against the brilliant blue sky. Rebecca, who had stayed with the younger children, now joins us with them for the last part of our walk home. Grace takes my hand, and although Josiah could walk well enough on his own, he insists that his father carry him on his shoulders the rest of the way.

I have been blessed today in so many ways, and none more so than having this moment here with my family around me. From the corner of my eye, I catch the flight of a hawk, swooping down low over the houses, his wings silhouetted against the evening sky. He cries out as he flies by, as if calling to us on the ground below, before he soars up into the night sky toward the trees. Nintisqua said once that he knew his wife was near after her death because the hawk would visit him to comfort him and let him know that all was well. I can't help but smile, and somewhere deep in my soul, I feel that indeed, all is well.

CHAPTER EIGHT
INTO THE DARKNESS

Another healthy child has come into the family, a girl for Patience and James, whom they have named Eliza Sarah. I am most grateful to God for her health and her mother's. Eliza's birth was an uncomplicated one and for that I am also thankful. Any time I tend the birthing bed, memories of my dear Mary Crippen are never far from my mind. I know only too well that the outcome can be unpredictable and that only God holds in his hands the fate of mother and child. Patience is a good mother, and with two young children now, she will be most busy and our visits less frequent. This is as it should be.

The house seems strangely empty without Wills in it. He and Rebecca Smith were married a few months ago, and he has moved to the house he and Phillip built by the furniture shop. It is a lovely home and Rebecca's dowery contained some beautiful linens and dishware, and I have enjoyed being their guest for evening meal. I still see him every day at the shop, but it is not the same. Isaac has now finished his schooling and has joined his father and Wills in the family business. He is becoming a fine furniture maker in his own right, his skills even surpassing those of Wills at that age. I see James every day as well at the tailor shop, which is nearby, but Patience no longer comes to bring his mid-day meal.

Isaac today has asked Phillip to allow him to build a small living quarter on the back of the shop where he can stay, a big step for such a young man, but I'm sure we will still see him at the house regularly, as he's most fond of his mother's cooking. But he is not the only one who has news today, and Wills's news I was much surprised to hear.

"Wills, I am sure I do not understand what you are saying, what do you mean you and Rebecca are going to Boston?" Phillip stands silently in front of the fireplace, his hands clasped behind his back. "Did you know about this plan?" I ask him.

He seems reluctant to look me in the eye. "Yes, Mother, I was aware, we have been talking about it, Wills and I, for some time. We want to expand our shop to Boston, where the town is growing so quickly. It is a great opportunity for us," he replies, finally looking up from the floor.

I look at my son, realizing now what this means. "So, you are moving away?"

Wills takes my hand in his. "Yes Mother, we are. Tis only a one-day trip by wagon, and I will come to see you regularly, and you can come to visit us as often as you would like."

"But what of your home here?" Elizabeth clears her throat, and I look over at her, suddenly realizing she was in on this plan as well.

"Mother, I believe that Peter Smith has been talking to Wills about renting the house from him while he and Rebecca are in Boston," replies Phillip.

I look about the room. "Clearly, there has been a great deal of discussion within this family to which I was not privy, although exactly why is simply not clear to me. Now if you will excuse me," I say as I remove myself to my room, quietly shutting the door behind me.

I lean my back against the door, feeling each beat of my heart in my chest and small beads of sweat forming on my brow. Wills and Rebecca moving away and Peter Smith taking on their house, which can only mean that Elizabeth's betrothal to him will be the next change to come. I'm going to be alone; my children are all to be married, striking out on their own, and I am relegated now to the role of old woman, the grandmother who tends her garden and fusses about with her herbs. When did I get so old? I walk across the room and sit on the edge of the bed, feeling every year of my age. I gaze down at my hands; the knotty veins and knurled fingers suddenly look like the hands of a stranger.

Wasn't it only a few years ago that these hands clasped William's as we said our vows? It seems like only yesterday they felt the squeeze of my newborn babes' fingers. My life has been moving so quickly of late; every few months it seems a grandchild is born, and another grows up to take on a new challenge. Ah, life is changing once again, and so must I. The role of grandmother has always been one of great joy to me, and I must find a way to embrace it more fully. My children are grown and so now I must focus on the next generation, the children of my children, who will plant our family's feet even more firmly in this new world. My own children have never seen England; the New England Confederation will be the only land they will ever know; it is their birthright now. This is truly their home and there will be no other, and so it is for me as well. I hear a soft knock on the door. "Mother, may I come in?" Elizabeth says quietly.

I smooth my apron across my lap and straighten my back. "Come, my dear."

Elizabeth slips into the room, closing the door behind her, and sits next to me on the bed. "I'm sorry, Mother, we should not have excluded you from our conversations, but we did not want to cause you any pain. I know it must be hard for you to think of Wills being gone and my..." her voice trails off.

"Being married?" She nods in agreement. "Oh, my dear, you all do not need to be concerned for me, it is the natural order of things that your children grow and marry. And yes, sometimes there is separation from one another, as I separated from my family. But there is never a parting in our hearts," I say as I pull her close and nestle my cheek against her silky hair.

"It's just that the last year has had not been without its discomforts, and you've done so much for all of us. We did not want you to think that we are not most appreciative or that our affection for you had lessened in any way."

"I would never think that, not of you nor your brother or sister. Yes, life has had its trials to be sure, but I have never doubted the support of my family. I have been most blessed in this world, and being your mother has been truly one of the happiest circumstances of my life." I wait patiently to see if there is more to come.

"Mother, I would like you to meet Peter Smith. He has spoken with Phillip regarding his intentions, but I would very much like your blessing," says Elizabeth softly.

"I would think so, my dearest, and I'm sure I will find him most agreeable if it is what you wish." I kiss the top of her head. "Now go, and leave me to my rest. We will talk in the morning and make a plan for me to meet this Peter Smith of yours."

The weeks went by quickly, too quickly, as Wills and Rebecca packed up their belongings in their new wagons, one for his woodworking tools and one for their possessions. Wills has rented for them a small house near his new shop, not as nice as the house he had built for them here in Plimouth, but it will be a start. Rebecca, already with child, will make it a home for them while he spends his days tending to his furniture-making in the shop. He hopes to take on an apprentice right away, and Phillip will visit for a few days after they are settled in to see that the shop is running well. I'm sure he will have no concerns; Wills has become quite accomplished and has a good head for business.

"Mother, it is time for us to take our leave," Wills says finally, having tied down the last bundle. We have not talked much about his going. I know it is as he wishes and so I have not said anything contrary, but I do not relish the thought. I wonder if I will see him again, if I will see his children. Boston is not the other side of the ocean, but in some small way it feels almost as far. As a woman alone, I cannot go at my leisure and will need Phillip or Isaac or perhaps James to take me, and this will not be easy.

"My son, may God watch over you and Rebecca and your children and keep you safe," I say, hugging him close to me.

"Thank you, Mother, I know this is not what you would wish but I appreciate your blessing, and I promise we will visit you after Rebecca is safely delivered," he replies as he hoists her up onto the seat.

I stand and watch as the wagons move along the road toward the gate, their wheels creaking and groaning liked the bones of an old woman worn from years of labor. As the gate closes behind the wagons and I turn back toward the house, I cannot help but wonder if I will see my son again. Abraham and William had both left through that same gate never to return. Perhaps it will be so again, but I must turn my attention now to what remains around me. A walk in the woods tomorrow to gather some tree bark and wild mushrooms might do me some good, and as I lie down in my bed, my thoughts turn to Wills and Rebecca, hoping they are now secure in their new bed in Boston.

My sleep is broken with dreams of days past and my childhood adventures. Thoughts swirl around my mind like autumn leaves blown about by the wind, but I cannot make sense of what I see, and in the morning when I awake, it is still dark. I quietly gather up my things for the day—my satchel, a small knife, some biscuits, and a few small bottles. I hear Phillip up and stoking the fire, but wanting no conversation this day, I slip quietly out the back and head off to the forest, looking forward to a day of solitude and quiet work. I see no one as I walk toward the gate except for the two young men on guard, who open it up enough for me to slip through.

A sliver of light as thin as the blade of a knife along the horizon announces the start of another day. It is clear and cool, and I am grateful for the warmth of my cloak as I pull it more tightly around me. While the sun tries its best to make an appearance, the birds rouse themselves from their slumber, and their chirping begins to fill the air as I reach the path at the end of the forest. I know this way well as it passes Coles Hill, where I often visit the graves of those I have lost, but I will not stop today. It is a pleasant walk when the weather is clear as it is on this day, and I have covered a good distance before the sun fully rises above the bay.

Having found a small glen of the willow trees I sought; it is quick work to peel away the bits of bark. The occasional sound of the wind whistling through the trees is my only companion, and I work quickly. Several hours pass before I realize it. The sun is now high in the sky, and I sit down next to a small stream to get a bit of water, filling two of my small bottles. I wash my face and hands with the cool, clear water and gaze at the reflection of the woman staring back at me. Her hair is starting to turn a bit gray, her face still mostly unlined, but her eyes are tired as she blinks back at me through the ripples of water.

A twig snapping behind me startles me to my feet, but I see nothing. I quickly gather up my things and head back toward the path to town. Again, something rustles in the bushes. I reach into my bag and take out the knife I brought along, suddenly realizing how small it is. Animals prowled mostly at night and certainly not during the heat of the day, but if it wasn't an animal, what was it? A trapper or Indian, perhaps? If it were someone from Plimouth, they would surely recognize me as one of them and show themselves. I take a few more steps toward the path and again hear the sound of rustling, but this time on my left rather than my right. Whatever it is, it is moving. I wait, so still I'm barely breathing. Hearing nothing, I slowly continue my way up the small hill, where I can now see the path ahead of me.

Although I hear nothing, I am aware that I am being watched, by something or someone. I continue to move quietly and carefully. And then I realize it is behind me. I turn my head slowly, and out of the corner of my eye, I see it. Its eyes are black as night, its fur gray and matted with what looks like blood around the ears and mouth. It bares its teeth, water dripping from its muzzle. A broad, bushy tail twitches to and fro like a broom sweeping the floor as it lowers its head and begins to growl. I have never seen a wolf this close before, and even in what seems to be its injured and more frail state, it is a large animal to be sure. Too big to be a female, a male surely, injured and afraid, I quickly realize he will do anything to save himself.

"Be gone," I yell at him, waving my arms in the air as William had taught me. *They are more afraid of you than you are of them*, I remember him saying. But this animal is clearly not afraid of me, and his response to my yelling is to simply crouch further toward the ground. I can see that he will attack, and I know I will not be able to outrun him even in his weakened condition. I hold the knife out in front of me, realizing I will not be able to use it until he pounces. My bag becomes my armor as I move it in front of my chest to help cushion the blow.

Now I can only wait. He will run or he will attack; I do not know which. Our eyes lock on each other, and for a moment, he seems to hesitate, but then without warning he is in the air and hurtling toward me. He seems even larger than he had on the ground, and his claws and teeth are aiming for my head. I raise one arm to protect myself and with the other thrust with all my might. The knife finds the animal's belly, and it screams in pain as it knocks me to the ground.

His teeth have sunken into my left shoulder and the pain sears through my body as I withdraw the knife and thrust again. This time, the animal falls off me, and I quickly scramble to my feet and run as fast as I can up toward the path. I am not sure whether he's following but I dare not stop to look. A short-cut through the woods would make it harder for him to follow me, and I turn away from the path, running as quickly as I can. He is behind me, I am sure, but not moving very fast. The thick branches tear at my cloak and scratch my face, but I keep moving, too afraid to stop. The pain in my shoulder is piercing and I can feel blood running down my arm, but I dare not stop to bind it. Suddenly, the earth gives way beneath my feet, and I feel myself falling into a void below. The wet, damp earth surrounds me, and the light fades away.

I do not know how long I have lain here, but when I open my eyes again, it is complete darkness, just a dim light from above, and I can see a few stars in the sky. My body aches and burns with a fever that feels as though it will set me alight. I try to sit up, but the pain is more than I can bear, and I realize that my circumstance is very dire indeed. I seem to be in a cave of sorts, or perhaps an old bear trap, not much larger than the space in which I lie. The walls of dirt rise on all sides to a height that would be well above my head were I to stand. It is small enough that were I able to reach out, I could touch the walls on either side of me with my hands. But my left arm will barely move, pain coursing through me whenever I attempt to use it.

Thankfully my bag is still on my chest, and I am able to reach inside for one of the small vials of water. After what seems like an eternity, I can finally hold it strongly enough in my left hand to uncork it with my right. I sip sparingly, knowing that once my water is exhausted, there will be no more. Not that it may matter, as clearly the bite from the animal is festering, and it will no doubt cause my demise long before running out of water becomes a concern. As I lie on my back looking up at the stars, I am thankful for the dew forming on my face to ease the burning, but the dampness now causes me to shiver, and there is no way to ease the shaking.

Will this be how I die? I have survived many things in my life, but I can see no way out of this place. I veered off the path, so even if someone came looking for me, they would not know where I might be. I need to sit up, to get a better look at my shoulder and see if I might be able to ease the pain. I take off my bag and roll onto my right side. The pain is like being driven through with a hot poker and sweat pours from my brow, but I cannot stop now. My breath comes in great gulps as I struggle, rocking to and fro and trying to get enough movement to bring my body upright.

A tree root of some sort protrudes out of the dirt wall, and I realize I might be able to use it to help pull myself up. I inch my way over to the wall, only a foot or two away, but it seems as if it takes hours to get there. Now on my back again, I grab the root with my right hand and test it. It seems strong enough, and I know I cannot hesitate once I start. I take a few deep breaths and pull. My screams echo through the night sky as the pain tears through my body, but I am sitting up now. I ease my way back toward the dirt wall until I can lean against it for support.

In the distance, I hear the call of the wolves, perhaps a response to my own pitiful cry. Their howls echo through the night as they are repeated over and over from one pack to another. In the darkness, I cannot see my wounded shoulder, so further inspection will have to wait till daylight. I place my bag under my left elbow to support my arm and lean into the cool walls of my dirt prison. I rest my cheek against the cool dampness of the soil, soothing and somehow familiar, and I sleep.

Birdsong fills the air, and I open my eyes to find rays of brilliant sunshine filtering through the leaves and branches to illuminate my surroundings. I can see the edge of the hole now, what looks to be some six or seven feet above me, and the space just large enough to hold a dozen standing men. On one side I see a few bones sticking up out of the soil, whether man or beast I do not know, but I fear my bones will become part of this place as well. My cloak is badly torn, but I might be able to use it to bandage my shoulder, which, while no longer bleeding, oozes a foul-smelling pus that is soaking through my dress. I lay my head back against the wall and my mind drifts. A sip of water perhaps. Digging into my bag I realize I have water, bark, and other herbs I could use to make a poultice for my shoulder. If only I could use both hands.

I lift my left hand with my right and carefully place it in my lap, and while painful, it is not as bad as it was last night. Working carefully and slowly, I manage to assemble the things I need, using my bag as a table to scrape the bark and chop the herbs. Thank goodness I had not left my knife in that poor creature, and it had somehow found its way into my pocket as I ran. I carefully put the bark and herbs into one of the remaining vials of water. In a few hours it will be ready, and I rest, knowing that the process of removing my dress from my shoulder will be a painful one indeed.

The sun has shifted when I open my eyes again; I must have dozed off. There is no more time to avoid what must happen next since the sun will be gone soon. At least there is no one to hear me cry and scream as I work to pull the fabric off my festering wound. I could not waste what little water I had to clean it, so I didn't know the extent of the damage, but it is as bad as I had imagined. I am able to make a small bandage from my cloak, soak it with half the remedy I made, and place it on my shoulder where there is the most pain. The liquid both cools and burns. As best I can, I use the remainder of my cloak to tighten it against my skin. It is not ideal but perhaps it will do some good. I take a small sip of the tonic as well and settle back into the wall for another long night.

Overhead the buzzards have begun circling; I've watched them all morning drawing lazy circles in the sky. It seems an insult to me as I am not yet dead, but their presence seems to foretell my future. Occasionally one dips out of sight only to return to the sky a few moments later. The wound seems no worse today, and I use the last of the tonic to soak it once more. I have just a small amount of water left, and I ate my last biscuit during the night. My mind drifts from thought to thought and I can feel the fever still burning. "Sarah," I hear William calling to me in a dream—perhaps he has come to take me with him to the heavens.

"Mother," the cry comes this time, and I realize it is not a dream.

"Here, I am here," I yell out with all my might. I can hear voices calling out, but can they hear me? "Help me, please, I am here in this hole," I yell out again. The voices seem to have gone quiet; maybe it was in my mind after all.

"Mother, we are here," says the voice again. I squint as I stare up into the sun, and there at the edge of the hole, the face of Phillip.

"My son, I have never been so happy to see anyone in all my days," I say as I smile up at him.

"Are you hurt, Mother?"

I nod. "Yes. I was attacked by a wolf and my arm it is badly injured."

Soon there are four or five other men at the edge of the hole and a rope falls over the side, which Isaac quickly climbs down till he is crouched next to me. "Grandma, here, some water," he says, offering me his pouch. I drink greedily and the water revives me some. "We are working on a plan to get you out of here. Eat this tack, and I will be back in a few moments," he says as he starts to climb back up the rope. I hear hurried voices above but cannot understand all the words. The sun is starting to fade, and the thought of another night here in this hole is more than I can fathom. An answer soon presents itself, however, in the form of a hastily constructed ladder lowered down over the side.

This time it is Phillip who comes down. I look into his eyes as he crouches beside me, and he gently sweeps the hair from my face. "Mother, do you think you can climb the ladder? It is not far, and I will be here to help you," he says softly.

"I do not think so, my arm is of little or no use to me," I reply, the tears welling up in my eyes.

"You have to try," is the firm response.

"As you say, my dearest," I say, knowing the pain to come.

Phillip pulls me to my feet, but it takes several moments for me to stand on my own. "I'm going to tie your cloak tightly around your shoulder and arm, so it does not move," he says. I nod. The pain already sears through my bones, and it feels as if my very flesh were tearing away.

"Now try to go up one or two rungs, I will help you," Phillip says; placing my foot on the lowest bar. The faces peering down at me seem far away, much farther than I can imagine myself climbing. "Don't look up, just look straight ahead. When you get closer the men will help you out,"

Phillip says as he half pushes, half lifts me up onto the ladder. I hold on tightly with my right hand, my chest heaving from the effort. "Now another," he says, pushing me up again. Another, and another.

"One more, Grandma, and we will have you," says Isaac, so close now I can almost touch him. My legs shake and my stomach churns; I feel as though I may be sick. "Don't give up, I love you Grandma, please don't give up," says Isaac, his voice cracking. I push up once more and then the darkness pulls me in and holds me in its embrace; I can resist no more.

I smell stew cooking over the fire, and I feel the smooth coolness of linens beneath my hands, but I can barely wake. Rem comes every few hours to bring broth and change the bandages on my shoulder. The room is quiet, the bed soft, and sleep most welcome, but my mind will not be still. I see the face of the wolf in my dreams and hear his growl on the wind outside the window. Dark and light seem to come and go, and I know not how many days I've lain here in this bed, but I am sure that the wolf waits for me outside as he comes to me each night in my dreams.

The days quickly turned to weeks, but I am slowly recovering. My arm will never be the same, but the pus has stopped, and the wound is healing. It is a miracle I was rescued. "How did you ever find me?" I ask Phillip, finally ready to hear the story.

"It was the wolf," he says matter-of-factly.

I look at him, furrowing my brow in confusion. "What do you mean, the wolf told you where to find me?"

"Not quite so, but we were searching for you along the path when one of the men spotted some buzzards circling in the sky. We worked our way through the woods till we were underneath them, and there was the wolf, lying dead just a few feet from where you had fallen into the hole. The birds had been picking at his carcass."

I lean back in my chair. The very creature that had tried to kill me was responsible for saving my life. God works in mysterious ways, to be sure. "So, the buzzards—you thought it was me, that I was dead?"

Phillip looks down at the floor for a moment before lifting his head to respond. "Some of the men did, but not me. I knew you were not gone to be with Father; I could feel it in my heart," he says finally. I smile at him. At times I forget that this man is not of my flesh, he seems so much like my own child. He looks now very much like William did when we first met, and he has grown to be a strong and confident man, a good husband and father.

"From now on, Mother, when you need to go into the woods you will take one of us with you, Isaac or myself," says Phillip with a tone that assures me there will be no more discussion.

"I can help Grandma," Josiah says from his chair in the corner. "I'm a big boy now." Laughter bubbles up from around the room, the kind of laugh that shakes your body from head to toe. I grimace as the movement sends pain through my shoulder.

"Josiah, I think you will need to be in long pants before you can help your grandmother," Rem says as she hugs him to her.

"You are a very good boy indeed," I say, smiling at my him. I am so grateful at this moment, grateful to God, to Phillip, and to all the men who worked to save me. And in some small way, even grateful to the wolf.

In eight months', time, I am once again working in the garden and spending a few days a week at the apothecary. I move a bit slower, and I can no longer lift my left arm above my head, so Phillip and Isaac built a small table that sits below my work bench to hold my things, so I do not have to reach so often to the shelf above. Wills has come to see me and to attend his sister Elizabeth's wedding to Peter Smith. They are now living in the house Wills had built. He also brings the news that he is now a father to a little girl he and Rebecca named Alice, after her grandmother. Both are doing well, and he cannot stay long, but it does my heart good to see him and to know that life is good in Boston. The shop is prospering Wills is becoming known in the new towns springing up all around Boston, and there is a steady stream of people in search of his furniture-making skills.

All my children now married, and Patience and Wills with children of their own. I'm sure it will be so with Elizabeth and Peter soon, too. My life has changed in so many ways, both good and bad. The life of a widow had not been my dream, but my children, and now their children, have been a blessing indeed. I wonder what Jonathan would think about the world we have created here, a world he spoke of so many times during our crossing on the *Mayflower*. It is the great sadness of my life that he did not live long enough to see what we could become. This once strange new world is no longer new; it is now our home. My home.

CHAPTER NINE
BEYOND THE GATE

I have for some time now promised Wills and Rebecca that I would come to see them in Boston. Each time Phillip rides to see them he brings back news of this new town and the lives that they are building there. "Do you think they will ever return to Plimouth?" I ask him bluntly.

"No, I do not think so, they are happy there, and Rebecca's brother has now moved to Boston as well. Wills is talking with Peter about selling his house here to him so that he and Elizabeth can call it their own." Elizabeth and Peter were blessed with a son some months ago whom they named Abel. A chubby and happy child to join our ever-growing family. Wills and Rebecca have lost a child, a little girl who lived only a few days sadly, but God has blessed them with another child who will be born in a few months, perhaps finally a sibling for Alice.

"I should like to go and see them," I reply. "Perhaps you could spare Isaac to take me?"

"Of course, Mother, let me look at the orders we have and see when we can find a few days for him to leave the shop. I promise I will make it so, and soon." I sit back in my chair, excited by the thought of seeing Wills and meeting Alice, but I am also afraid. I have not been outside of the stockade since I was attacked by the wolf. Elizabeth, Isaac, and Josiah have harvested all of the bark, wildflowers, and herbs for my tonics. I have just not been able to bring myself to venture out again, even after all this time. So many towns and villages now dot the landscape around us, and I have not visited any of them. My life has been confined to Plimouth, but it is time now, I think, to venture out and see more of this place that has grown up beyond the gate.

True to his word, just a month later Philip has Isaac help me pack a few things into the smaller wagon, which he will drive to take me to Boston. He's clearly more excited to go than even I am. The journey will take a very full day, and Rem has packed a sack of biscuits and hand pies for us to eat along the way. Isaac will stay only a day or two before he returns to Plimouth, as Phillip cannot spare him for long. I will stay until Isaac can return for me in a few months' time. My life has been quite small in many ways since coming to Plimouth, my world shaped only by those around me. I must get past my fears if I want to see Wills and his family, which I very much do.

The sun is already oozing across the horizon this beautiful summer day, casting its light in shades of white and gold. As we set out on the road the breeze is cool, at least for now. We see several other travelers on our journey, and Isaac nods and tips his hat at each one in turn. The little wagon creaks along the path and the mule expertly sidesteps the large ruts and big stones. Once the full heat of the day sets upon us, we pull off under a tree to give the mule a rest and to eat from the sack that Rem has provided. The water from the little stream we find nearby is cool and crisp, and we are grateful for it. "Isaac, you've been most quiet on our journey, does something trouble you?" I ask.

"No, Grandmother, I am not troubled, just thinking about what Boston must be like and happy to be seeing Wills," he says.

"I am as well," I reply, and with that we return to our travels.

We are beginning to see more travelers and the road has improved, but a new obstacle has appeared. Isaac is ill, and we must stop regularly for him to relieve himself of the contents of his stomach. "Isaac, let me take the reins, perhaps you should try to lie down in the wagon and rest a bit." He nods his head in agreement, although reluctantly. His shirt is wet with sweat and his face is flushed, his cheeks as red as apples. I give him a bit of tonic that I brought with me, and it calms him for a small while, but it is becoming increasingly clear that he is getting sicker. Ahead on the road I see several buildings, so we must be close to Boston.

Isaac groans quietly behind me, and each jostle of the wagon seems to bring him pain. I know we have to stop to give him a proper rest and so that I can make some potion for his discomfort. I ease the wagon over to the side of a large building and stop. Isaac barely seems to notice we are no longer moving, and when I feel his forehead, it is clear he's burning with fever. I jump down from the wagon and tie the mule to a post nearby. There are a few horses and another wagon tied up in front, so perhaps this is an inn—I can only hope. Indeed, I am heartened to see my hopes confirmed by the sign on the door, and I open it and step inside. I can barely make out anything in the darkness. Once my eyes adjust, I see several tables and a few men as well as a woman at the back of the room. I've never been in a place like this before, and to be here without a man seems most strange indeed, but Isaac needs help and I must push past my reservations.

Everyone stares at me, and suddenly I feel as if my voice has left me. "My dearest, what are you doing out on this road alone?" says the woman as she walks toward me, wiping her hands on her apron. She is a large woman with faded red hair and a bosom that spills over the top edge of her dress. Her face is worn with fine lines, and she is tan from, I would guess, years of work in the fields.

"I'm Mrs. Tench," I say, finding my voice at last. "I'm not alone, my grandson is outside in our wagon, he is ill."

The woman steps back. "You come into my house bringing a sickness?" she responds with a tone of indignation.

"No, I would never, he is ill from something he ate or drank I believe; it is not the pox or the winter sickness. I know this because I am a healer and I make tonics and potions for those who are ill. He was well when we left Plimouth this morning," I reply.

I can see her face and shoulders relax. "John, go with this woman and see to the boy," she says as she motions to one of the men seated at the table.

"Thank you," I say as John follows me outside. He speaks with Isaac for a few moments as I stand nearby.

"He is right ill indeed," says John, walking past me in the darkness back to the inn. "We have a room in which you can stay, if you can pay," he adds. Phillip was worried about thieves and robbers along the road and so he did not give us much money to travel with; I hope it will be enough.

"I can pay," I say. The woman, whom John refers to as Bess, organizes the men to retrieve Isaac from the wagon as she leads me to a small room at the back of the house. It isn't much, two small beds and a wash basin, but it will have to do. I fetch some water from the well in the back of the inn and lay a damp cloth on Isaac to help with the fever.

I set about making a tonic as Bess watches with interest. "So, what are you doing there, dearest?" she says finally.

"Sarah, you can call me Sarah," I reply, not looking up from my work. "I'm cutting up bark from the willow tree and mixing it with some water to make a tonic, this will help to break his fever." Bess continues to watch as I add the mixture to one of the small bottles I always carry in my satchel, grateful I had brought a few herbs and bark along with me. Isaac is quiet but he's able to take a few sips of the tonic, and

I wring the cloth out in the basin and place it on his brow again. Now we will have to wait.

"Would you like something to eat, Sarah?" asks Bess.

"That is most kind of you, but I have just a small amount of money as my son did not want to risk our being robbed, and I owe you for the room," I respond.

"You never mind now about that; we will see what can be done. For now you should eat something," says Bess as she guides me toward the main room in the house and sits me at a small table in the corner. There are a few other men eating and talking, but they pay me little mind. Looking around the room, I realize there are stairs leading to a space above, where I assume some of the men are staying in other rooms. Never having been in a place such as this before, I find it both strange and interesting, and, without Isaac by my side, more than a bit disconcerting.

The bowl of stew is just what I need, and I eat heartily, saving a bit for Isaac in case I can get him to eat something. Bess is a good cook, and the men compliment her food as she refills their mugs with ale. This place smells of smoke and leather, a smell that reminds me a bit of William. The ale is strong and comforting, and for a moment I almost forget our peril. But I must check on Isaac. He is still quite warm with fever and refuses to eat any of the stew Bess provided, yet he is able to take a bit of tonic. I must speak to her and figure out how to get a message to Wills, but for now, the day's events have taken their toll and I lie down on the other bed to rest, my body sore and aching from the journey. Before I know it the sun is streaming underneath the door—I slept the whole night away. Panicked, I leap from the bed to check on Isaac, and I am relieved to see that he slept and that he seems a bit cooler to the touch.

The hustle and bustle of the morning has begun, and I hear the rattling of pots and pans from the kitchen on the other side of the wall. I slip quietly out the back door to fetch some water from the well with which to wash. In just a few moments the water turns brown as the dust and dirt from our journey washes away. Feeling much better, I sit down on the bed to count our money. One piece of eight and a tanner might be enough to keep us here until Wills can come, but I can't be sure. Isaac is better but clearly far from well and certainly in no shape to travel. I knit my brow together as I look at the coins in my lap. Perhaps I could offer some labor to Bess in exchange for our room and board? I could wash, or cook or clean, surely there must be something she would value.

Bess is in the kitchen preparing the morning meal for the men who spent the night in the inn. I see three or four of them already at the tables waiting on the porridge that steams above the fire. "How can I help you?" I ask Bess, who is already sweating from the day's labors.

"I'd be most grateful if you could take these two bowls out to Mr. Morse and Mr. Johnson, they are at the table in the corner by the door. I'll follow with the other two in just a moment," she replies, clearly grateful for the help. I take the two bowls out to the men as she asked, and they are appreciative although clearly surprised by my presence.

Once the men have been served, I take a small amount of porridge to Isaac, but after just a couple of bites he can eat no more and returns to his fitful slumber. I finish off the rest and then return to the kitchen to help with the washing of dishes and baking of bread. "Bess, I need to get a message to my son in Boston. Is there someone here who can help me?" I ask, my arms up to their elbows in flour.

"Of course, let me speak with John. He may be able to go himself or he will know if someone is going that way."

"I can pay for his services, but I do not know how long our funds will hold out before my son can come help us," I say, unsure how to broach the next subject.

"You need not worry." Bess puts her arm around my shoulder. "We won't throw ye to the dogs," she says, laughing. I smile, although the thought of being thrown out of the inn is terrifying indeed. "Perhaps you wouldn't mind continuing to help out around here until you can get to Boston?" Bess cocks one eyebrow up, reinforcing her question. She must have read my mind. "For room and board for you and your grandson, of course," she clarifies.

I stop kneading the dough long enough to hug her, minding my sticky hands. "Oh, thank you Bess, I was thinking that also, but I was unsure how to ask." She smiles broadly, and something about her reminds me of my mother, although surely, we are close to the same age. It is her smile perhaps, warm and genuine even if a few of her teeth are missing.

"I get little help around here from these men to be sure, so it's most welcome indeed," she responds as she heads out to fetch more wood for the fire.

I feel as if the weight of the world has been lifted from my shoulders. At least now we will be safe here, fed and sheltered until Isaac is well enough to travel or until Wills can come. I've given John three pence and a note for Wills, and he will ride into Boston in a day or two and do his best to find him. I know on which street his shop is to be found, and I hope he will make quick work of it. Otherwise, I've no choice but to continue to work while we wait for God to help us in our plight. I don't mind really; Bess is always on the move and most organized, so it makes light work of the day's labors and I enjoy her company. Some of the men seem quite surprised to see a Puritan woman working in this place, but no one questions me, and I spend as little time as I can outside the kitchen.

We have been here now some four days, and Isaac is able to sit up and eat and drink small amounts before lying back down to sleep. His brow is still warm to the touch, but he does seem to be on the mend. This morning Bess asked if I could gather the linens from the two rooms upstairs for the wash. Reluctantly I agreed and hoped I wouldn't encounter anyone there. Relived to see no one, I quickly gather up the linens and take an armful downstairs. I hastily return for the remaining linens but am startled to find Mr. Morse coming up the stairs just as I am trying to go down. Quickly I retreat to the landing to allow him to come up, and he mumbles something under his breath as he pushes rudely past me, flattening me up against the wall as he does so, his arm brushing against my breast.

For a moment I can hardly breathe. Had he meant to assault me in this way, or was it simply the close quarters and his general lack of regard? I hurry down the stairs and run out the back door and into the yard where Bess has set up the wash tub. The air fills my lungs, and the breeze dries the beads of sweat that had formed on my brow. It was nothing, I'm sure; perhaps it would be better to keep this to myself. If Bess knew she might demand that we leave, and I can't risk Isaac's recovery. Focusing on the task at hand is most helpful, and it is mid-afternoon before I stop again to take some bread and cheese. I gather up the dry linens and take them in, hoping very much that I will not be tasked with returning upstairs into put them back on the beds. As I turn the corner into the kitchen, I see Mr. Morse standing to the side of the fire. Bess is nowhere in sight, so I move quickly to go to our room; perhaps he will not try to follow me in there. Before I can reach the door, he grabs me by the arm and pushes me against the wall. I hold the linens close to my chest, trying to shield myself from the weight of his body, which now presses against me, preventing me from moving. "Sir, I must insist that you let go of me at once," I say with as much authority as I can muster.

His breath smells of ale and rotted teeth, and his blue eyes have a milky quality to them that makes looking at him most unpleasant. He smirks at me. "So what is a woman such as yourself doing in this place?" he says, his speech slow and slurred.

"I am traveling to Boston if you must know, although my business is surely my own." He strokes the stubble of his beard with his free hand, still holding my arm tightly with the other, his knee pressing in between my legs. His eyes are dead, as if there were nothing behind them, no conscious, no godliness. The seriousness of my situation becomes clearer with each passing second: he is going to rape me. "Isa—!" I try to call out for my grandson, but before I can get the words out, he clasps his other hand over my mouth.

"Now, now dearest, this won't take long. No need to be calling for help and all, and if you do, I'll have to hurt ye," he says, leaning into me harder and loosening his grip slightly as he begins pulling up my dress and pushing me to the floor.

I feel his filthy, rough hands tearing at my clothes and tears welling up in my eyes. This could not be happening to me, and yet it is. I close my eyes, not wanting to look at him, and I turn my face toward the wall to escape his fetid breath. I can feel him tugging at his pants, and I know my fate is sealed. Then suddenly there is a loud bang, and he goes limp on top of me. I open my eyes to see Bess standing over him with a cast iron skillet, blood beginning to run down his neck from a wound at the back of his head. Bess grabs his feet and drags him off me and across the floor, closer to the fire, before coming back to help me up. "Oh, my dear Sarah," she says as I wobble to my feet. I throw my arms around her and weep like a child, clinging tightly to her.

Mr. Morse begins to moan as he tries to get up from the floor, and I look at Bess with panic in my eyes. "Never you mind, dearest," she says, walking calmly over to where he lies on the floor. She raises the skillet above her head and hits him again. It is clear now that Mr. Morse will not stir again, ever. The next few hours are a blur. The magistrate is summoned, and he speaks with Bess and me as well as Isaac (who had heard nothing) and the other man, Mr. Johnson, who had returned for the night. Thankfully they took Mr. Morse's body away, and Bess is busy scrubbing the floor where his blood pooled. Wrapped in a blanket, I sit in the corner next to the fire, still shivering despite its warmth. Bess has given me some ale and I drink it heartily.

When everyone has gone and the inn is quiet, Bess pulls up a chair next to me by the fire with an ale for herself and another for me. "How are you?" she says quietly. I reflect for a moment on this day. God had surely blessed me when he brought Bess to my rescue, yet how could he have let this happen to me at all? I know there is evil in the world, but how could God have allowed this evil to touch my life? Was it God I should be thanking, or Bess? I look at Bess, who for all her life has toiled and labored—a hard life to be sure, much harder than mine, I imagine—and yet she looks to me like an angel sitting there.

"Bess, I cannot express to you my most sincere appreciation for saving me today from that heinous man."

She nods. "This can be a rough life. Sadly it isn't the first time I have had to deal with such depravity, and it will likely not be the last," she says, shaking her head as if in disbelief. "I'm just glad I returned when I did, before...." her voice trails off.

Nothing more need be said, and we sit in silence until I can bear it no more and finally go to bed. I am sure I will not sleep but the trials of the day and the many mugs of ale have exhausted me, and I fall asleep more quickly than I imagined.

"Grandmother?" I hear in the distance. Then "Grandmother?" again, closer, but I cannot make sense of it. I realize there is a hand on my arm, and I recoil for a moment, my mind returning to the events of yesterday. "Grandmother, you are having a bad dream, it's me, Isaac."

I open my eyes to see Isaac kneeling next to the bed. My head pounds and my arm is sore, but it all fades away as I realize that Isaac is up and dressed. "My dear, you are well?" I ask as I struggle to sit up on the side of the bed.

"Yes, much better today, I think I might have something to eat," he replies. I hug him close.

I mend my dress as best I can. Bess gives me another apron to wear, and it covers most of the damage so hopefully no one will notice. Perhaps I can see about a new dress in Boston. Isaac and I sit together this morning for some porridge, and it does my heart good to see him eat so heartily. "Isaac, this is Bess. She and her husband John have been taking care of us the last few days as you lay ill," I say as Bess brings another serving for him.

"Thank you, ma'am, for your kindness to my grandmother and I, we are both most appreciative," says Isaac as he greedily eats up his second portion.

"I was grateful to have your grandmother's help," Bess says. Isaac looks up at me over his bowl, clearly surprised.

"Yes, I've been helping out around here to pay for our room and board," I say. "Don't look so surprised, my son, I'm a strong and capable woman not afraid of work, as you well know."

"Indeed, you are, Grandmama, indeed you are," he says as Bess winks at me.

By evening meal, the chores are done, and the inn is quiet. Isaac and I have agreed that we will set out for Boston in the morning. I must admit I am a bit sad to be leaving Bess. She has been a true friend indeed, and I hope I will see her again on my return to Plimouth. Just as we are about to blow out the candles, the door opens and in walks John, followed closely by Wills. I leap from my chair and hug my son tightly to me. There is much to say, but right now I am just happy to see him. Isaac chatters away while I listen, asking all about Boston and Alice and catching Wills up on all the news from Plimouth. Before we head to bed the three of us discuss our plans for the remainder of our travels, and Wills gives Bess a crown for our stay and for his night as well. Most generous on his part but certainly no more than she deserves.

In the morning, as the inn fades into the distance behind us, I can't help but wonder if I would be here continuing my trip had it not been for Bess. I try to shake the memory from my mind and focus on the road ahead, but it hangs in my thoughts as a cloud hangs in the sky. Buildings loom against the horizon, and the road quickly becomes clogged with wagons and horses and carts and all manner of man, woman, and child. The city, for it is truly a city, teems with an energy and noise I have not heard in some thirty years, since traveling through London to reach the Mayflower. As Isaac drives the wagon through town behind Wills on his horse, I cannot help but marvel at the shops and markets—butchers and bakers on every corner and farmers out selling their fruits and vegetables. As we pass the wharf I see several large ships docked with both English and Dutch flags swaying in the breeze. While the thought of this many people and the noise of the city had unsettled me in Plimouth, I now find it most exhilarating.

Cattle are being brought onshore in large numbers from one of the ships, and their bellowing and snorting adds to the sounds swirling through the air. On our short ride through town, I see not one but three mills, which both surprises and amazes me. Women here have merely to travel a few blocks to get their corn or wheat ground, which makes me truly jealous, I must admit. The clothes too are a surprise, with many women wearing colorful, adorned dresses and hats that are much more elegant than anything we see in Plimouth. "So, Grandmother, what do you think?" asks Isaac as we stop at a crossroads to let some other carts pass.

"It is quite marvelous, is it not!" I say, smiling at him. He nods in agreement, and we chatter about the sights all the rest of our journey.

By evening meal, we are well settled in Wills's home, and my countenance lightens considerably after meeting the charming Miss Alice, who looks very much like her father. She smiles and laughs as she plays, and I very much enjoy her company. Isaac seems fully mended, although I still feel strongly that he should try to rest for a few days before making the return trip to Plimouth. "I will stay one more night, Grandmother, as you insist, but then I must get back. Father will be waiting on me and I have already been gone much longer than he imagined," Isaac says, placating me with his agreement.

"I sent word to Phillip as soon as John arrived here," says Wills.

"Very good, my son." I nod. "See Isaac, you have nothing on which to worry, I'm sure your father very much understands that your illness was out of your control." Isaac seems reassured and a bit relieved, as he had been hoping to see a bit more of Boston before returning home.

I awake in the morning to the sound of bells ringing in the streets, more than seems fit for a normal day, and I hear voices in the main room although the sun is barely above the horizon. I dress quickly and by the time I've joined the others, I can hear shouting and yelling in the streets. My heart races as I pull my shawl tightly around my shoulders. "Wills, in God's name, what is happening?" I ask, my voice sounding thin and stretched. I am not prepared for his reply.

"It's King Charles, Mother, he has been executed, word arrived just early this morning." I sit down in the nearest chair, my mind struggling to comprehend what Wills is saying. The King of England is dead by the hands of his people—what a strange turn of events indeed.

I'd known, of course, about the troubles with the King, everyone did. The early years of his reign were fraught with constant quarrels between the King and the Parliament of England, which sought to curb his royal prerogative. Belief in the divine right of kings had waned, and the Parliament opposed many of his policies, especially those that levied taxes on his subjects without parliamentary consent. The King's religious leanings were also of great concern since he'd married a Roman Catholic, which both we as Puritans and the Scottish Covenanters found most disturbing. By 1642 civil war had broken out between England and Scotland, and eventually Charles I was defeated by the Scots, who turned him over to the English Parliament. In and out of prison since then, he was tried and convicted of treason just a few months ago, and now, apparently, he has been put to death.

Many in Plimouth were very loyal to the King, while in Boston many lean more in favor of the parliament—the bells ringing throughout the city a celebration of the end of Charles's reign. "What will happen now?" I ask no one in particular.

"We are now the Commonwealth of England, Grandmother," replies Isaac, who is clearly delighted with this turn of events, "and we shall be governed by Parliament."

"It is not so simple," responds Wills quickly, and I see the consternation in his eyes. "Some will remain loyal to the crown and declare their allegiance to Charles's son as the rightful King of England."

Isaac appears surprised by this revelation. "I thought everyone would be glad to see the King gone and for ordinary people to have more of a say in how things are done?"

Wills laughs, and Isaac's cheeks turn bright red as he looks down at the floor. "Isaac, it is not so simple. I do not expect you to understand, but this could hurt our business."

I look at Wills quizzically. "I don't understand Wills, why would this have anything to do with us or our business?"

Isaac, Rebecca, and I all stare at Wills, who rubs his eyes vigorously with his hands as if to wipe away a vision he does not want to see. "If we support the Parliament, we will be seen by those loyal to Charles as traitors; it we support the King's son retaking the throne, we will be seen as traitors by those that prefer to see a Parliament in control. No matter which side we choose, there will be consequences."

I lean back in my chair, quickly realizing that he is right. And how would a resolution be reached? Would there be a civil war here in the colonies? More critically, what if there were disagreement within our own family—would we be at war with each other? My mind races, crowded with thoughts I cannot completely understand or control. One thing I know for certain is that once again God has brought to our family a hurdle we must overcome.

Wills and Isaac decide to venture out to see that the shop is secured and to speak with others to gauge the mood in town. For now, Rebecca, Alice, and I will stay quietly inside, shuttering the windows from the clamoring in the streets around us. We do our best to entertain Alice with games and songs, which helps distract us all as we wait for the men to return, although it is no easy feat to keep a child of nearly four years inside on such a warm and sunny day. No matter, the men will return soon, and we will know just where things stand and whether it is safe to venture out. For now, the house feels safe and comfortable and we've plenty to occupy our time.

Alice seems to be a clever child and a great help to Rebecca, who is now close to birthing another babe, by God's grace. A boy this time I'm sure would be most appreciated, especially by Wills. But no matter, if the child and mother both survive and remain well, more children will surely come with time. Rebecca is a quiet woman with little to say, and silence hangs over us like dust in the air as we wait, the hours seeping away one after another but the noises from outside continuing unabated. The sun is nearly down before the door opens, and I am relieved to see Isaac and Wills safely inside the house once more. While I am bursting with questions, it is clear that the men need to wash and eat before much will be said. I wait patiently by the fire, running my hands along Wills's fine carving on the arm of the chair.

At last, with Alice put to bed, Wills seems ready to talk. "For now, it is mostly confusion and speculation that drives the talk in the tavern, but it is already clear to me that sides will be chosen, although I cannot tell how quickly," says Wills in between attempts to light his pipe. Isaac nods in agreement.

"Are we safe here?" asks Rebecca as she gently strokes her rotund belly, her brow knitted with consternation and concern.

"Yes, my dearest, we are safe here," replies Wills, smiling, and at once Rebecca relaxes.

"Do not worry yourself," I add. "It is not good for you or the child to stress." She nods and excuses herself to go lie down, clearly not wanting to process any more of the day's events.

"Isaac, I think you should leave for Plimouth in the morning. If things should become more unsettled, your father will need you there," says Wills.

"But I've barely gotten to see any of the town, must I go so soon?" replies Isaac, sounding less like his nearly twenty years and more like a lad of half that age. He reminds me of Henry in this moment and I can't help but smile.

"Isaac, I know you are very disappointed, but I'm sure Wills is right, you need to be getting back. After the delays of our travels here, your father has been left to tend the shop on his own for some time now. But perhaps just one more day wouldn't hurt?" I say, looking at Wills.

He can't help but smile. "Mother, you always seem to find a way to make everyone happy. Yes, Isaac can stay one more day."

That resolved, we talk for hours, catching Wills up on the news from Plimouth and planning the boys' day tomorrow. Boys, children—it is odd in some way to call a grown man my child, but my child he will always be. So much now like his father, I can see William in the way he walks and the way he holds his knife; even his laugh is so much like his. It is a comfort but also reminds me of what has been lost. William would be so proud of his children, all of them. Patience and James with four babes now and another on the way, the years have gone so quickly! Wills and Rebecca with Alice and another soon, Elizabeth and Peter with their babe Abel, and Elizabeth already with child again. My family, once so small with such an uncertain future, has grown and grown and does my heart good, but it is hard not think of Mary and Henry gone so young. I wonder what would have become of their lives.

The noise outside the windows has died down with the passing of the hours, and with the quiet comes much needed rest for the household. I sleep soundly except for the occasional murmurings from Isaac on the floor nearby. Excited to start his day, no doubt, and perhaps already dreaming of the adventure he believes is to come. As the early morning sun begins to peek through the window, I rise quietly so as not to wake him and dress in haste so that I can help Rebecca with the morning meal. To my surprise, only Wills is at the hearth stoking the fire and hanging the porridge pot. "Is all well, my son?"

"Oh, good morning Mother," he replies, coming to kiss me on the cheek. "Yes, Rebecca is drawing near her time and she was quite restless last night, so I thought perhaps you and I could manage."

"Yes we can, how very considerate of you," I say. I set to making the porridge as Wills rouses Isaac to fetch some fresh water. We have a bit of pork and some biscuits that Rebecca made yesterday, some jam, and the table is set. Wills, Isaac, and Alice all dig in happily and I take some porridge to Rebecca, but as she's fast asleep, I return it to the pot. No sense in waking her as sleep will be a most precious commodity very soon if Wills is right. After the boys depart, I bathe Alice and dress her with the intention of exploring the streets nearby the house, but by the time we are ready to go, it is clear that Rebecca is indeed going to deliver, and her pains are coming quite regular.

"Alice my dearest, I'm afraid we will have to postpone our adventures today in order to stay home and care for your mother," I say as I stroke her long brown hair.

She nods. "Is mother hurt?"

Rebecca is moaning now with each pain, and Alice in her youth has found the most likely explanation.

"No, she is not hurt, she is going to have a babe, a wee one—a brother or sister for you," I reply, hugging her to me tightly.

"Then why is she crying?" says Alice with the hint of a tear in her eye.

"Oh, my little one, this is very hard to understand but your mother is going to be fine. There is some pain when you bring a child into this world, but with a little help and the grace of God, all will be well soon."

"Can I hold the babe?" asks Alice hopefully.

"May I," I correct her.

"I don't know if Mother will let you," replies Alice, "but you can ask her."

I cannot contain my laughter, and Alice joins in, not really understanding why but happy to be laughing, nonetheless.

Not knowing when Wills and Isaac will be back, Rebecca suggests I take Alice next door to Mrs. Brown, which I do without delay since her pains are coming more quickly now. I brew some birthing ale and broth, and Rebecca consumes both easily as I gather the things she has prepared for the birth. She has sewn a new gown—her stitching is accomplished and it is most lovely indeed. As the day wears on, it becomes clear that the child will be born soon, and I boil some water and clean the sharpest knife I can find. I wish Wills were here, as this still unfamiliar house makes each task a bit more difficult for me. But Rebecca is doing well and using the birthing straps I tied to the bed some time ago.

Just as the sun reaches the horizon a boy is born into this world, my new grandson. He is quite large, perhaps the largest babe I've ever seen born, and he is healthy and suckles quite vigorously. Rebecca, although tired, is well, and I take the babe from her breast when he falls asleep and lay him in the cradle Wills made, which stands next to the bed. "Get some rest, my dear," I say. "I will be nearby should you need me." I slip quietly into the other room. Rebecca did a marvelous job, leaving little for me to do, and I'm certain many more children will come to them. Surely the boys will be home soon as darkness is not far away, and so I set about making the evening meal before going to fetch Alice. Sure enough, before I can finish, a very excited Isaac comes through the door with Wills following behind.

"Grandmother, you should see it, you should see everything, it is quite glorious, oh I have so much to tell you!" says Isaac, nearly skipping about the room.

"In time my dear, but right now I have something to tell the two of you," I reply as I wipe my hands on my apron. "Wills, you should go and see your wife and meet your son." Wills lets out a whoop as he quickly heads to the back room, and I hear him and Rebecca chattering excitedly. Isaac is less interested in the babe but instead regales me with descriptions of all the things he saw today. Our evening meal is a celebration, and Alice at least is duly impressed by the babe and most excited to hold him on her lap, with a bit of help, as promised.

"So, Wills, have you and Rebecca decided on a name for this child?"

He smiles. "Yes we have. He is to be called John William Tench, after our fathers," he replies. I can feel the pride bursting from him, and I could not be happier for my son and his dear wife.

After this eventful day, my weariness lies on me heavily and I sleep most soundly, dreaming that I am sailing on the water, the breeze swirling my hair around me like a cloud. But suddenly I am awakened by noises from the other room. Isaac is up instantly, now my ever-watchful protector, and he returns in just a moment with the candle. "Grandmother, please come, it is Rebecca." I hastily throw my robe over my nightdress, not even stopping to grab my cap. Wills is wiping Rebecca's face and neck with a damp cloth, but I can see even from several feet away that she is burning with fever. I run back to my bag to grab some tonic only to realize that there is no more; I used all that I brought with me on Isaac when he became ill.

My stomach twists into knots and I struggle for breath. I am in a strange place with no access to the plants and tools I need and no idea where to find them. "Wills, is there a local apothecary near here?"

"Yes, on Sims Street. Isaac, it is next door to the tavern where we had our ale today, do you think you can find it again?" Isaac nods and runs to fetch his coat and hat. I quickly provide him a list of things I need and send him on his way, knowing that it could be several hours before anyone arrives at the shop. In the meantime, I search the pantry for anything I might use.

There is no more bleeding than I would expect, especially with such a large babe, but there is also pus, which is beginning to smell most foul. John wails to be fed but it is unsafe to let him feed at Rebecca's breast for now, so we also need to find a wet nurse and quickly. "Mrs. Brown!" exclaims Wills, and without another word he gathers up the infant and is gone. Once again, we are indebted to Mrs. Brown in the house next door, who is feeding her own little boy, born just three months ago. I soak all the linens on the bed and wrap Rebecca in the cool cloths, gently wetting them with water every few minutes to try and keep the fever at bay.

In her delirium she calls out for the babe but does not understand what is happening around her; perhaps that is for the best. The minutes seem to pass like hours, and there's no sign of Isaac. Wills paces the floor, stopping to glance at Rebecca from time to time, but she has become quiet and still, and my prayers to God for her safety become more urgent as they run through my mind over and over. There must be something I can do to save her, but I can think of nothing. Without the willow bark and other herbs I sent Isaac for, I have nothing other than cool water to offer her, which has little effect. Morning arrives and not long after Isaac with the things I required from the apothecary. As quickly as I can, I set about making the tonic and feeding it in small amounts to Rebecca. Now we can only wait.

The day is a never-ending routine of drawing water, cooling the sheets, and giving Rebecca sips of tonic. Wills has gone to the Browns to check on the wee babe, who seems to be doing well, sleeping and feeding at the breast of his savior. Isaac makes himself useful by chopping wood and tending to the garden, which has been neglected these last few days. In between my ministrations, I prepare a stew that we leave on the hearth to eat from as we can. No one seems to have much of an appetite save for Alice, who often repeats my own words to me from the day before that her mother is going to be fine. Not wanting to be separated from her mother, Alice makes herself a pallet next to Rebecca's bed and lies on it from time to time, singing softly to herself. My heart aches for her, and my fear grows as the hours pass.

Sometimes it is hard not to feel that God is most angry with me, that I am being punished somehow for something I have done or said, or perhaps for something I didn't do. Could this be punishment for my lack of sorrow at the death of Mr. Morse? I had prayed for his soul but not very heartily, and perhaps God has chosen to punish me for my lack of piety. Punish me if he must, but why must he punish my son and his children for surely, they live a blameless life. But only God knows his own mind, and we must keep our own council as best we can. I cannot pretend to know why some live and some die. Rebecca hangs on for nearly three days but never speaks again. I am bereft at the grief I must now bear witness to, and the little girl on my lap who doesn't understand. "You said Mother was going to be fine," says Alice in a tiny whisper, her tears streaming down her face as I rock her in my arms. How can I explain it to this poor child when I don't understand it myself?

Wills takes her from me and holds her tightly. "I know you did everything that you could Mother, and I am most grateful," he says as his own tears flow. He drops to the floor, still holding Alice as he rests his head in my lap, and the three of us cry together until we can cry no more. These children now without a mother, and Wills with the shop to look after.

I know at once what I must do. "Wills, I'm going to stay, I'm going to stay here and take care of you all. Alice, my dear, we will be fine; as God is my witness, we will be fine."

CHAPTER TEN
THE CITY ON THE HILL

The wharf is unusually busy this morning; a ship came from England just yesterday and the men are busy unloading its precious cargo. Sugar and spices, seeds for planting, ale, wine, and even a few cows. Each time a ship arrives it is like unwrapping a present when you simply can't guess what is inside. The smell of the sea and the bustle of the wharf always reminds me of my time on the *Mayflower*, and of course thoughts of Mary Crippen are never far from my mind when I think of those days. I keep a close eye on Alice, who loves to skip among the rows of wooden crates from which the sellers ply their wares. It's been nearly eight months since her mother died and she seems to have accepted this new arrangement. Wills speaks to her of her mother and how wonderful she was each night before putting her to bed. It is most touching and still brings me to tears more often than not.

We walk slowly along the water, making our way back to the house. Perhaps we will wander by Wills's shop on our way home and give him a bit of the bread and wonderful cheese we found this morning. Alice loves to visit the shop and entertains herself with all manner of tools, pretending to make furniture of her own just as she sees her father do. It is a beautiful day and the sun is warm on my face, but the breeze has a hint of coolness, an omen of the winter to come. From a distance I hear a church bell tolling its sweet sound. Then another bell, and another. The wharf becomes still except for the sounds of the bells and birds squawking overhead. Then suddenly, all the men are moving quickly toward the common houses as if drawn there by a force they cannot see but also cannot escape.

"Alice, I'm afraid we will have to go home, your father will probably be there soon, and I think it would be best if we wait there for him."

"Whatever you wish, Grandmama," she replies, seemingly unaware that something is amiss. We move quickly along the wharf and run across the street at the grainer's, keeping close to the buildings and away from the streets, which now team with horses and wagons, all headed toward the center of town. "Slow down, you are going too fast," cries Alice, and I realize I am nearly dragging the poor girl.

"I'm sorry, I will slow down, but we must go as quickly as we can, please try your best," I reply more harshly than I intend. Alice begins to cry at my tone, and I realize I've done more harm than good. I stop and take her face in my hands.

"Alice, I am sorry my dearest, but we must hurry home," I say, drying her tears on my apron.

"Why?"

I move her into a small doorway and kneel beside her. "There is something happening in the city. I am not sure what, but to be most safe we should go to the house. Do you understand?"

She nods. "What about John?"

"We will stop and get John from Mrs. Brown, don't you worry. Now we must go." I hear voices yelling and shouting behind us near the wharf, but I cannot make out what they are saying. My heart pounds in my chest as we hurry the last few blocks, and I only began to relax when the house is in sight.

Hannah Brown is standing outside, John in her arms and her Daniel sitting beside her. "Sarah, are you and Alice well?" she asks, her voice tense and high pitched.

"Yes, we are fine, we were at the wharf. Are the men here?"

"No," she replies, "I have not seen Wills, and my Samuel has gone to the common house to see what is happening."

I take John into my arms. "Come with me to our house, grab what you need for Daniel and come quickly, we should stay together until the men return." She nods and scoops up Daniel. By now Alice has run ahead and opened our door.

After setting John and Daniel into the cradle, Alice and I close all the shutters against the increasing clamor from outside. Then Hannah and I make a quick trip outside to gather additional wood and bring more water into the house. I also dispatch a chicken; we can pluck it inside, but we will be feeding more mouths than usual this night and it will be most needed. Finally I grab a handful of carrots and a few onions from the garden before nearly running back into the house. The garden is in its infancy but there are a few things we can harvest now, and we have plenty in the larder still. Hannah and I work as one to feed the children, pluck the bird, and churn some butter. We sing songs and do our best to keep Alice amused and distracted from the noise outside. The bells have stopped, but even with the house closed, we can hear the voices from outside. I have to know what is going on.

"Hannah, if you can manage for a few minutes without me, I'm going to go out and see if I can find anyone who may have some news about what is happening."

"The boys are asleep, and Alice and I will be fine, won't we dear?" she replies with a soothing tone, although her face tells a different story. "Do be careful," she adds in a whisper so as not to alarm Alice.

"I will," I say, hugging her before slipping quietly out the door. Even though God had seen fit to take Rebecca from us he has blessed us with Hannah, not just to nurse John but as a true friend to me, and she has done much to help me adjust to my new life here. She's taught me to find my way around the city and introduced me to all the best shops and markets. Nights when Wills and her Samuel are at the common house, she often brings Daniel over and we sew and talk until the men return. I have not had such a friend since my dear Mary died so many, many years ago.

I encounter only a few people on my way out to the main street, and no one I meet seems to know what's happening—most are doing their best to scurry quickly to their homes. When I reach the main street I see a man I recognize from the market standing at the corner. I do not know his name, but I know he works unloading ships. "Sir?" He turns in my direction, and I can see his face is worn and lined from years of work in the sun.

"Ma'am, you should not be out unaccompanied by a man. Where is your husband?"

"I live with my son and his children. He has the furniture shop near the common house, William Tench is his name. Do you know him?"

"No, I've no need of furniture and I do not know your son, but you've no business out alone this day," he replies in a gravelly voice worn with age.

"Do you know what is happening?"

He smirks. "Virginia has declared loyalty to the son of Charles I. They want to see him, Charles II, become King of England."

I can hardly comprehend what I'm hearing and shake my head in disbelief. Wills had predicted this when Charles I was executed, and he was right, a fracture had begun.

"Do you know what Boston will do?" I ask, almost afraid to hear his reply.

"They will stay the course I suspect, and support parliament's rule." The weight of his words hangs around my neck like an anvil. For years there has been civil war in England, the Scots, Irish, and English all at odds about who will rule and to what degree. We have escaped the fray here in the Colonies for the most part, but perhaps our luck is about to change. "Best ye go home, ma'am. Your son I'm sure will be along soon. There will be no fighting today, but time will tell." He tips his hat as he slowly turns and walks away. He is right of course, and I quickly make my way back to the relative safety of the house.

Hannah and I can only wait now, and the minutes seem like hours as we entertain the children as best we can. Alice as always is of great assistance, and I focus on completing the stew, lest the men come home and there be nothing to eat. The sun is nearly gone beyond the horizon when Wills and Samuel Brown finally appear. They wash their hands and faces quickly, and we serve the evening meal with little conversation, as Wills clearly does not want to talk in front of Alice, who by now is old enough to understand more than we care for her to. Finally, with the wee ones settled in the other room, Wills confirms what the man on the street had told me earlier, that Virginia has declared its loyalty to the crown and formally recognized Charles II as the rightful ruler of the English Commonwealth.

"So, what does this mean for us, for Boston?" I ask finally.

Samuel shrugs his shoulders and looks at Wills.

"I'm not sure, Mother, I don't think any of us are sure at this moment," he responds matter-of-factly. "While there is no doubt Massachusetts is an English colony, it appears that it will stand firmly on the side of Parliamentary rule, as we always suspected it would."

My mind races and I must ask the question that keeps swirling around it. "Will there be a war between us and Virginia?"

"No, Mrs. Tench, I don't think so," replies Samuel, and Wills nods in agreement.

"The issue will be less about what happens here in Boston and more about how parliament responds to Virginia. However, I do think some men and their families might move to Virginia and vice versa, depending on their own convictions," adds Wills.

"And what will we do?" says Hannah, looking closely at Samuel. The glance that Wills and Samuel exchange tells me this is a question they have already decided.

"We will stay here in Boston and support parliament," comes the response almost in unison.

"Well then, we at least know our way forward," I reply. I feel a jumble of fear, uncertainty, and confusion. We've been removed from the day to day of England's troubles for so long that I no longer know how I feel about what is happening. At the end of day, I suppose it should trouble me no more whether the Commonwealth is ruled by King or Queen or someone else entirely, but in some small way it feels as though the England I had known had died along with Charles I.

By the following spring it is clear that whatever might be happening in Virginia will have little or no effect on us here, and our daily lives carry on without much change. Phillip comes to visit Isaac and brings the sad news that our dearest Rem had become ill and passed on to her heavenly reward. I feel great remorse wondering if I would have been able to save her had I stayed in Plimouth. Patience and her husband, James, have taken Josiah and Samuel into their home, while Grace, now nearly thirteen, stayed with Phillip and Isaac to help with the house. The children all spend every Sunday with Phillip, and in another year, when Grace is a bit older, they will be under one roof again. Perhaps Phillip will marry another, but for now his heartbreak is nearly more than he can bear.

Elizabeth and Peter have been blessed with a baby girl, Martha, and they are a family of four now, with little Able having left behind his leading strings, running through the house daring his mother to try to catch him. It brings me joy to see our family continue to grow, but I have moments of pain when I think of my darling children who rest in God's care instead of my own arms. Had Mary lived she would be a woman now, married and perhaps with children of her own, and my dearest Henry would surely be a man as wonderful as his brother Wills has become. But it does me no good to think on what might have been; I must focus instead on what is before me.

"Wills, we must think about starting Alice in school soon, perhaps the school by the common house near the dock?" I say as I set his plate in front of him for evening meal.

He nods in agreement. "She has grown up so fast mother," he replies, shaking his head in disbelief.

"You all do," I say, chuckling at my son's observation. To further prove his father's point, John chooses this moment to shout out "mama," which causes us both to respond with peals of laughter. Poor John, such a sweet babe, and me, the only mother he has ever known save our dear Hannah Brown. We have started weaning him and it won't be long before his visits to Hannah and Daniel are simply for play, and I'm sure Hannah is most ready. She weaned her own babe a few months ago and soon her task will be done, until she has another of her own at least. I've been most grateful for her in many ways.

"So, what will I do at school?" asks Alice, excited about the prospect even in her uninformed state.

"You will learn to read, cipher, and study the bible," I reply.

"Did you go to school, Grandmama?" she asks.

"My mother taught me and my sister and brother in our house, each afternoon in between our chores."

"Do your brother and sister still live with your mother?" she asks. I lean back in my chair. The innocence of her question catches me quite off guard and takes me back to memories I have not allowed myself to visit for some time.

Wills looks at me thoughtfully. "You don't speak much of your family, Mother, you never have," he observes. I realize he is right. Perhaps it has been my way of coping with the loss, the uncertainty of not knowing what had become of my family.

"No Alice, my mother, father, and brother are in heaven with God, and I am not sure what became of my sister," I reply.

"Maybe she is in heaven too with your mother and my mother," she responds matter-of-factly.

"Perhaps she is," I say, feeling a tear form in the corner of my eye.

That night we talk about England, Leiden, and our journey on the *Mayflower*, and I find it does me good to talk about the past. The loss, yes, but also the love and laughter that we found along the way. Even after Alice and John have gone to bed, Wills and I sit talking into the wee hours of the morning. "Mother, I had no idea how very much you endured to bring us to this life here," he says as he kisses the top of my head, finally on his way to bed. "Thank you for all you have done for me, and especially for staying after Rebecca died to care for Alice and John. You will always have my undying love and gratitude."

I hold his hand up to my cheek, warm and a bit rough like his father's. "My son, you and the children are my precious gifts from God, and I will be here for you until my very last breath," I reply. My heart is full, but my eyes are tired, and I quickly fall asleep where I sit in front of the hearth.

Life has become routine here in Boston, and Alice is taking well to school. John is walking and keeps me busy chasing after him as he runs from one piece of furniture to another. Phillip has visited again and filled us in on all the news in Plimouth and of course the birth of more grandchildren, so many now it is hard to keep track! While I miss us all being together in Plimouth, my time here in Boston has been most enjoyable. Hannah and I have become very close; she is nearly like a daughter to me, and she and Daniel visit with us almost every day. Today, Hannah will stay with the boys while I run to the fish market before evening meal. The walk to the wharf is one I have come to enjoy very much, and I stop along the way to talk with several of the street vendors I have come to know.

The streets are busier than usual today, and the harbor is full of ships that have arrived in the last few days. The breeze is strong, blowing in off the bay, and it lashes my dress around my legs as I tighten the strings on my cap. The bracing air brings with it the smell of the sea. The fish monger, Mr. Bowers, and his dear wife are most pleasant, and he always holds the very freshest of fish for me, knowing I will pay a good price. We talk about the weather and the stoutness of the breeze as I look through today's offerings. So many people bustle around the wharf it feels nearly like the docks in London now.

I decide to walk down to the open grass just past the market to sit and eat the apple and cheese I brought with me while enjoying the sound of the wind and the waves. The sun is warm on my face, and I feel peaceful and at rest. Lying back on the grass and looking up at the blue sky takes me back to a moment years ago when Rem and I did the same as we watched the children splashing in the stream. It is a good memory, even though Rem and Henry are no longer here. As I lie here lazily watching the clouds race across the blue, I realize there is something else in the sky, a darkness that was not there a few moments before—smoke from what must be a very large fire.

I immediately bolt to my feet and look around to find the source of this dark column of smoke rising into the air, and it quickly becomes clear that it's coming from the far end of the wharf. No need to worry, I tell myself, being so close to the water they will surely have it out in no time. I sit back down and watch for a few minutes, but soon the clamoring of voices tells me I am wrong, this is indeed a worrisome fire, and men are streaming toward the wharf. I quickly gather my things and head up the grassy slope toward the street. The wind is whipping the flames, and now several stalls along the wharf are burning and sailors are working frantically to free their ships before the fire spreads to them. Men and women are forming bucket brigades to bring water from the bay to douse the flames.

I stand and watch in disbelief as I see Mr. Bowers, the fish monger, run toward the bay, his coat and hair ablaze, and dive into the murky water. I do not see him again. The wharf has erupted into chaos, and it feels almost as a dream as I watch the flames moving from place to place as if dancing their way across the wooden structures. It seems only a few moments before the fire has spread across the street and the inn at the corner where I usually cross to the wharf is burning too. Panic sets in as I hurry to make my way toward the house, going as fast as I can. Surely Hannah must be aware of the fire by now, as the smoke billows across the sky, becoming thicker by the moment. Women and children are running away from the fire, men running toward it. If the fire cannot be brought under control, the whole city could burn to the ground.

My dear god, Alice is at school not far from the wharf. I stop, unsure of what to do. John is with Hannah, and surely she will protect him, but what of Alice? I turn just east of the inn and quickly start making my way toward the school; I must ensure Alice is safe, and Wills is much too far way to get to her. The streets are full of men carrying buckets and women clutching small children as they scurry along the road, fear and panic evident in their faces. The roar of the fire is becoming louder and I can barely hear the men shouting over it now as the snapping and crackling fills the air. As I pass a well, I stop for a moment and raise enough water to dampen my clothes, hopeful this will keep any stray sparks from burning the cloth. I remove my cap, praying for forgiveness as I do so, and soak it in the water then tie it at the back of my head across my nose and mouth, as my father had taught me when I was a young girl. I immediately feel relief from the hot, acrid smoke that had already begun filling my lungs.

I can barely move now along the crowded streets, and the screams of women and crying of children become deafening. The fire is continuing to move, almost like a shadow I can see it racing along nearly the same path I am following just two streets over. It is like a monster, feeding on homes and shops at a tremendous pace, as if it cannot get enough to eat. At this rate, I fear it will reach the school before I do. The black smoke has nearly blocked out the sun, and it feels as if I am running through a fog that swirls around me. I can barely see the buildings in front of me, but the spiral of the common house catches my eye and I know I am close now. My head is pounding and my legs are burning, but I must keep moving; I couldn't bear it if something happened to Alice.

The heat now is becoming more intense, and as I turn the corner to the school I see that the monster is close. I reach the door but quickly realize it is locked, bolted from the inside. I pound on the door with my fists. "Alice, Alice!" I scream with all my might. I hear the scraping of wood from inside, Mr. Arnold carefully cracks the door, and I slip inside, quickly closing it behind me.

"Mrs. Tench, the fire, I didn't know what to do with the children," he exclaims as Alice wraps her arms around my legs. Poor Mr. Arnold, barely a grown man, the fear evident in his eyes as sweat pours from his brow and drips onto the floor.

"We cannot stay here, we must leave, the fire is coming closer," I reply as calmly as I can. There are seven or eight children huddled in the corner of the classroom; most are crying and asking for their mothers and fathers.

"It isn't safe, we can't leave," says Mr. Arnold, wringing his hands, his eyes wide with fear.

"We cannot stay, the fire will trap us here and all will be lost if we do not go and go now," I respond firmly. Taking his elbow, I guide him to the children at the back of the room.

"Children, we are going to leave. You must stay together and stay close to me and Mr. Arnold, do you understand?" The crying begins in earnest as smoke begins to waft in under the door. "You must stop now," I say firmly.

"Listen to my grandmama, she is going to help us," Alice says, much calmer than the other children, perhaps because I am here. I hope I do not let her down again. I once promised her everything would be fine, and it must be so this time. The children seem reassured by her words, and we use what little water we have to wet cloth to tie over each of their faces. Mr. Arnold is trembling so hard I fear he will not be able to walk, but we must go.

"When I open the door, follow me quickly. Do not let go of each other's hands, we must stay together, and do not be afraid, God is with us," I say, taking one last look at Mr. Arnold, who nods in agreement. "Alice, stay close to me and do not let go of my dress, no matter what, do you understand?"

She looks at me with those big brown eyes so much like her father's. "Yes, I understand."

When I open the door the heat and smoke make it feel as though we are in hell itself. Ash rains down from the sky like snowflakes on a winter's day. The smoke is so dense I cannot see my hand in front of my face. I quickly push Alice back inside and slam the door. It is too late to go out this way. Perhaps the window at the back? "Quickly, Mr. Arnold, the window," I say as I run to the back of the room and lift the plank from across the shutters. I open one just a bit to look outside, and much to my relief, while it is smoky, it is not as bad as the inferno I had encountered at the door. "Help me through the window and then pass the children out one by one," I say as I climb up on the small table I had pushed next to the opening.

In seconds I am on the ground, Alice follows, and then one after another the children scramble through the opening, most of them crying but some just silently staring at the scene around them in disbelief. I hear the hissing and snapping of wood all around us, and I know we have only moments to make our escape before it will be too late. But I am wrong; it is already too late. The roof of the school comes down in a crash of flames, and the force of it throws me to the ground. I scream out in agony, knowing Mr. Arnold and one of the children were still inside. It is impossible to see anything but flames and smoke inside what is left of the school, and I know in my heart that no one could have survived. I have no time to grieve for those who have been lost, as our own time is drawing short. I quickly gather the children and we begin to make our way along the street, staying close to the buildings to help guide our way.

The fire roars behind us, the monster constantly nipping at our heels, bellowing its smoke and flames at our feet. I try my best to move the little ones along quickly and they follow without tears or complaint. The smoke is lessening some, and I know we are now only a minute or two from the house. For the first time I allow myself to think of Wills—would he be there, or would he be lost to me forever? I cannot dwell on it, God is in control now—but glancing back over my shoulder toward the bay, it looks more like the work of the devil himself than anything God would do. As we turn the corner onto our street, I catch a glimpse of Wills's horse and wagon out front, already filled with things from the shop, and relief floods over me. Alice runs ahead and the other five children thankfully follow her lead.

Once safely inside the house, I allow myself to breathe. Wills hugs Alice and then wraps his arms around me and holds me tight. "Thank you, Mother," he whispers in my ear as he squeezes me tight. "I will never be able to thank you enough."

"If I never do a thing in my life again, my dear son, I will die happy knowing that you, John, and Alice are safe," I say as I hold on to him tightly.

"We are not safe just yet, I'm afraid," says Wills. My heart sinks as I see his face. I had so hoped the fire would not reach us, that perhaps the wind would die down or change direction. "We must go and quickly; I've no doubt the fire will be here soon," he continues matter-of-factly. "Hannah and Samuel are coming too, with Daniel and John. They are packing up now, and we must do the same."

"But what of these children?" I ask. I look around the room at their little dirty faces, covered in soot except for streaks washed away by their tears.

"They will have to come with us. There is a meeting place in the woods north of the city on the other side of the river; everyone who can will go there, as will we. Hopefully we will find their families there," says Wills.

I've never moved so quickly in my life, running from room to room gathering up the few precious things we could take with us. In addition to Wills's wagon and horse we are fortunate to have a small donkey and cart, and I fill the bottom of it with linens and bedding and perch three of the children on top. I will drive this cart. The other two children will go with the Browns, and Wills will drive his wagon with Alice. Wills had managed to grab many of his tools and has just enough room for a few pieces of furniture, some dishes, and a few of Rebecca's things that he's saving for Alice. I grab the fire pot from the hearth and some food stores as well. Alice has gathered a couple of the chickens and puts them in a crate. Wills ties the cow to the back of wagon, but all the other animals must simply be let go.

I had already seen horses, dogs, pigs, and cows running through the streets as we made our way home, and the exodus continues as everyone releases their animals so that they might make their own way out of the hell that surrounds us. Samuel and Hannah take the lead, and I follow them with Wills behind me. I hear one of the children crying softly in the cart, but there is no time to stop and comfort them. The roads are choked with people and animals all fleeing in the same direction. We move along slowly, the fire all the while creeping closer and closer. The smoke had filled the sky to such an extent that we did not see the dark clouds forming above us, but in an act of God's grace I did not anticipate, it begins to rain. A soft, gentle rain, only enough to clear the air and perhaps to slow the fire, but a blessing nonetheless. We hear the voices of people around us ringing out with praise for the rain and the dying down of the wind that came with it. Perhaps the fire would not reach our house after all.

By nightfall we have made it to the river, but the crossing is slow with many, many wagons lined up to use the only bridge, and we can do nothing but wait. Thankfully, one of the little boys with us spotted his family also waiting to cross, and he was most gratefully reunited with them. That leaves us still with four little ones whose families' fates are unknown and whom we must care for until… I cannot think about it right now. Mr. Arnold's face flashes before my eyes. As the roof began to cave in, he looked at me for a moment, his eyes filled with fear and regret for the life that he instantly knew would not be. My heart aches for him and the child, that poor child. I cannot even recall if it was a little boy or a little girl. So many people, so many children, so much death and destruction. It hurts to breathe, it hurts to think, it hurts to live.

The rain has stopped and the clouds' part, revealing a full moon that reflects off the river and illuminates the night. I am surprised to see how many people surround us, thousands of people perhaps on both sides of the river. I feel a bit of relief—perhaps the destruction was not as bad as I feared. We finally manage to cross the river and find a place on the west side of the gathering to bed for the night. It is a relief to finally hold John and see Samuel, Hannah, and Daniel safely with us. The children, whose names I now know are Mary, Beatrice, Jone, and David, are sound asleep along with Alice, exhausted both in body and soul after this grueling day. I too am most tired and happy to lie in the back of the cart to get some much-needed rest. I have nearly fallen asleep when a sound wakes me. It is a sound too familiar to my ears, the sound of mothers wailing for their lost children.

The cries rise from all around us and drift up into the night sky much like the smoke in the distance illuminated by the moon. My own tears begin to flow, for all who have been lost today and for all those mothers and fathers who will try to find the will to live on the morrow. I have been in that place, that place of darkness where it seems like there is no light. The place where memories wound like shards of glass, causing more pain than comfort. But I also know that the love of those around us can bring light to that darkness and help us to find our way forward. A pack of wolves in the distance joins in to share their own sorrow, and the woeful song becomes a lullaby as I finally drift off to sleep.

The sun brings light to the misery around us; so many fled with nothing but the clothes on their backs and have no place else to go. Wills has spoken with many of men, and it seems as though both the shop and the house have been lost, as we feared. We are by some grace the lucky ones; we will make our way to Plimouth, where we will have food and shelter and the chance to begin again. I'm pleased that Hannah and her family will be coming with us. Returning to Boston feels like more than they can face, and I'm happy for their company and help. I'm sure we can find something for Daniel in Plimouth, even if it is only helping Wills and Isaac in the shop, for surely others who lost everything will also eventually make their way there and need to replace that which is now gone.

We have found a family who wishes to take Mary in; they lived next door to her family, who sadly did not survive. David has found his uncle, who will keep watch with him, hoping to find his parents and sisters. There are so many searching the faces hoping to see someone that they know, someone that they love. Beatrice and Jone will simply have to come with us. We cannot leave them, and we cannot stay here, as food and water will become scarce very quickly. Beatrice seems happy to go along, but Jone has not spoken since we were at the school. She was the last one to make it through the window before the roof collapsed, and I fear she has been deeply frightened by what occurred. With God's help, perhaps time will heal her little broken soul. Alice has made it her mission to look after the poor thing, and that has been of great help. She has said very little about the fire other than to tell Wills how happy she is that I rescued her and the other children. She didn't mention Mr. Arnold or the other child; perhaps she doesn't realize what happened, which would be a blessing indeed.

As we make our way along the road with the others, I realize that the building I see ahead is the inn of my dear friend Bess, and despite our plight, it does my heart good knowing I will see her again. Hordes of people are here and we must tie up some distance away to find a place for all three wagons. There are people lined up out front to get inside, so I slip around to the back while the others wait near the well. Stepping inside, I realize my heart is beating a little faster than it had been, and I have to pause and take a deep breath. Mr. Morse isn't here; he can't hurt me, but being in this place again brings the memory back in a way that feels as if someone had driven a hot poker into my heart. I see no one in the kitchen, but dirty dishes are piled everywhere. Bess must truly be at her wits' end, as I have never seen this kitchen in such disarray.

I retrieve an apron from the wall and set to washing the dishes and tidying up the kitchen as best I can. Wills and Samuel bring in fresh water and wood for the stove, and I cut some meat and cheese for them to take back for Hannah and the children. "As I live and breathe, my dearest angel!" exclaims Bess as she rounds the corner into the kitchen. I can't help but laugh at the sight of her, as disheveled as the kitchen and a bit grayer than I remembered.

"My dear friend, I am so very happy to see you," I say as I hug her tightly.

"You are not hurt, you and your family, you are well?" she says, looking me up and down.

"No, we are not hurt. My son Wills and his daughter Alice and son John are here with me, as are our friends the Browns and a couple of children we rescued during the fire," I reply.

Bess brushes back a loose strand of hair and tucks it into my cap. "Ye've had a tough go of it my dear, but you know you are welcome to stay here as long as you like," she says reassuringly.

"Thank you, Bess, that is most kind of you, but we are going back to Plimouth. My other children and grandchildren are there, and we wish to be with them again," I say, squeezing her hand. "But, for now, let me help you." I return to tackling the pile of dishes. The two of us work quickly, and before long things are orderly once again and Bess turns her attention to making more stew and porridge for the never-ending line of hungry travelers. Wills and Samuel make camp for the night just outside the inn; the children and Hannah and I will sleep in the back room that Isaac and I shared on our first visit. Thank God for Hannah, who watches the children while I help Bess, who, as usual, has no one else to ease her burden. The sun is fading in the evening sky before I rest, sitting on the edge of the cart and enjoying a cool cup of water Alice brought me from the well. I can still see the smoke in the sky in the distance and our clothes smell most strongly of it, my white blouse now streaked with gray as the ash had mixed with the mist of rain. I have one other dress in the wagon; perhaps I can wash this one before we set off again. But for now, I only want a bit to eat and some rest.

I sleep soundly that night, Alice, Jone, and Beatrice curled up on the floor between me and Hannah. John at the end of my bed and Daniel with his mother, we manage to make the small room work for the seven of us. My bones ache in the morning when I awake, but there is no time for hesitation as many who had slept both inside and outside of the inn will be looking for a meal before making their way to their next destination. I know Wills will want to get on the road before the sun rises too high in the sky, but I can't leave without helping Bess get through one more meal. I enlist the help of the girls, who, despite their ages, are of more assistance than I had anticipated. Beatrice is quite skilled at making dough; her mother had taught her well. Her mother, had she survived? Did she know that Beatrice was alive? I'm not sure if we shall ever know.

As we pack up the wagons Bess appears at the back door, wiping her hands on her apron. "My dearest, you have no idea how much your help this last day has meant to me," she says sincerely.

"While I wish I had seen you under better circumstances, I am glad I was here to help," I say, smiling back at her.

Bess motions for me to come closer. "What will happen to Jone and Beatrice?" she says in a voice just above a whisper. I look over my shoulder at the girls helping Alice to get the boys settled back in the wagon.

"We will take them with us to Plimouth for now, and then I simply do not know," I say honestly.

Bess looks at them and back at me, and I see her eyes glistening. "Let them stay with me?" she asks expectantly.

"Truly?" I say, surprised by her request.

"You know John and I, we never had babes of our own, and these two, well they need a family, and they are hard workers," Bess says.

"Give me a moment," I say and then gather Wills, Samuel, and Hannah a short distance away so as not to be overheard by Bess or the children. After several minutes, we agree that if Bess wants to keep the girls, it might well be in their best interest to let her do so, providing they both agree. After all, we would have to find homes for them in Plimouth, and given the number of children who could also be in need, that might be difficult. I take Jone and Beatrice by the hand, lead them to a spot of shade, and sit down with them on the ground. "Children, we do not know what has happened to your families or if they have survived the fire. Do you understand what I am saying?" I ask gently.

"Yes, my mother and father are dead," says Beatrice bluntly. Her forthrightness nearly brings me to tears, but I work hard to maintain my composure.

"It may be so, my dear, I do not know for sure," I reply. Jone looks at me with her blank stare, still saying nothing.

"Are you going to be my mother now?" asks Beatrice.

I pull her to my breast and hug her. "My dearest child, I would be most honored to be your mother, but there is another who I would like you to consider," I reply. Beatrice looks at me thoughtfully. "Bess would like you and Jone to stay here, with her and her husband John," I say. Jone looks at me but says nothing.

"I like Bess," says Beatrice. "She gave me a sweet before we went to bed last night." Oh, in the mind of a child, life is so simple and easy. This little one has been nothing but helpful and almost cheerful since we fled the city. I wonder how much of the situation she truly understands.

"Jone, what of you my dear, would you like to stay here with Beatrice and Bess?" I ask.

"Come on now, you must come with me," says Beatrice, taking Jone's hand as she pulls her up and runs back toward Bess.

I watch as Bess hugs both girls and strokes their hair, and I know that she will take good care of them. As I stand up and smooth my skirt, Jone is suddenly in my arms, hugging me tightly. "Thank you," she whispers before turning and running back to Bess.

As we continue our journey toward Plimouth, I can't help but think of the last time I traveled this road. So much has changed since then: Rem and Rebecca are both gone, but there is new life as well, grandchildren I have not even met yet. In some ways it feels like going home, but I also feel strange and unsettled in a way I haven't before. What would life be like for us in Plimouth now? I do not know, but I know that I am glad to be going home.

Chapter Eleven
In Times of Old

Our little town has grown so much in the last few years. Many of those displaced by the fire in Boston have settled here as well as other newcomers who seem to arrive each month now. Wills, Alice, John, and I have settled in with Phillip and Grace in the house William and I built so many years ago. Grace, Alice, and I sleep in my old room, and Wills has taken what was once the nursery with John. Isaac and his wife, Suzanna, and their daughter, Sarah, live behind the shop in a house they built last year. Isaac is such a fine young man and a good father; Rem would be so proud of him. She would be proud of all the children. Grace is betrothed to one of the Samuelson boys, yet I fear she's reluctant to leave her father. She is the last one to go and I know she feels a duty to care for him; perhaps my presence will ease her mind some. Josiah has been apprenticing with a shoemaker in Duxbury for the last few years and seems happy doing so, according to his letters. His brother Samuel has taken on with his Aunt Patience's husband, James, in the tailor shop, which James now owns in partnership with his brother.

Alice is now nearly as tall as I am, and she helps her father, uncle, and cousin in the furniture shop each day. She is quite accomplished with numbers and is learning much from Phillip about the nuances of managing a shop. The business is doing very well, and Phillip and Wills are, I think, happy to be working together again. Wills has been courting the widow Mary Amsden, and I am sure they will marry soon. Mary's children did not survive the winter sickness a few years ago, sadly, but she is quite taken with John, and Alice adores her. I know the men have been talking about building another house, and it would sadden me to not have them about all day, but I'm sure Wills would much rather have a home of his own, as he should have. Patience and James are here often with William, Eliza, Job, Samuel, and little Hannah.

Elizabeth and Peter were kind enough to take the Browns in for a few months while they built a new house, next to Isaac behind the furniture shop on land that Phillip graciously gave them. Hannah has given birth to another boy and a little girl since settling here in Plimouth, and we still visit nearly every day. She and Elizabeth have become fast friends as well, and their children often play together. There are now so many of us it is a challenge to get everyone in the same room to share a meal, but we make do. My many grandchildren are truly a blessing from God, and I so enjoy my time with them. Most days I tend to the garden with help from Alice and John, and evenings I help Alice with her sewing and John with his schooling. He is smart like his sister and a bit cheeky, often finding things to laugh at instead of studying. No mind, he will certainly follow in his father's footsteps, Wills having already given him some small woodworking tools of his own.

This morning, like most mornings, I walk down to the market for a few things for our evening meal. I nod and smile at the people passing by—some familiar faces, but more and more strangers I do not recognize. There is a line at the butcher, but I'm in no hurry and the gossiping of the women while they wait can often be amusing. I'm sure God does not approve of this pastime, but nonetheless, it is common when more than a few women gather in one place. As I wait patiently, I hear a voice that seems familiar, but I simply can't place it, my mind a bit puzzled. I pay no further attention to it until the woman standing a few paces in front of me turns to talk to the woman behind me. She has the face of a ghost, a face I never imagined I would see again.

My head spins and I feel my knees getting a bit weak, and then the ghost grabs ahold of my arm. "Ma'am, are you well, do you need to sit down?" she says.

I look at her blankly as she and another woman lead me over to a bench in front of the butchers. I want to speak, but my mind struggles to find the words. I peer into the woman's eyes and finally I'm able to say it. "Mary?"

The woman smiles. "No, I'm sorry, my name is not Mary. Is she someone I can get for you?" she replies. That voice—hers is the voice I recognized.

"No, I mean…" I do not know what I mean. I look at her again. "I'm sorry, it's just that you look and sound very much like a woman I used to know, a dear friend who died many years ago," I say finally.

"Well, I'm sorry if I startled you, what did you say the woman's name was?" she asks.

"Mary, Mary Crippen," I say.

The woman leans against the wall and closes her eyes for a second as if gathering her thoughts. "Mary Crippen was my mother; my name is Mehitable Crippen," she replies, smiling.

I shake my head in disbelief, and then without hesitation I wrap my arms around her and hold her tightly to me, which she does not resist. She is so much like her mother, the mother she had barely known.

"What is your name?" Mehitable says finally, and I can't help but laugh. Here I am holding this woman close to me, and I have not even told her my name.

"Sarah, Sarah Tench. But when your mother and I came here on the *Mayflower* it was Bailey, Sarah Bailey."

"You're Sarah?" she asks, wide eyed.

"I am, but how is it that you know my name? Surely you can't remember me. You were just a child when you mother died and your father moved away."

She nods in agreement. "No, I don't remember you, but I do know of you. My father spoke of you often when he would tell tales of my mother. He said that you were a dear friend and that my mother loved you like a sister," she replies.

I feel my hands trembling. All these years I'd thought Edward must have hated me and that he blamed me for Mary's death. "Your father, he spoke of me?"

Mehitable nodded. "Yes, he still does from time to time, although he speaks seldom now."

"He is alive and here in Plimouth?"

"Yes, we came back here when Virginia declared for King Charles, my brother Daniel and his family, my father and me."

"What of your brother Samuel?" I ask cautiously.

"He stayed behind in Virginia, as he swore an oath to Charles II. Father felt strongly that Parliament should rule and so he decided we should return here, to Plimouth," she explains. I have a hard time understanding that for the last few years Edward and the children have been right here, in Plimouth, and I did not even know.

"Where is your home, my dear?"

Mehitable points north to the area of town that had sprung up outside the stockade near the river. "We have a house there, in the new side of town. Daniel works at the mill, and I help care for father and Daniel's children. There are six of them."

Laughter bubbles up from a place deep inside me—Mary's grandchildren, what a blessing indeed!

"What are their names?" I ask.

"Enoch, David, John, Abraham, and daughters Mary and Sarah," she replies. My heart catches in my throat; surely Daniel had not named his children after my family.

Mehitable must have read my mind. "Mary after our mother of course, Abraham after your first husband's son, and Sarah after you. Daniel remembers you and Abraham and your many kindnesses to him when he was a child and how much our mother loved you," she says softly.

I do not know what to say. "And you, my dear, you are married, children of your own?"

She shakes her head. "No, I've never married. My step-mother died some time ago and so I have been caring for father and helping with the children ever since," she says with just a tinge of regret in her voice. "You must come and see father, and Daniel!" she adds suddenly. The thought of seeing Edward again after all these years is a bit daunting, and while I want to see him, I am hesitant.

"I will, of course I will, but perhaps you should speak to your father and Daniel first," I suggest.

Mehitable nods in agreement. "They will be so happy to see you, as I am. It is beyond wonderful to meet you after all these years. I have so many things to ask you about my mother."

I smile. "It would be my honor to share my memories of your mother with you." We sit a few minutes more, not saying much, just basking in this moment. Finally, we agree to meet here again in two days. This will give Mehitable a chance to speak with her brother and father and for me to tamp down my trepidation about seeing Edward. To say I am on pins and needles does not do justice to my concerns. Could I have really been so wrong about Edward's feelings after Mary died? Perhaps it was just his grief that made him act with what felt like such disdain for me. I look back on those days now with a memory more clouded than it once was, but still, it is hard to imagine I had misunderstood him so fully.

The day started dusty and cloudy, but as I walk to our agreed meeting place, I see Mehitable already waiting, a man with her. As I get closer, I know immediately that he is none other than Daniel Crippen. While certainly no longer the little boy I once knew there is no mistaking him, and his broad smile when he sees me warms my heart. He hurries toward me, reaching out his hands for mine. "Mrs. Tench, I'm oh so very happy to see you again," says this booming voice I do not recognize. I laugh and squeeze his hands, which seem nearly twice as big as my own. The little boy of eight I had last seen is now a handsome man with a bit of gray starting to show around the temples and the same twinkle in his eyes I frequently saw in Mary's.

"Sarah, you must call me Sarah," I say, feeling myself smile from ear to ear. We find a place to sit under a nearby tree and chat for hours, Daniel filling me in on all the details of their lives after leaving Plimouth.

I am enchanted by their stories and so pleased to hear that God has blessed them and that their lives, for the most part, seem to have been happy and healthy. It is clear they feel pain around the separation from Samuel but also a recognition that we each choose our own path. "Father would very much like to see you, Sarah, and I do believe if you are open to it, you should do so soon," Daniel says.

I look at him, a bit taken back by his words. "Is your father that ill?" I inquire.

Mehitable nods. "I'm afraid he is coming to the end of his time here with us, and perhaps soon," she replies. "He eats very little now and sleeps most of the time."

"Of course, I will come, I will come today if you think it best," I reply. My heart flutters, but I know that I must see Edward before it is too late. God has given me this window, this chance to perhaps make amends with him, and Mary would have wanted it to be so.

"I think it would be best to come now if you can," agrees Daniel. We gather up our things and chat as we walk along the road to their home. I have never been in this part of town, and I'm amazed at the number of shops and markets that have sprouted here. Only bits of the original stockade now stand as walls have been removed to allow the town to grow, and now there is more here than in the part of town where we had first settled.

When we arrive at their home, a lovely but frail-looking woman whom I understand to be Daniel's wife, Lydia, and a little girl with lovely brown curls meet us. "Sarah, meet my daughter Sarah," says Daniel.

"It's lovely to meet you," I say to the little girl, who looks to be about ten.

"My name is Sarah too!" she says with a big smile that reveals a couple of missing teeth.

"My dearest, this is Mrs. Tench; she is the friend of your grandmother Mary's I told you about and the woman for whom you were named," Daniel says as he strokes Sarah's long hair.

She looks at me rather wide eyed and somewhat confused. "You must be very, very old," she finally says, shaking her head in disbelief. Daniel looks quite horrified at his daughter's directness.

"Indeed I am my dear, I am very, very old and very happy to be so," I say, laughing as Sarah and the others join in.

I meet all the children in turn, before Daniel finally says, "Why don't you go in and see Father by yourself, we will stay out here and give you a few moments alone."

I nod and slip inside while Daniel holds the door.

It is cool and dimly lit inside, the shutters closed against the brightness of the sun. Near the hearth against the wall is a bed and a man whom I would never have recognized as Edward. He is gaunt and has little hair left, his cheeks are sunken, and his skin has the grayish hue that comes on as death draws near. He is, as Mehitable and Daniel had suggested, quite ill and not long for this world. I quietly pull up a chair next to the bed and hold his hands in mine. He does not stir right away, but after a few moments, his eyes flutter and he turns his head toward me. "Lydia, I am most thirsty," he says faintly. I find the water and hold a cup to his lips, and he drinks slowly, barely lifting his head from the bed.

"I'm not Lydia," I say when he has finished. "It's Sarah, Sarah Tench."

He stares at me for a moment as if trying to understand what I have said. Then he closes his eyes and a small tear runs across his cheek and onto the bed. "Mehitable told me she had seen you, but I couldn't quite believe it," he says finally. "I am most thankful to see you again, as I'm soon to be with God and I will rest more peacefully in his grace given this chance to apologize to you."

I lurch back in my chair, stunned by his words. "Oh Edward, whatever would you have to apologize to me for?" I say as I take his hand in mine again. He looks at me, his eyes watery and milky with age. His voice is raspy and weak, but it is clear he needs to talk.

"When Mary died, I was angry, angry with God that he had taken her from me, and angry with myself for not having gotten help for her sooner."

I squeeze his hand. "Edward, you could not have known what would happen. You did as you thought best in the moment, and that is all we each can do," I say.

"But that is not all," he replies. "I felt so responsible for Mary's death that I could not bear to look at you, knowing how much you loved her and how much she loved you, as a sister."

My tears began to flow freely. "Edward, I thought you blamed me for Mary's death, that you were angry with me?" I cry out between sobs that I can no longer control.

"No, no Sarah, I never blamed you, ever, I know you did everything you could to save Mary and the babe, it was me, it was my fault," he replies breathlessly.

Our grief and pain had obscured the truth, and we'd both ascribed feelings to the other which were wrong. We'd lost our ability to see and understand one another, the last thing that Mary would have wanted for Edward, for the children, and for me. My heart aches for all the years lost, for all the time I could have had with Mary's children, and I feel immense regret. But I also feel something I never imagined I would: absolution, the force of Edward's words truly cleansing my soul and removing the stain of guilt I have been carrying for so, so many years. He did not blame me for Mary's death and neither did the children; he had blamed himself all this time. We talk quietly for another hour or so, but then he falls asleep and I feel it is too much to wake him.

When I emerge into the sunlight the world seems different, as if I were looking at it with new eyes, and perhaps I was. As I say goodbye to Mehitable, Lydia, and the children, I know they will never again be distant from me. Daniel walks me back to the house and kisses me on the cheek before saying goodbye. At night I sleep more soundly than I have slept in many years, dreaming of happy times. In the morning, I awake to a message from Daniel. Edward died quietly in his sleep during the night, calling out Mary's name. As I stand with the family on Cole's Hill, I cannot help but remember all the times I have stood here before. I lay flowers on the graves of Jonathan, William, my lost children, Mary, and Edward. As I look around, I see the names of so many we have lost, and I know my own time here is now closer than it is far away. I have no fear of death; I can only hope God will bless me with his mercy in my hour of need.

I've decided to open the apothecary shop again but just for a few days each week. Many who remember me still come to the house to call for tonics and preparations, and it is probably best to have them call at the shop instead. It's a pleasant distraction, and Alice seems to have taken an interest in learning about the herbs along with her cousins Eliza and Martha, the daughters of Patience and Elizabeth. It does my heart good to see the girls spending time together, and it makes me think of all the family I left behind when I came to this place. Is my sister watching her grandchildren tend the garden? I wish I knew for certain, but other than a few letters many years ago, I have heard no news from her.

Life is busy and full of the grandchildren I have come to adore so much. Many nights the house is nearly full of children playing games, telling stories, and singing songs. Daniel and his children are frequent guests as well, and it's clear that many friendships are being formed. It warms my heart so to see it, and I know Mary must be smiling down on us. This summer has been most hot, and we spend as much time as we can near the bay basking in the cool breeze and enjoying the even cooler water. The children splash and play as Patience, Elizabeth, and I sit on the banks mending or washing, and the days go by like a lazy stream floating along.

"Look Grandmama, a crab!" says Daniel, holding the small wiggling creature carefully between two fingers.

"Yes it is, perhaps you should put it back near the water, I fear it's too small to eat," I say, smiling. He and the other boys run back to the water's edge and splash about, looking for more treasures. Patience's three younger boys, Samuel, Job, and Daniel, run from one place to another with Elizabeth's two not far behind. The girls sit along the banks tending to the smaller children while drawing their letters in the sand with sticks. The children's laughter fills the air and it's been a wonderful afternoon indeed, but the men will be returning home soon and so we must get back for evening meal. I send Patience's daughter Eliza to fetch the boys, who are playing just beyond the dunes.

Suddenly a scream shatters the calm and Eliza comes running back over the hill. "Mama, mama," she cries out. Patience is on her feet instantly.

"Stay with the other children," I say to Elizabeth as I run after her. By now Eliza has reached her mother and buried her face in her apron, sobbing uncontrollably. While Patience tries to calm her, I hurry on to find the boys, then stop suddenly, realizing what had frightened Eliza so. There at the edge of the water is Job, face down in the sand, his little body contorted and battered, one arm missing. He had clearly been attacked by some large creature from the water or perhaps from the forest behind us. The other boys are father down the dunes beyond him and seem unaware of what has occurred.

I turn back and see Patience coming over the dune just as she realizes what has happened. It is a horror for a mother to lose a child, a pain that you cannot understand unless you have endured it yourself. I know that pain, and now my daughter will too.

"Job!" Patience cries out, and the sound of her anguish rings out across the waves.

I grab her and hold her tightly to me. "Child of mine, your son is gone, and there is nothing you can do for him save pray to God for mercy on his soul and his grace for you and your family," I say softly. She crumbles to her knees, her face in her hands. By now the boys have realized something is amiss and are headed back towards us. I do not want the younger ones to see Job in this way.

"Patience, go to your son and cover him with your apron. I will get the other boys, but they should not see their brother and cousin in this way," I say firmly. She nods, unable to even speak, but does as I ask. I watch as she removes her apron and gently turns Job over, wrapping him up in the white cloth and holding him close to her. I walk briskly toward the boys and gather them together. "Children, there has been a calamity, and I need you all to go to where Elizabeth is waiting and stay with her, do you understand?"

"Is Mama well?" asks Samuel, his eyes welling up with tears.

"Yes, your mother is fine, it's your brother Job. Now go on as I asked, we will explain everything later," I say, hugging each boy in turn.

Elizabeth takes the children home while I stay here with Patience, who is still sitting in the wet sand holding Job. The apron, once white, is now mostly red, and what had been sobs of pain are now just quiet tears. The sun hangs low in the sky by the time James, Wills, and Phillip arrive, and the waves have begun lapping at Patience's feet. James carefully takes Job from his mother and holds him in his arms while his own sobs shake his body. It hurts me so to see my daughter and her husband in such pain, and I bury my face in Wills's arm as he holds me tightly, my chest hurting from the weight on my heart. We walk slowly behind James and Patience as they carry Job to our house, where we lay him in Phillip's room so that I can prepare him. As I wash and wrap him in linen, I hear more and more voices in the other room, and more crying. I sit down on the bed next to my grandson, now tightly wrapped in his burial shroud.

Pain is a part of life; I have learned that over and over, and yet the pain I feel now is magnified by my own first-hand knowledge of what Patience is feeling. It was in this same house on this same bed that my Henry and sweet Mary lay so long ago. I feel old at this moment, as if my life were already over, filled so full that it can take no more. I know I need to go and comfort my family, but I don't know if I can. I walk over to the window and open the shutter to let in the fresh air, now starting to cool as the sun sets behind the few clouds that remain. The light is pink and gold, the rays of sun reflecting off the clouds like so many jewels. Just then a hawk flies overhead, dipping down low over the garden and squawking as it goes by. I can't help but smile as I turn away from the window and go out to join the others.

Life is resilient, it will always be, and Elizabeth has blessed the family with a new babe, a boy they have named Job Peter Smith in honor of his cousin, now in the new burying ground some eight months. Patience and James have learned, as so many have, that you can survive the unthinkable. Samuel has been most melancholy these past months, feeling somehow responsible for his brother's death, but I hope time will heal his little heart. Patience would like to have another child but in the time since Job has left us no child has come—perhaps God's way of saying that one child cannot be replaced with another.

Alice has taken more and more of an interest in my herbs and potions, and when I am at the shop, she often takes breaks from the accounts to sit with me at my bench. She has become quite skilled at making the willow bark tonic, and I trust her to make it now whenever it is needed. Each morning we spend some time looking over various plants I have collected and discussing each one. She has a razor-sharp mind and easily remembers each of them and what they are for. Alice and Abraham Crippen, Daniel's youngest boy, have been spending much time together as well, Abraham having taught Alice to play chess. Most nights after chores are done the two of them can be found playing and talking until it's time for bed. I know many of the congregation frown upon this game of chess, but I find no harm in it and the children seem to enjoy it very much.

I can see that the two of them are becoming more than friends, and it warms my heart to think that our two families might be united. I'm sure Mary must be smiling down from heaven at the prospect that our grandchildren might be wed. Time will tell, but I can see the way that Alice looks at Abraham, and while she is too young for formal courting, it won't be long now. Wills seems to like Abraham, and he works at the mill with his father, a fine living for a young man. Mehitable is also a frequent visitor, and I enjoy talking with her about her mother and our early adventures. She is a fine woman; it is sad to me that she has not married but that seems to be her wish, and she is certainly busy helping with her nieces and nephews. I had thought perhaps that Wills might take an interest in her, but he is betrothed to the Amsden widow. I think it is a good match, and preparations for the wedding have begun. Wills is building a house next to Isaac's behind the furniture shop. Only Phillip and I will remain here when he, Alice, and John leave us in a few weeks.

The winter is full upon us now and the bitter cold brings such pain to my shoulder, which has never properly healed. As I sit here in front of the fire pulling my shawl tightly around me, I can't help but think about the many years I have sat in this house. William would be so proud of our children and grandchildren. They have grown to be fine men and women, and he would be most pleased. I have done my best to raise them well and hope as he looks upon me from heaven that he approves of my efforts. The weather today is most bleak, and the snow is falling at a steady rate. I scurry out to the larder and gather up a few things in case we are not able to get out for a few days. Phillip has come home early from the shop, knowing that few will go out as the snow deepens, and I bake some bread while he plucks a chicken.

We have seen many a snow here in Plimouth, but none such as this has ever come to pass. It has snowed now for some three days, and the wind howls as if it were trying valiantly to blow it all away. The snow, now over knee deep in some places, has brought the town to a stand-still, and the quiet is unnerving. Not even the children have ventured out in this to play, and no voices can be heard. I hope our livestock will be well in the barn, as we are not able to get out to feed them or bring fresh water. Our provisions will hold us for a few more days, but I have started taking a mental inventory of what we have left in the house, thinking about how to stretch what we have should this go on for much longer. I can only hope that the others have stocked up as well and that they too are enjoying the warmth of a fire safely inside their houses.

Phillip has used a plate to clear some of the snow away from the back door so that we can get to the firewood, but it is too much labor to try and reach anything else. The snow has stopped falling from the sky, but drifts have come up over the shutters and it feels as if we are almost encased in a blanket of white. We have no more meat left, so it will be only porridge and biscuits until we can get back to the larder. I eat very little, hoping to save what we have for Phillip, but he has caught me and chastised me soundly for not eating my full share. Thankfully he does not notice that I scrape back into the pot nearly half of what I ladle out for myself.

Today is the fourth day we have been trapped inside the house and the bitter cold means that the snow will not be melting soon. Phillip and I take turns at moving the snow so that we can reach the larder and the barn. It takes us nearly three days to reach the barn, but Phillip is finally able to get in, which is a relief. Around us, we see every family doing the same. I've never seen so much snow in all my days and I hope I never will again. The house smells of wet wool as we dry our clothes near the fire. At least now we have more food stores and milk from the barn. Our poor cow has suffered from not being milked for so many days and it is unclear if she will survive.

I managed to clear a bit of the snow away from the front door and the windows, so the house is not so dark. Outside, men are starting to use spades to try and clear paths from their homes to other homes nearby to barter for wood or food, depending on their needs. I hear more voices being raised around us, but they are muffled, and I cannot hear what is being said. My sewing helps to pass the time, and Phillip is working on carving some bed posts for a new bed. The days become nearly ten in number very quickly, and before we know it the thaw has begun and with it our first chance to get out of the house and see to the rest of the family.

It is not far to the shop, but even in that short distance we pass two buildings that have suffered from the weight of snow. One lost part of its roof and the other simply toppled over as if it were made of small sticks. My heart begins to race, wondering if the children are safe. The shop has suffered no damage; Phillip and William built it most strongly, and Isaac and Wills are there working to clear snow from the front. They and their families are well, but they have not yet been able to get to Patience and Elizabeth and certainly not to Mehitable and Daniel on the far edge of town. Wills and Isaac will try to get to Patience in the morning if they do not see James at the tailor shop before then.

I spend the day helping to set things right in the store, sweeping the dust that has accumulated out onto the snow, which grows dirtier by the minute. A few men brave the streets on horseback, and several stop to speak with Phillip. He learns that the Widow Thomson died in her home; unable to get to her larder and unprepared for the length of the storm, she starved to death. Phillip and I stay with Wills overnight rather than return to our house, and they plan to leave at first light to go check on Patience and Elizabeth. I sleep restlessly; my mind will not be quiet as I worry about the children and their families. Prayer does not quiet my mind, but it does my soul some good. My slumber is interrupted repeatedly by the sounds of a hawk, but each time I wake I realize it was only in my dreams.

As Phillip and Wills make their way to Patience I can only wait impatiently for word, and Alice and I busy ourselves with making tonics and cutting the dried herbs. The sun is nearly down now but the men have not returned, so we withdraw to the house to start preparations for evening meal. Darkness has fallen and I'm sure no one will come tonight; they must be staying with Patience and James. I eat sparingly. I've simply no hunger for food, only for some word on the children. Alice does her best to keep me entertained and the evening passes quickly, but the night goes slowly and I sleep little. By first light I begin to have that gnawing feeling that something is not right. Alice senses my discomfort and does her best to reassure me, but the feeling does not leave.

The sun is shining brightly and the snow melting, the streets now a sea of mud mixed with ice and chunks of snow. More people are out today, and several have stopped by the shop to enquire about new furniture, some having been forced to burn chairs or tables to keep warm. There are no wagons moving yet but many more horses can be seen, which gives me reason to believe that the boys will return soon. By mid-afternoon I have nearly given up hope when I hear someone coming through the back door. When I see Wills I know at once that something is terribly wrong.

He crosses the distance between us in a few quick steps and wraps his arms around me, holding me to close to him. "What is it, my son?" I say quietly.

I feel him trembling and his voice cracks as he tries to speak. "There has been a misfortune at Patience's home," he says haltingly.

"What do you mean?" I step back to look in his eyes. I see the pain before he even says another word.

"A part of the house collapsed from the weight of the snow," he replies finally. I gasp, covering my mouth with my hand as the horror of what he's saying starts to sink in.

"They are hurt. How badly?" I ask.

"After the roof collapsed there was a fire. Mother, they are all dead..." Wills says quietly. The rooms seems to spin around me and I sink to the floor, unable to hold my own weight on legs that have failed me entirely. My darling firstborn, Patience, the babe that made me a mother. James, a wonderful husband and father, William, Eliza, Samuel, and Hannah just a babe, they can't all be gone? I simply cannot comprehend what Wills has said as he helps me from the floor into a chair. I heard the words; I hear them over and over as if they are an echo or a cloud that hangs in the air.

Alice appears then with a mug of ale. "Please Grandmama, have a sip of this," she says as she holds it up to me. Tears stream down her face and her father does his best to comfort her. But I cannot take the mug, my arms will not move, only the tears come as I feel sobs tightening my throat.

My child, my grandchildren gone in an instant. Phillip has stayed behind; Peter having gone to help him remove the bodies from the blackened hull of what had been Patience's home. Thankfully he and Elizabeth and the children are safe. They had seen the fire from their house, but they had not known that it was Patience's home. No matter, they would not have been able to get there and could have done little. The bodies have been wrapped and lie on the floor in the barn until we can bury them with Job, uniting the whole family again. The picture of them lying there in the straw haunts my every waking moment.

For days people come by the shop to offer their prayers and condolences. Many knew James from the tailor shop, and of course I and my children are well known here even by those who have arrived more recently. Daniel was able to ride in and he has been most kind, bringing little biscuits and sweets baked by Mehitable for us to eat. It is most thoughtful of her, but I find I'm unable to swallow even the smallest bits; I drink only a bit of ale and some broth. This loss has hit me most hard, and most days it is a labor to simply get out of bed and dress. Sadly, nearly forty souls were lost in this storm, the worst in memory for all of us who have been here so long.

At night I lie on my bed thinking about that night, the night before I knew my family was lost. I kept hearing hawks in my dreams, and I wonder now, were those the spirts of my dearest Patience and her children saying goodbye? My mind swirls with memories and pain, an aching pain that shakes me to the bone. Tomorrow, Phillip says, the weather will be such that we can bury our dead, but I don't know if I have the strength to face it. I am tired, most tired, but sleep will not come. Tomorrow I will say goodbye to another child, and my grandchildren, precious babes just barely starting their lives.

God in his infinite wisdom surely knows his plan, but I cannot comprehend it.

The day is cloudy and damp as we walk to the new burying ground. The sky matches my mood, dark and foreboding with no glimmer of sun in the sky. Phillip and Wills have already dug the graves and taken the bodies up to the hill. It shakes me to my core to see them all lying there together, and my breath comes in small gasps as the enormity of what has happened bears down on me like the weight of an ox. Many of our dear friends are here, for which I am most grateful. It is a relief to finally see Elizabeth and her family, and I hold her tightly to me. Daniel is here with Mehitable, Hannah Brown, and James's brother and sister too, feeling the same loss we all feel. I can barely hear the words the Elders are saying; it's as if they are far away rather than standing just next to me.

My grandchildren are all close to me, Alice and John; Elizabeth's sons Abel and Zachariah and daughters Ruth and Martha; and of course Job, still in his mother's arms. Isaac is here with his wife Suzanna, heavy with child, and his son and daughter. Phillip with Grace and Josiah and his wife, having just married before the storm. I can feel Wills right behind me, perhaps to be there in case I should fall again. But I will not fall…I will be strong for these children; these grandchildren will hold me up with their love and light. I will mourn, we will all mourn, but I could not feel more blessed when I look at these faces around me. As always, God takes and gives in his own way, in his own time, and it is not for me to understand but to simply accept that this is the way of life.

There are several other families at the burying ground today, but my eye catches on one woman, standing off to the side all alone, as if she is waiting for someone. She looks to be about Elizabeth's age, of modest means, but I simply cannot place her. I do not think that I know her, but she seems familiar somehow; perhaps I have seen her in the market. I think on it no more as I say my thanks to those who have come today, but then I find that she in in front of me, although rather hesitant. "Sarah Tench?" she says with a Dutch accent.

"Yes, I am Sarah," I reply.

She smiles. "I am sorry, I don't mean to intrude, but I arrived late yesterday and was told I would find you here," she says with a slight smile. I cock my head as I study her face, which is somehow becoming more familiar. "I'm Anne Anglesey; your sister Margaret was my mother."

CHAPTER TWELVE
LOVE AND COURAGE

Even now after several months have gone by, I find it hard to believe that Anne is here, and that my sister, the last of my first family, is gone. I see so many little things of Margaret in her, the way she plays with a lock of her hair, the way she laughs, and it makes me smile, but it also brings on a sadness. Margaret and Richard had four children, two boys and two girls, but sadly Anne is the only one who survives. Thankful, their second born, died when she was just seventeen of the sweating sickness. Margaret, Richard, Job, and Stephen all died last year from the pox. Anne was also ill, as evidenced by the many scars on her face, but she survived. Sadly, Anne's husband, Jacob Rayner, his parents and siblings, and her only child, a son named Ephraim, also died from the pox. Within two months' time Anne had lost her entire family and was left completely alone.

While cleaning through her mother's few possessions she ran across my last letter to her, kept all these years in a small box along with a lock of our mother's hair and my father's quill. Deciding she would take a chance on finding her cousins in the Colonies, she boarded a ship with what little money she had and sailed to Boston. There, stuck by the harsh winter, she worked at a baker's until she could make her way to Plimouth. Not expecting to find me still alive, she was most surprised when her inquiries directed her to me rather than one of the children. It has for the most part been a very happy reunion, and she is living with me and Phillip. We spend most nights talking about my dear sister and learning about their life in Holland.

While I still ache over the loss of my dearest Patience and her children, having Anne here has helped to fill the void left by their passing. Phillip too seems to enjoy her company, and I often find them talking late into the night. Wills and his new wife have had a child, a little girl named Mary, a sister for John and Alice. I sometimes doubt however that Alice even knows the child is alive, for her every waking thought seems to be of Abraham, and I've no doubt that he will soon ask for her hand. It is hard to imagine that Alice has already reached marriage age, but I confess time seems to move faster and faster these days as I measure its passing by the lives of my blessed grandchildren.

I am finding it harder and harder to walk to the shop each day, so Alice has taken over managing the apothecary and she is doing a fine job. The doctor who lives a few doors down has become acquainted with her and often sends people to her for remedies, and he gives her ideas for new tonics and poultices. I have found them to be most helpful myself as my shoulder still pains me terribly many nights, making sleep elusive. Having Anne with us has been a blessing as she has taken on most of the household chores, easing my burden considerably. Grace has finally married, trusting her father can care for himself and perhaps thinking that Anne will stay on with him after I am gone.

Word reached us yesterday that England and Scotland, united, now have a new king. King Charles II has taken the throne, and "Long live the King" rings out from nearly every home. I hope we will finally be united among the Colonies once again. What was once land settled by those willing to risk their lives in the new world has now truly become part and parcel of England. We are under direct authority of the English, subject to their laws and of course their taxes. Young men may even be conscripted to fight in the standing army and ship-born military that the English have set up throughout the Colonies. The New England Confederation continues to be strong, and more and more defined colonies have arisen, including a new colony to be called Rhode Island. New groups of people have joined us as well; those calling themselves Quakers have been arriving for some time now, and they are a welcome addition to the town.

While the colonies may be united once more under the flag of England, tensions here between settlers and the native Indian tribes are rising once again. We were welcomed when we first came here, but now we come in droves, month after month taking more and more of their land, the best land, for ourselves. Our homes and markets push them farther and farther away from the shore and the rivers where they trap and fish. Once there was talk of paying the Indians for the land, and in some small measure some do, but certainly not what it is worth. I heard a man was found dead near the mouth of Town Brook; he had been scalped. Phillip says there is no reason for concern, but still, it unsettles me as I think about what the future will hold for my grandchildren.

For a few weeks now the sky has been cloudless, nothing but blue, the wind starting to carry with it the smell of drying tobacco and dying leaves. This is my favorite time of year, and the beauty of this place cannot be overstated. The leaves on the trees turn every shade of gold, brown, and red, coloring the landscape as if with a painter's brush. Perhaps I should take one last walk to collect some bark and plants before the winter comes; I'm sure Alice would like to come along. We'll bring Abraham just to be safe, and of course that will delight Alice beyond measure. I'll speak to Wills and see if he agrees, which I'm sure he will. I think he has grown most fond of Abraham and proud of Alice's work with the herbs and tonics.

So it is agreed, and we watch the weather, deciding that tomorrow will be a good day. It has been pleasant and dry, and we will take the wagon to a spot to the south which I've not explored in some time. Alice and I set about gathering up all the things we shall need, and she chatters on most excitedly about the prospect of spending the day with Abraham. "Alice, need I remind you that we have things we must accomplish tomorrow, this is not simply a walk in the woods for you and your beloved," I say, smiling.

She blushes a deep shade of crimson. "He is not my beloved, Grandmother," she replies, but her face tells another story.

"You do love him, do you not?" I ask, already knowing the answer.

She looks down at the floor for a moment but then turns her face to me and, with a great deal of confidence and solemnity, says, "Yes, I believe I do love him," before hiding her laughter behind her hands.

I hug her close, laughing along with her. It does my heart so much good to see her happy.

Our work finished, John walks with me back to the house. He is a fine boy, so much like Wills but also more like his mother than one would have imagined. Quiet and a bit shy, but when he speaks, he does so with authority, and like his sister, he is very smart. We talk often of his mother and my memories of her, but it is not with sorrow, and I am careful to not make him feel guilt over her passing. Bringing children into this world is a most precious gift from God, but while it is blessed work it is not without its dangers for both the mother and child. I think of the many who have died in this way and the number is not small, but the child is never to blame.

Abraham has fetched Alice on the wagon, and they pull up in front of our house just as the sun is coming over the horizon. Anne helps me load the basket with our biscuits, some meat, and water into the back. Before I can get up into the wagon, Phillip emerges and pulls me aside. "Mother, can I speak to you for a moment before you leave?" he says in a voice just above a whisper.

I nod and follow him around to the side of the house. "Whatever is it my son, are you well?" I ask, the concern rising in my voice.

"No, I mean, yes I am well, I mean…" he stumbles through his words. I try not to react and, as I often did with his father, wait while he gathers his thoughts. "While you are gone today, I'm going to speak to Anne, to ask her, to be my wife," he says finally. "I am asking for your blessing. If it is not to your liking, I will not proceed," he adds.

I put my hands on either side of his face as I look into his eyes, so much like William's. I could not love this man more if he had come from my own body. He has truly been a son to me and looked after my welfare most ardently since his father died. I think Margaret would be very happy at this turn of events. Anne is most dear, and I can see that she truly cares for Phillip. "Of course, you have my blessing Phillip, it would make me very happy to see you and Anne united through God's grace," I reply, smiling broadly. He kisses me on both cheeks and then hugs me tightly, and I can feel his happiness. Our dear Rem has been gone a long time; it is good that Phillip will have a wife again and someone to share his burden.

We finally set off, Phillip and Anne waving goodbye from the front porch. It is a glorious day, the sun shining like a bright crystal in the sky and the breeze just starting to hint at the cold weather to come. The three of us squeeze together, Alice next to Abraham, of course, and we laugh and talk all the way to my chosen spot. Alice even regales us with a song, and I'm amazed at what a lovely voice she has. The two of them smile at each other constantly, and Abraham is very attentive to our needs, making regular stops along the journey so we can relieve ourselves or snack on the food we brought with us. It seems a long time since I've had a day when I felt so carefree and happy. It is wonderful indeed.

By late morning we have reached the place where we intend to tie up the horse and wagon so that we can continue on foot more deeply into the forest. We gather up the things we need from the wagon, and Abraham manages to stuff some of the food into his many pockets. We walk silently, listening to the songs of the birds and the gentle rustling of the leaves in the trees. This valley is even more abundant than I had remembered, with foxglove, jewel weed, skunk cabbage, and a great deal of willow bark. Alice and I set about collecting what we need while Abraham keeps an eye out for bears and other animals. I have never fully recovered from the attack by the wolf some years ago, and I feel much safer knowing that Abraham stands watch with his new rifle, a gun I have not seen before. He assures me it is accurate and that he is a good shot, and I know he would protect Alice with his life.

The sun is starting to move across the sky, and we must go back soon. "Alice, please put everything we have collected into the baskets, we need to head back to the wagon," I call out to her, picking foxglove just on the other side of a small creek.

She waves to signal her understanding and I turn away to finish my own work when I hear Abraham cry out, "Alice, Alice, what has happened?" I look up to see him running toward her sitting on the bank of the creek, and it is clear she is in pain. I follow quickly behind him. I hear Alice crying and Abraham doing his best to comfort her.

"My dear, whatever happened?"

"I don't know, I was starting to cross the creek and next thing I knew, I was on the ground," she says, the anguish clear in her voice.

"Where are you hurt, child?" I kneel down to examine her.

"It's my foot Grandmama, it hurts very badly," she says, choking back tears. Abraham looks at me with concern on his face, but his words are reassuring and Alice seems to calm some. I remove her shoe and stocking and see her foot has become quite large and is already turning blue. Thankfully there is no blood, but I know it will be difficult for her to walk back to the wagon, and too far, perhaps, for Abraham to carry her.

"Abraham, let's see if we can get Alice up and move her over here under this large tree and out of the sun," I say. He nods, and we each take an arm and help her hobble over to the tree, where we gently settle her on the ground. "Alice, I'm going to go back and grab my basket where I left it on the ground. I have some willow bark, and if Abraham can get me some water from the creek, I will make you a tonic to help with the pain."

My mind races as I walk to get my things. It's clear she cannot walk, at least not now. Perhaps she'd be able to after some tonic, but that would mean we would have to spend the night here. I look around to see if there might be a good place to shelter for the night, but I see only trees and brush. Never mind, for now I need to tend to Alice, then Abraham and I can talk. I quickly make the tonic and tear some strips from the bottom of my underslip to bind Alice's foot. We fashion a bed from the leaves and cover her with Abraham's coat. "My dearest, try and get a little rest," I say as she closes her eyes, exhausted from the pain.

I motion for Abraham to follow me a short distance away from where Alice lay so that we can talk without disturbing her. "Is she going to be good, Mrs. Tench?" he asks, his voice trembling a bit.

"Yes, she's going to be fine, however I think it might be best if we do not try to walk back tonight. Let's give her some rest and more tonic and see if she can manage in the morning." Abraham nods his agreement and I can see he is thinking. "Will the horse manage?" I ask.

"Yes, she will be fine, I'm sure, I was just thinking about where we might best bed down for the night. It should be in a place where I can watch over both of you easily, perhaps protected on one side," he responds.

"Yes, I was thinking the same thing."

We talk for a few more minutes and agree that Abraham will leave us and look around to see if he can find what we need. "Here, keep my rifle Mrs. Tench, I know you know how to use it," he says, holding it out to me.

"Oh no, you need to keep it with you, we will be fine I'm sure," I say, trying to hide any fear I might be feeling.

"No, I insist, I couldn't bear it if anything happened to Alice, or you," he adds. Mary would be so proud of this man standing here, doing his best to protect and care for us. I finally agree, and Abraham sets out to look for shelter. I sit next to Alice, who is still sleeping, and I am relieved to see that her foot has grown no bigger and the tonic seems to be helping her pain.

The snapping of a twig wakes me from a light sleep, and I grab the rifle, suddenly most grateful that I had kept it. "It's me, Mrs. Tench," Abraham says as he walks up from behind me. Relief washes over me that it's not a wild animal, and that Abraham is safely back. Alice sits up and drinks some more tonic.

"I found a small cave not far from here that I think would be a good place for us to stay for the night," says Abraham.

"What do you mean?" asks Alice with alarm. "We can't stay out here; we need to go back."

"My dear, I think it's best if we wait until tomorrow to try and walk back to the wagon; it's too much for you now and too far for Abraham to carry you," I reply, trying to soothe her.

Alice looks at Abraham. "It will be fine, Alice, you'll see. I'll be here to watch over you and your grandmother, and tomorrow, we will go back to the wagon," he says, kneeling down next to her. She nods her agreement. "Let me help you get up," he says. Once on her feet, it is clear she can only take a few steps without significant pain, but that is a few more than she had been able to do earlier. I gather up all our things, walking laden like a pack mule so that Abraham only has to carry Alice. "I'm sorry," he says as he lifts her up and puts her over his shoulder like a sack of flour. Despite our situation Alice finds this predicament quite entertaining and can't help but laugh sheepishly.

Thankfully we do not have far to go, and Abraham manages admirably, only resting once along the way. The cave is not large but will protect us from any wind and the morning dampness. Someone else had sought refuge here some time ago, as we find the remains of a small fire and even a little wood. Alice and I settle in while Abraham goes out to see what he might find for evening meal. We have very little left of the food we brought with us and even less water. I gather a bit more wood but never venture far, as Alice seems quite anxious about being alone. I do find a few small berries, but this late in the season there is little left to be had.

Abraham thankfully is very successful and brings back a rabbit and a bird. I set about cleaning those while he makes a small fire at the front of the cave on which we can cook. He crafts a small spit with some twigs, and it works quite well. We each manage to eat a bit and drink the last of the water. At first light, Abraham will go back to the creek and get more for our journey back to the wagon. Alice is once again asleep, and Abraham and I step out beyond the edge of the cave to talk without waking her. The sun has dropped below the horizon now, and only a few golden rays cast their light into the sky. Soon it will be very dark indeed, with only the moon and fire for light.

"Mrs. Tench, is Alice going to be able to walk tomorrow?" asks Abraham, clearly concerned.

"Honestly, I do not know. We will just have to hope that some rest and more tonic is enough," I reply.

"I'm sure the men will come looking for us tomorrow when we don't return tonight," says Abraham, speaking more to the great darkness beyond us than to me.

I reach over and take his hand in mine. "I'm sure they will, and either way I know you have done, and will do, your very best to care for us until we can get Alice home."

He nods, clearing his throat, and his voice cracks just a bit as he speaks. "I love her very much," he says.

"I know you do, and I know she loves you as well," I reply. That makes him smile, and I know he will sleep better now.

The ground is hard, and sleep eludes me as I fret about Alice and what we will do if she is unable to walk tomorrow. I finally get up to relieve myself just outside the cave, and something catches my eye in the distance. We are up on a hill so I can see for some distance, but I cannot determine what I just saw. I wait and watch for a few more moments, and when a slight breeze blows through the trees I see it: a fire. I can't tell how far away it is, but it is there. I quietly wake Abraham, and he follows me outside. "There," I point to the small swirl of smoke in the distance, illuminated by the moon. "Perhaps they can help us?"

Abraham hesitates. "But they may also hurt us; we don't know who it is or why they are here," he says. He's right of course; an old woman and a young girl who can't walk, we are not in much of a position to defend ourselves.

"What shall we do then?" I ask.

"Let me go alone and see if I can get close enough to determine if it is friend or foe," he says as he turns back for his rifle.

"Be most cautious my dear, do not risk yourself if it seems too dangerous. Please return here. God's blessing on you, Abraham, I'll be praying for you," I say as he walks away into the darkness. I sit down on a large rock at the edge of the cave, watching and listening, but I have no sense of where he is or what might be happening. The sun is just coming over the horizon when Abraham returns. He brings water with him, which is most appreciated, and another rabbit. I wait patiently as he catches his breath and quenches his thirst. Alice stirs. I help her up, and she hobbles out of the cave to relieve herself. She is walking better but still not where she needs to be to return to the wagon.

"Well, what did you see?" I ask finally. Alice seemed puzzled, so I quickly explain to her the events of the night. Abraham's face betrays no sense of what he is thinking or clue to what saw.

"Indians," he replies. I feel my heart skip a beat. "It was a tribe I did not recognize, there were perhaps three or four of them, a hunting party maybe." There was a time when I would not have hesitated to approach an Indian for help. Nintisqua and his tribe had helped the colony and my family, and I never saw them as a threat. He was a friend. But now, things have changed; there is more conflict and more killing, on both sides. We could not know if they would be friendly toward us or not.

"There is more," says Abraham. Alice looks at him wide-eyed, and I sense her growing fear. "Their camp is near the trail we must follow to get back to the wagon," he says bluntly. Alice begins to cry quietly, and I do not object when Abraham puts his arm around her to console her.

"We could go a different way?" she asks.

"Perhaps," I reply, "but with your foot we need to go the most direct way we can, as you can only bear so much."

"This is my fault," Alice says as her tears became a torrent, her guilt almost palpable.

"It is not your fault," says Abraham reassuringly. "It's not like you wanted to fall and injure yourself, it just happened, and I find no fault in you for it."

I agree with Abraham and together we do our best to calm her.

"I suggest we stay here another night. Hopefully they will move on, and if not, then I pray that Wills, Phillip, and Daniel can find us," I say, glancing between the two of them.

"I concur," Abraham says, and Alice nods in agreement, unable to bring herself to speak.

"Let's eat something and work on gathering what we need for the day before darkness comes again," I say, getting to my feet and wiping my hands on my dress. I feel dirty and my clothes are soiled and damp, as I'm sure Alice's are as well, so I might try to clean them a bit by tearing off more of my underslip to use as a cloth to wash with. Abraham sets about gathering more wood and hunting more prey so that we can eat again later in the day. We keep ourselves busy; even Alice manages to help a bit, and the day passes quickly.

"We must keep the fire as small as we can," Abraham says as we cook the wild turkey he had found for us.

"Why?" replies Alice.

"We saw the Indians from their fire last night; we don't want them to see us from ours," he responds. I have been impressed with him. He has stayed calm and been very resourceful in our time of need, and very brave. I'm sure all will be well and tomorrow we can make our way back to the wagon. Hopefully it is still there. Abraham and I agree that we'll take turns standing watch during the night.

He went first, as my lack of sleep from last night quickly strained my ability to stay awake, and now it's my turn. I slept fitfully, but at least I slept. I had given a tonic to Alice to help her sleep, and I can hear her breathing heavily at the back of the cave. The fire is now not much more than a few embers—the air has cooled since last night, but we can't risk making it larger. I see the Indians' fire still there in the distance as I settle my back against a rock, the rifle across my lap. In the darkness, the stars fill the sky like so many jewels in the heavens. "William, if you are there, if you can see us, send us help my love, we need your help," I whisper to the night sky. I close my eyes to pray and when I open them, I see a star streak across the darkness before its light dims. I smile. Perhaps William heard my plea—but pleas won't be enough. If help does not arrive early tomorrow, I know what I must do. Alice might be able to walk but it won't be quickly, and she will need to rest often. Abraham may be able to carry her some of the way, but even as strong a young man as he is, he can't carry her all the way, and a litter would be impossible to maneuver in this brush.

When morning comes, I watch carefully for any signs of help, but there are none. I can still see the smoke from the Indian camp in the distance, and so I put my plan into motion and wake Abraham. "I am trusting you to get Alice home safely, can you do that?" I ask.

"I don't understand," he says.

"I am not going with you," I reply.

He knits his brow and shakes his head. "Why, why would you not go with us?"

"Alice will only be able to walk slowly, and she will need a great deal of help. I am going to set out to the north of the Indian camp and try to draw them in my direction while you and Alice make your way to the wagon on the south side," I say firmly.

"No, no, Mrs. Tench, you can't do that, Alice would never forgive herself," he says, choking back the tears.

"I would never forgive myself if I didn't do everything in my power to save her, to save you both. I risked my life for her once before and I will do it again," I say calmly. "I must go now. I'm not going to wake her, as my conviction may be shaken by her tears and pleas and I cannot risk it. I've put most of my things in the basket, but I will keep the knife and a bit of flint. Please tell Alice how much I love her, and that I'm sorry I could not say goodbye."

"You are sure about this?" asks Abraham, hoping I will change my mind.

"I am. Wait for a bit before you depart, and God's speed." I hug him quickly and glance back at Alice, still asleep in the cave. When I reach the bottom of the hill, I turn to see Abraham still standing at the mouth of the cave and wave goodbye before heading into the forest. The air is cool, and the sun has not yet risen above the level of the trees, so it is shadowy and quiet underneath the canopy of leaves. To keep my bearings, I must go slowly until the sun rises higher in the sky. If I am not careful, I will veer too far south, defeating my purpose, or worse yet, I will walk directly into their camp.

William taught me a great deal about finding my way in the woods, as he was always concerned that I would stray from my path when collecting my plants. I never imagined I would use those skills in this way, but I am grateful for them, for without that knowledge I could not attempt this diversion. The walk is easy enough and I move quietly through the forest, stopping only now and then when I find a clear spot to check the position of the sun. I pray that Abraham and Alice are making progress, although I know it will be slow. I sit to rest a bit under a tree and the enormity of my situation begins to become clear. I feel as if I am carrying a heavy weight in my heart. If the Indians are not friendly, it is doubtful I will ever see my family again. They might kill me, or perhaps worse in my mind, they might take me. I have heard of some women and children who were taken by the Indians, most to never return.

I have lived a good life, a better life in some ways than I ever imagined I would live. If God decides that this is my time, I will be happy to give my life in the protection of my family. Alice has been like a daughter to me, and I could not bear to lose another. I only pray that this works and that she remains safe. As I walk further on, I hear a sound up ahead—voices I think, but I am not sure. I move more slowly, careful to not make any noise. I want them to follow me, but I mustn't be discovered when I am too close to them, as I would have no chance to escape. I can hear them more clearly now, men's voices. I hear no women, which means Abraham was right that this is most likely a hunting party. I recognize a few of their words, Nintisqua having taught us some words that he felt might be useful.

Carefully I slip out from behind the brush I have been hiding behind to check the position of the sun. North is to my left and the Indians seem to be nearly straight ahead of me, so I turn and make my way due north for some time before I begin going a bit more east again. I can still hear them talking and laughing, and the sound of their voices helps to orient me as I walk. Finally, I reach a place where I think I am close enough to be heard but far enough away to hopefully escape. Now what? I hadn't really thought through what I would do to get their attention, but I suppose the easiest thing to do is simply yell out. "Kew-Kew," I yell loudly, the Algonquin word for *hello*. The sound seems to echo all around me, and their voices fall silent.

They are coming… I can hear them, talking as they make their way toward me, and I turn to run as fast as I can to the north. The bushes and brambles tear at my hands and face, but I don't dare slow down. I must keep going as fast as I can, though I fear it will not be fast enough. I can feel they are getting closer, and I know now I cannot outrun them; I need a place to hide. I see a very heavy thicket ahead and lie down next to it, doing my best to slide up inside of it without disturbing the outer layers. The branches are rough, and my hands become bloody and dirty as I claw my way farther and farther into the thicket. I gather up my dress and tuck it under me as I curl up as small as I can. I cover my head with my arm to hide the white of my cap. Now to be quiet.

I must slow my breath, I cannot make a single noise, perfectly still and perfectly quiet. I can hear them; they seem to be all around me and moving slowly. I hear a twig snap nearby, which means at least one of them is close. Nothing moves except my eyes as I try to peer through the heavy brush. There he is, just a few feet away. I can see his legs but nothing more as he walks past me. Suddenly he stops and turns back toward me. My heart is pounding so hard surely he can hear it. He stands there for what feels like an eternity before he continues. I want to cry, I want to sing praises to God, but I know I must remain quiet. The sun is fully overhead now; I'm not sure how long I have been in the thicket, but the voices have not returned. I slowly begin to move my legs, stiff and numb from lying still for so long. Still hearing nothing, I slowly crawl back out from under the brush and sit up.

My whole body aches and I can barely get to my feet. I need to find some water soon. I hope it is safe to head south now, and I know there is a creek not too far away, back the way we came that first day. If I can make my way to where we left the wagon, I'm sure there will be rescue, although I am now too far away to make it there before dark. I continue to move slowly, stopping to listen from time to time for any sound, but there is none. It is slow going but I push myself to keep moving. At last, the creek appears in front of me just as the sun is dropping below the trees. I cross the water, which is only up to my knees, and drop down on the other side to drink heartily. The cool water soothes me and I begin to wash the dried blood and dirt from my hands and face.

When I look up from the creek, I see him standing there on the opposite bank. He is an older man with much gray in his hair, which is braided and decorated with a few beads. His clothes seem to be made of deer skin but there is no adornment, just the arrow pouch on his back. In his left hand a bow, in his right, what looks like a hatchet. I should not be surprised that he has tracked me—the Indians are masters of the forest, and their skills are legendary. I stand up, wiping my hands on my dress and drying my face with my sleeve. "Nitpom," I say, trying not to sound as frightened as I feel. The Algonquin word for *friend,* or when you meet someone from another tribe who does not know you.

He looks at me and points. "Nitpom," he replies.

"Yes, yes, I am nitpom," I say again, pointing at myself and then at him. I know there is nothing to be gained in trying to run; he could close the distance between us in short time.

He looks at me as if trying to see my soul, to somehow understand me, staring without moving. He says something I do not understand and motions to his head then points at me. I'm not sure what he wants, and my mind searches unsuccessfully for more of the words Nintisqua had taught me, but I can find none that seem to be right. Again he speaks, pointing to his head with a lifting motion and then pointing at me. He wants me to take off my cap! I quickly remove it, and my hair, which is now nearly all gray, falls about my face and down to my shoulders. I don't know why he should want to see my hair—perhaps he's trying to decide if my scalp would be to his liking—but he has made no move to cross the creek. Finally, he nods his head and says something I do not understand before disappearing into the forest.

My knees are weak and I am shaking as I drop down onto the sandy bank of the creek and finally give in to the tears I have been holding back. Relief washes over me in waves like those cascading over the large rocks in the creek. A beaver runs along the water's edge on his way to his lair. If there are beaver here, then no doubt the Indians are here trapping, as their hides are very highly prized for their warmth. The Indians probably never intended to hurt me, perhaps they even would have helped us, but I will never know for certain. Before I can bring myself to get up the sun has gone behind the trees, and I know I must find a place to sleep for the night, as it would be too easy to get lost in the dark. I walk on for a bit, scouting for a place to spend the night. A little outcropping of rock I find seems good enough; at least I will be protected from one side. I'm hungry and have nothing to eat, but I manage to make a small fire.

The darkness is complete, with clouds now covering up what little light the moon might have offered. I hear various animals calling out to each other as the fire crackles and snaps, shooting sparks into the air. I lean against the rocks, which are cold on my back, and draw my knees up to my chest. I wonder if Alice and Abraham are home safely sleeping in their beds. Will someone be looking for me, or will they just assume I have not survived? Either way, tomorrow I must try to get back to the trail we came in on. I have no intention of just sitting here dying in these woods. I want to go home to my children and grandchildren, to my family. I keep the knife clutched tightly in my hand all night, sleeping very little, and the darkness seems to go on and on without end. I hear noises all around me, but I see nothing. I hear the howling of the wolves in the distance, but thankfully they are not close.

A little mouse runs in front of the fire; if I were faster, I could have caught him and had something to eat, but he simply runs too quickly. I'm cold so I add another log to the fire and warm my hands over the welcome heat. There are no stars to be seen this night, and in the distance, I can hear of bit of rumbling in the sky. If it rains, I will have no fire and no shelter, so I pray fervently that God will at least spare me that. I finally fall asleep and wake to dampness, not true rain but a heavy mist in the air and a sky solid white with clouds. I cannot see the sun at all and so I walk around a bit, trying to find some moss on the trees. William always said moss grows on the north side, and I could use that to orient myself to keep walking.

I am not well; my head aches, I feel that I have a fever, and the cool air is causing me to shiver. I wish I had kept a small bottle of tonic with me as I could very much use it. I started off in the direction I thought was right, but after walking for some time, I do not see anything that looks familiar. Perhaps it is just the gray dreariness that makes it seem different. One of the cuts on my hand is angry and red and becoming quite painful. After some time, I come to terms with the thought in my mind that I had been trying to avoid: I am lost, unsure where I am or which way I should go. I sit down on a fallen log and contemplate what to do, but my mind finds no solution. For now, I must simply sit and wait. Perhaps if I build a large fire, it will help them find me. I'm sure they must be searching; I can't imagine that my family would abandon me easily, but I may no longer be where they are looking.

I find an open clearing and begin dragging branches and small limbs into it to build a fire. My flint is a bit damp, and it takes several tries, but finally a spark lights the dry grass I have placed under the wood. There is a great deal of smoke, everything a bit damp from the mist in the air, but finally the flames take hold and the fire roars to life. Its warmth soothes me, and I find a place to lie down, praying that I will be found soon.

The sound of an animal nearby startles me and I realize I have been asleep. It is nearly dusk, and the fire is now just a few embers. My throat is dry, and my eyes burn. My hand has grown much larger, and the cut has become more enraged and most painful. Slowly I get to my feet and place a few more limbs on the fire, which catch quickly.

Food, I don't know that I have ever been this hungry, and I need water, but I can barely put one foot in front of the other. Even though the air is cool, water is forming on my forehead and running down the sides of my face and back. I am sick clearly, from what I am not certain, although I suspect this cut on my hand may be to blame. Without my tonics I've no way to treat it other than to clean it with water when I can. I sit down on the grass near the fire and realize I am simply now at God's mercy. I will be found and returned to my family, or I will not; it is no longer within my control. I knew the chance I was taking when I decided to do this, and I am not sorry. If my life should end this way I will go to heaven without regret.

The night has fully engulfed me in its arms, and I can no longer get up to tend the fire, so it will be out soon. My mind drifts in and out, thoughts swirling around like the circles you see in the water when you drop a pebble. The wind is getting stronger, and I think I can hear voices carried along on its whisper. Perhaps help is finally coming. But I cannot keep my eyes open any longer, I must sleep, I must give in to this pain and find some rest. "God, please have mercy on my soul and bring to me your comfort and blessing in these my final hours," I whisper at the sky before closing my eyes.

How long I have been asleep I cannot say, but I can feel the warmth of furs around me and hands that hold water from a gourd to my parched throat before I fall into the abyss, the darkness engulfing me once more. The smell of smoke hangs in the air, and I hear voices around me, but I cannot make sense of what is being said. After what feels like days, I open my eyes to find I am in a teepee and sitting there across from me, the Indian I saw on the bank of the creek. When he realizes I am awake he brings me a gruel of some kind, feeding it to me with his fingers. I can barely swallow but manage to get a small bit of it down. He points at himself. "Nen Atiska," he says, then he points at me. "Howan?"

The words are coming back to me. "Nen Sarah," I say, pointing at myself.

"Wuttat," he says as he lifts my head up slightly to take a drink from the gourd. He pulls a deerskin up to my chin and tucks it around my shoulders before adding another heavier fur. "Wuskesuk," he says as he gently closes my eyes, and I gladly fall back into the darkness.

Too weak to be afraid, I accept whatever kindness Atiska offers me most gratefully. My hand is bound in some kind of wrapping but it is still quite painful. After he has fed me some meat and bread he unwraps my hand, washing it with water. He looks at me with what seems like sorrow in his eyes. "Matchet nutcheg," he says finally, shaking his head. I think for a moment. *Machet* is bad and *nutcheg* must mean hand. He's right, my hand is quite bad, I am sure. He leaves the teepee but returns quickly with a twig, which he whittles slightly with his knife. He hands it me and gestures to his mouth. I know what this means; I have seen it many, many times throughout my life, and I put the stick in my mouth and bite down hard.

Atiska takes his knife and slices through the angriest part of my hand, blood and pus running down onto the dirt floor. The pain courses through my whole body and tears begin to trickle into my hair, but I keep biting on the twig. He cuts again, just slightly in another direction, and then washes my hand once more and binds it tightly. I am exhausted beyond measure and Atiska gives me something warm to drink, and in a few moments, I am drowsy and in less pain at last. I must find out what it is that he has given me, I think to myself as I fall asleep. My dreams are confused, full of William and Johnathan and others I have known who have passed; perhaps this is God's way of preparing me to die.

But it does not yet seem to be my time. Today I have been able to get up and walk outside the teepee. Atiska has warmed some water, which I use to clean myself. He also gives me a cloak of sorts to wrap myself in while I clean my clothes. My modesty means less to me at this moment than being able to wear something not covered in dirt and blood. Atiska has been most respectful of me, and I don't know now why I was ever afraid of them. I have not seen the other men who I assume were with him, and I cannot speak to him well enough to ask many questions, so we spend much of our time in silence. He has been teaching me some words and I have taught him some English as well. I'm not sure how long I have been here, but I feel I may be strong enough to try again to walk to the start of the trail. "Moonchek wekit otan, I want to go to my house in the town," I say while looking at him to see how he might react. I have no idea if he intends to let me go or not. He has been most kind to me, but perhaps for his own purposes rather than just concern for my welfare.

He looks at me and shakes his head no. "Noondtit papaum," he says as he gestures with his hands.

"Too far to walk?" I say.

"Yes," he responds, one of the words he learned quickly, and then he scrambles to his feet and heads out into the forest. I do not know what to think—does this mean he is going to keep me captive here? Is he expecting me to become his wife? Maybe I should try to escape while he is gone, but I've no idea how quickly he might return, and I don't want to risk making him angry. While he has showed no sign of ill intent toward me so far, I cannot know how he might react. I look around the teepee to see if there are any weapons I might use, but I find nothing. Even if I had, would I really be able to use them on the man who probably saved my life? I'm not sure, but it makes no difference now, he has returned. I feel very guilty and ungrateful for all that Atiska has done for me, but while I might not be able to hurt him, I also do not want to spend what is left of my life with him here in the forest.

"Sepu Mohtompog otan," he says as he sets down a wild turkey he had brought with him. *Otan* is town and *sepu* is river, but I'm not sure what he means. The town of the river, the town on the river? But what is the other word?

"I'm not sure what you are saying, Atiska, what is mohtompog?" I reply. He takes a stick and draws in the dirt, a sun and moon and an arch going from the sun to the moon. Suddenly I realize what he is trying to say.

"Sepu river, mohtompog tomorrow, otan town, we will take the river to town tomorrow?"

He smiles and nods yes.

Dear God, I thank you for this blessing, I think as I take his hand and squeeze it tightly. "I do not know the word for *thank-you* Atiska," I say, "But I will never forget your kindness and care for me." I touch my chest above my heart and then touch his chest. "Nitpom," I say quietly.

"Nitpom," he replies.

At first light we set off. I slowly follow Atiska along a well-worn path leading to a river, where he has a small canoe. I am already tired from just this short walk so it is clear he was right; I would never have been able to walk back to the trail. He puts some food and blankets into the center of the canoe and makes me a chair of sorts in the front with a piece of wood and some blankets, then he picks me up and gently sets me in. My hand still tightly wrapped, I will not be able to help with the paddling, but I'm sure Atiska is used to maneuvering the boat alone. I am grateful for the blankets as we glide through the water. I do not know exactly what town we are going to, but it makes no difference to me; once there I can get word to Wills. I have no money, but surely, I can find someone who will help me for the promise of a payment to come.

We talk little during our journey, but I revel in the sunshine and the wildlife along the way. I see deer, beavers, foxes, and even a small bear as we float along the river. For the most part the water is calm. Beavers have built dams in a few places that cause the water to churn up, but it is not impassable. I do not know how long this journey will take, but given the number of blankets and provisions we have brought, I've no doubt we will be spending the night somewhere along our path. Once the sun starts to sink below the trees, Atiska does indeed stop at a sandy bank and pulls the canoe ashore. I'm a bit unsteady on my feet, having sat for so long, but Atiska once again picks me up from the canoe and carries me onto dry land. There is not much I can do with one hand, but I work to gather some wood for the fire while Atiska brings everything up from the boat. It appears to me that he has stayed in this place before, as he seems to have hidden some things here for his use. Quite ingenious really, knowing he could always come here in a time of need with little preparation.

Our meal is mostly hard tack and petukquannuk, a bread Atiska makes in a small clay pot. The fire is warm, and though we talk little there is an easy comradery between us now. Once the fire dies down a bit, Atiska points out various stars in the sky. I'm not always sure what he is saying but he seems to know them well, and I've no doubt he could use them to navigate on a clear night. It is hard to believe that when I first arrived here, I thought of Indians as savages, uneducated, with no redeeming qualities. Nintisqua proved I was wrong about that, and all these years later Atiska has reinforced it. It is true the Indians have murdered settlers, but we are certainly not without shame and have killed many, many Indians with our diseases and with our swords. There is plenty of blame to share. They did not ask for us to come here but still welcomed us with open arms, and we have often betrayed them. It is something I deeply regret, and I sometimes wonder if it might have been best if we had stayed behind in Holland.

But one cannot hold back change; it is as constant as the rising and setting of the sun. The Dutch, English, French, Spanish, they are all here, and if not us, someone else would surely have come. As I lie down for the night, I cannot help but wonder if tomorrow I will be home. It is a comforting thought and I fall asleep quickly.

I'm not sure what awakens me, but I'm aware that Atiska is not lying nearby as he was earlier. Sitting up, I peer into the darkness and finally spot him standing at the edge of the forest behind a large tree. He turns to look at me, puts his hand over his mouth, and shakes his head no. He is warning me to be quiet so I do not speak, but I do stand up, ready to run if need be. The forest seems very quiet, and I do not hear anything until a twig snaps nearby. Atiska immediately runs back to my side and, loading an arrow into his bow, he hands me his hatchet. We stare into the darkness, waiting, watching.

Another sound, and I see in the trees a bit of moonlight reflecting off something. I point in that direction and Atiska nods; he has seen it too. Then without warning a white man steps out of the trees, his rifle pointed at Atiska. "Mrs. Tench?" the man says.

My heart leaps. "Yes, I'm Sarah Tench," I say.

"Come toward me, ma'am, please, away from the Indian."

"No," I say loudly, stepping in front of Atiska. "I am not his prisoner, and I do not want you to hurt him, this man has saved my life."

"Ask him to put down the bow," the man says.

"Atiska, you must trust me, this man is nitpom, he is from my village, he will not hurt you," I say, taking the bow and arrow from his hand. Thankfully the man in the shadows lowers his rifle and comes toward us.

"Mrs. Tench, are you well?" the man asks.

"Yes. Atiska, this Indian man, he is taking me to town on the river," I respond. "Who are you? How do you know me?"

He walks a bit closer. "It's me, Mrs. Tench, Jabez Howland. I was here checking my beaver traps when I saw the light from your fire." Jabez Howland, the boy I had once saved, now saving me. "The whole town has been looking for you, and your son asked everyone to be watchful when we were in the forest or along the river."

"Alice and Abraham?" I ask, almost afraid to hear the answer.

"They are well. Alice is nearly healed, and Abraham has been with his father and your son looking for you these past weeks," he says with a smile. I cannot help but embrace him, both in gratitude for this news and as a way to show Atiska that this is indeed a friend he need not fear.

"I have a boat just up the river a small distance. In the morning I can take you home," says Jabez. Home, I am going home.

Sleep eludes me and I spend the night talking with Jabez, telling him how Atiska had rescued me from what would have been certain death. Jabez seems most surprised but does his best to express his appreciation to Atiska for his kindness. He is also quite concerned for my welfare; my fever still burns and my hand is still wrapped, but he will fetch a doctor as soon as we get back to Plimouth. I've no cap, and my clothes are ill fitting, as my flesh has gotten much smaller these last few weeks. Still, I am alive, and I have Atiska and God to thank for that. I see that Atiska sleeps with his hatchet in hand, and it saddens me that we fear each other so. I was frightened of him, and he is now frightened of Jabez. It is sad that we could not have found a way to share this land more amicably, but I'm afraid that time has passed.

When the morning light breaks above the horizon, Jabez sets out to bring his boat here. I do my best to thank Atiska once again for his kindness, and I can only hope he understands how truly grateful I am. When Jabez returns and it's time to go, I cannot help but feel a bit of sadness, as Atiska has been a true friend to me. "Nitpom," I say once more.

"No, netompas wompi meesunk," he replies as he kisses me gently on each cheek. *Sister white hair*—I could not ask for a better compliment than to be called a part of his family, and I choke back tears as Jabez carefully helps me into the canoe. Atiska covers me with one of the blankets, and then we are on our way.

Our journey along the river is quick indeed, and before I know it, I am back at the edge of town. Still some distance from home, but I can almost feel my family close to me. I'm too weak to walk far, but thankfully Jabez has a wagon and horse nearby, and he and another man lay me in the back on the blanket that Atiska gave me. A woman offers me a cap for my hair, but I don't want it. For some reason, having my hair uncovered now seems important, although I'm not sure exactly why. This experience has changed me, I suspect in more ways than I now understand. We travel just a short distance to the doctor, and he and Jabez carry me into his house. He unwraps my hand, and it's immediately clear from the putrid smell that it has not healed well despite Atiska's efforts.

The doctor's wife washes my hand in hot water, the doctor covers it with a salve, and then his wife binds it again. "Mrs. Tench, I am not going to give you false hope, I do not know if your hand is going to heal. If it doesn't improve soon, we will have to remove it if you want to save your life." It is as I already knew, but it tears at my heart to hear him say it.

"I understand, I appreciate your honesty most sincerely," I reply. "We can wait a few days, but no more," he reiterates. I nod my agreement. Jabez is kind enough to pay the doctor for me; I must remember to have someone repay him for this and all his kindnesses to me. He also has sent word ahead to Wills and Phillip to let them know that I have been found and that we will arrive before sunset.

The journey is slow, and the jostling of the cart brings a great deal of discomfort, but I keep reminding myself it will be worth the effort. Jabez stops to procure some food and drink for me, which is very much appreciated although I find that I am not very hungry. The ale though is most welcome, as it both satisfies my thirst and calms my aching bones. I try to get some rest, but I find myself gazing up instead at the trees silhouetted against the sky. They have changed in my absence to the brightest of yellow, red, and brown, and the leaves look like little birds as they fly through the air toward the ground. The trees will be bare soon; winter is coming as it always does. I shiver a bit at the thought, remembering the bitter cold and snow that took the life of my dear Patience and her family. Let us hope this winter is not as bad, but it is only for God to say.

I am most sincerely thankful for his mercy in getting me to this day, but I cannot help but feel there are not many days ahead. I have already decided that the doctor will not remove my hand. No, I simply cannot do that. To become a cripple dependent on others is not in my nature and not something I could endure. If the salve does not work, then the ending is written. I wonder who will be waiting for me in heaven? So many precious souls have gone before me, and I can't help but look forward to seeing them again, when God makes it so. Homes and buildings I recognize are starting to come into view, and Jabez says it will not be long now. The weariness in my bones is most profound, but I'm sure seeing my family will give me strength.

"Grandmama," I hear a girl shout in the distance, and I lift my head to see Alice running towards us as fast as she can. Jabez stops the wagon, and Alice climbs in the back, wrapping me in her arms and weeping most profoundly. I hold her as tightly as I can with one arm and kiss her face, brushing away the tears.

"It's well my child, all is well, no need to cry now, I am home," I say. But still the tears flow, and soon the wagon is surrounded by my family. Wills with John; Phillip with Grace; Isaac and his wife and children; Elizabeth and Peter with their children; Daniel, Mehitable, and Abraham; Hannah Brown, and so many others. Everyone is shouting and some are crying, and the commotion brings others out of their homes to see what is happening. Before I know it, the street is full of people, yelling and shouting their welcome and blessings.

Abraham climbs up in the wagon with Alice. "It is very, very good to see you again, Mrs. Tench, you don't know how hard we have been looking for you," he says with a huge grin.

"Let's get you home, Mother," says Wills, reaching over the side of the wagon to squeeze my hand. Jabez starts moving again as the sea of people slowly parts to let us through. Abraham helps me sit up, leaning against him so that I can see all of those who have come out to welcome me. My heart is overwhelmed by this outpouring of affection, and it lifts my spirts to see all these faces. I have known some of these people for a very long time and we have seen many hardships together. It is good to know that they are here to see me through what may be my last.

Anne is waiting on the porch; she and Phillip were wed while I was away as there was concern from the elders that they were alone in the house for so long. A shame I was not able to see them make their bond, but no matter, I am most happy for them. The men gather round to gently pull me out of the wagon, and Wills carries me to my bed, which I am joyfully happy to see. Everyone wants to see me, and I do my best to talk a bit to each, but I am most tired now. Alice has brought me some stew and a bit of ale, and now I just want to rest a bit. I can hear them all talking in the other room.

"She has wasted away," says Wills.

"Her hand, why is it covered?" a woman's voice, I think Elizabeth's.

"Is she ill or just tired?" says Anne.

I can hear Jabez telling them how he found me, and I am pleased he is getting the appreciation he deserves. I hope he tells them about Atiska and his care for me.

On and on the voices go, but soon they fade into the distance as I fall asleep.

A few days have passed, and I am able to sit by the fire and enjoy the company of the steady stream of well-wishers who come to call. Wills has stayed here with Alice to help look after me. Daniel and Abraham arrived this morning; Daniel told Phillip it was most important that he speak with me as soon as I am able. He pulls a chair up next to mine and holds my good hand in both of his. "Are you in much pain?" he asks quietly.

"No, it is not very much," I say with a weak smile, but I'm not sure he believes me.

"I wanted to thank you, for what you did for Abraham and Alice in the woods. You might have all been lost if it had not been for your courage," he says. "I cannot thank you enough for helping my son get home to me and his mother."

I look into his eyes, welling up with tears. "I could not save your mother, my dearest friend Mary, but I am most grateful I was able to save your son."

Abraham and Daniel both embrace me, then Abraham kneels in front of me, Daniel and now Wills, too, standing behind him. "Mrs. Tench, I know you understand how much I care for Alice, and I have spoken to my father and to hers to ask their blessing on our marriage, but both have said that the blessing I require is yours," says Abraham anxiously. I look at Daniel and Wills, now smiling at me, their arms locked together. I do not let my face betray my thoughts and I can see that Abraham is growing most concerned, but I'm sure the others already know what my response will be.

"Abraham, I can think of no other I would rather see betrothed to Alice. You have my blessing, my child, with my highest regards. Alice might never have made it home if it were not for your care of her, and for that I will always be most grateful," I say, leaning forward to kiss him on the cheek.

Wills fetches Alice from the other room and Abraham begins his speech, which I'm sure he had practiced, but before he can even finish, she has already said yes. Mary and Edward should be here to see this; it would have made the moment complete.

But now, I must retreat to my room, for the doctor has come to look at my hand again to see if it has made any progress. He unwraps it carefully, and thankfully the odor is less than before, but otherwise it is unchanged, still angry with a redness that's now starting to extend up into my arm. "Mrs. Tench, I'm afraid it is not good news," he says solemnly. I nod; the pain has told me it was not healing as it should, so I am not surprised. "We need to remove the hand today," he says, clearing his throat as if choking on the words.

"I appreciate everything you have done, sir, and I trust your counsel, but it is something I cannot do," I say firmly.

"I understand, Mrs. Tench, but you know that you will not survive more than a few days if you do not."

"It is in God's hands now," I reply.

"I will speak to your son," he says.

"No, let me, I will tell him."

"I will pray for you," he says as he closes the door behind him.

The beginning of the end. A heavy sigh comes on me; I'm not sure if it is relief or sorrow, perhaps a bit of both. That night, I speak to Wills and Phillip, and while there are tears and pain, in the end they both understand and accept my decision. Tomorrow, I will speak with Elizabeth and the older grandchildren and leave it to their mothers and fathers to deal with the wee ones.

My conversation with Alice is most difficult, to be sure. She blames herself for this situation, but I have done my best to help her conscious remain clear. She would like to marry Abraham right away, while I can still be present, and I agree, I would like that very much. The women all gather to work furiously on a dress and the other things needed for the celebration, which is planned for the day after tomorrow. Anne, with help from Martha and Ruth, Elizabeth's oldest girls, works on the meal, and based on the smells coming from the kitchen it will be most fine indeed.

I spend my time in my chair in front of the fire, watching all the goings on and offering my advice. It is an effort, but I do my best to make sure the others do not see the pain I am in. The fever has returned, and I have no desire for food. Alice glances up from her sewing and I can see a tear running down her cheek. "Come here, my child," I say, motioning her to my side. "Alice, this is a most happy time, do not cry," I say, wiping her face with my apron.

"I don't want you to go," she says softly.

"I will not be gone as long as you remember me, speak well of me, and tell your children of me," I reply.

"But I won't be able to talk to you," she says.

"You will, my love, I will be on the wind that's all around you. I will never be far away, just talk to the sky and listen for my voice in your heart."

The day of the wedding has arrived, and Alice and Abraham look most handsome in their best clothes. The celebration is grand, and I have never seen Alice so happy. It has been a joy to spend this day with those I love, and I am most grateful for it. If it had not been for Atiska I might have died weeks ago and missed this opportunity to see my family again. I do not feel sadness; I feel only a completeness, as if I have done all that God intended for me to do with my life. My family will carry on, and years from now, I hope they will speak of me and remember.

Wills carries me back to the house; the morning has exhausted me, and I am too weak to walk. We spend a few hours talking quietly, just the two of us. "Mother, can I get you some ale or food?" he asks.

"No, just stay here with me, my son, your presence is a comfort," I say quietly.

The sun is going down, the light changing in the window. "Wills, I would like to go outside, would you take me?"

"Of course, Mother," he replies gently. Wills wraps me in the blanket Atiska gave me and carries me outside, holding me tightly. The air is cool, but it feels good on my face and soothes my fever. The sky is ablaze with the last light of the day, rays of sun poking through the clouds in brilliant shades of yellow and pink. A few white clouds drift by on the breeze, and the leaves blow across the ground like little mice running in every direction. A sense of peacefulness descends on me just as a hawk flies' low overhead, tipping his wing to me before he turns skyward and heads into the sun.

ABOUT THE AUTHOR

Gail Combs Oglesby was born and raised in the western Detroit suburbs and lived for many years in California, and Texas. She now calls the mid-Atlantic area her retirement home which she shares with her husband and fur kids. She earned her bachelor's and master's degrees from the University of San Francisco in Human Resources, as well as a Doctorate in Business Administration from California Coast University. For over thirty-five years she worked in leadership roles in the Human Resources function in a variety of industries and from that experience published, HR Confidential: An Insider's Guide to Finding and Getting a great job which can be found on Amazon.

When not working, the passion that has bewitched her for the last fifty years has been genealogy. Originally the spell was cast while trying to solve a family mystery, which took nearly forty-years to uncover. Today, access to online databases and DNA has helped her, and thousands of others to make those connections to the past and Gail can often be found helping others with their search. Through that work she developed a deep admiration for what our ancestors, especially the women, have endured so that we could be here today. It is now her mission to bring their experiences to life through her writing and to celebrate the ordinary women whose accomplishments were anything but ordinary.

She can be reached at GailOglesby.com